ONLY
GLORY AWAITS

Only Glory Awaits

Ambassador Emerald International

427 Wade Hampton Boulevard
Greenville, S.C. 29609 U.S.A.

and

Ambassador Productions Ltd.

Providence House
Ardenlee Street
Belfast BT6 8QJ, Northern Ireland

www.emeraldhouse.com

Cover design, Sam Laterza page layout by A & E Media, Sam Laterza, Katherine
Rodriquez

ISBN 1 889893 95 1

Library of Congress Cataloging-in-Publication Data

Nuernberg, Leslie S.
  Only glory awaits : the story of Anne Askew, Reformation martyr /
Leslie S. Nuernberg.-- 1st ed.
     p. cm. -- (Seasons of grace ; #1)
Includes bibliographical references and index.
  ISBN 1-889893-95-1
 1. Askew, Anne, 1521-1546--Fiction. 2. Great
Britain--History--Henry
VIII, 1509-1547--Fiction. 3. Christian women martyrs--Fiction. 4.
Lincolnshire (England)--Fiction. 5. Protestants--Fiction. 6.
Reformation--Fiction. I. Title. II. Series: Nuernberg, Leslie S.
Seasons of grace ; #1.

 PS3614.U86O55 2003
 813'.6--dc21
                                          2003007421

Seasons of Grace • 1

ONLY GLORY AWAITS

Leslie S. Nuernberg

AMBASSADOR
EMERALD INTERNATIONAL

Greenville, South Carolina • Belfast, Northern Ireland
www.emeraldhouse.com

In Loving Memory of my mother,
Gladys P. Nuernberg
Who always believed this book was possible

My deepest appreciation to
Dawn Abels and Gail James,
whose constant encouragement brought this book into
existence. Without their enthusiasm and gentle prod-
ding, I never would have made it past Chapter 1.
Thank you both so very much!

Special thanks to
Doyle Perkins,
who started as my agent and became
my friend.

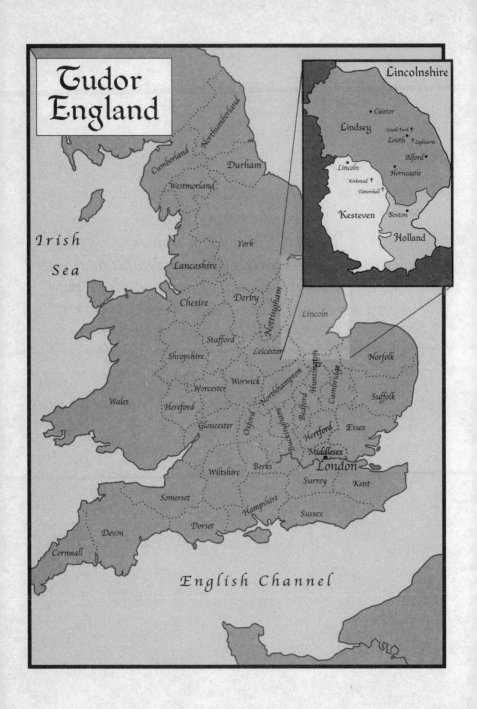

Tudor England

Irish Sea

Cumberland
Northumberland
Westmorland
Durham
York
Lancashire
Chesire
Derby
Nottingham
Stafford
Shropshire
Leicester
Lincoln
Worcester
Worwick
Northhampton
Huntington
Norfolk
Wales
Hereford
Oxford
Bedford
Cambridge
Suffolk
Gloucester
Buckingham
Hertford
Essex
Middlesex
London
Berks
Wiltshire
Surrey
Kent
Somerset
Hampshire
Sussex
Dorset
Devon
Cornwall

English Channel

Lincolnshire

Caistor
Lindsey
Louth Park †
Louth † Legbourne
Alford
Lincoln
Horncastle
Kirkstead †
Tattershall †
Kesteven
Boston
Holland

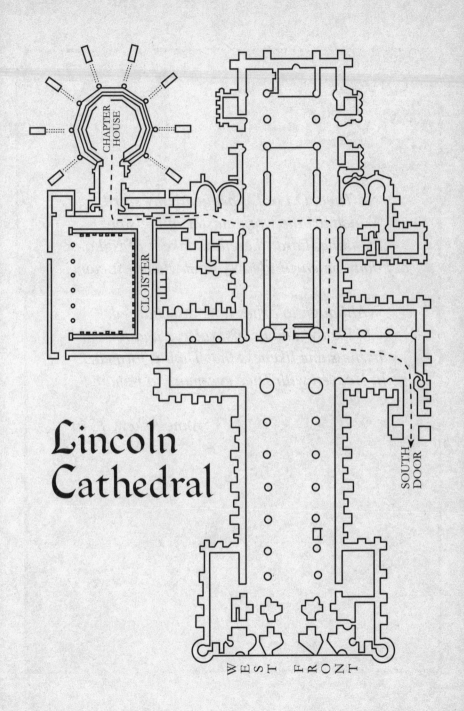

CHAPTER HOUSE

CLOISTER

Lincoln
Cathedral

SOUTH DOOR

WEST FRONT

To Thee, O Lord, I bequeath my spirit,
Which art the work master of the same.
It is thine, Lord; therefore, take it of right,
My body on earth I leave, from whence it came.

Although to ashes it be now burned,
I know Thou canst raise it again
In the same likeness that Thou it formed,
In Heaven with Thee evermore to remain.

Anne Askew, 1546

Chapter I

Newgate Prison, London, England
July 16, 1546

The young woman huddled on the musty straw mattress, trying in vain to settle herself in a position that would mitigate the racking pain in her weary body. Though she struggled fervently to keep her thoughts off her pain, every muscle and every joint reminded her of the agony she had recently endured at the hands of her captors. It was July, yet she lacked even the comfort of being warm as dampness from the thick, cold limestone walls invaded her, sending shivers through her slender body. She lay still a moment in hopes of quieting the constant throbbing, but started when somewhere in the bowels of the prison, iron gates clanked and a wail erupted, then faded into sobs.

Once more, she shifted her body slightly and winced as searing pain shot through her limbs. Muscles quivered in revolt. She vainly tried again to reposition herself, holding her breath against the agonizing onslaughts. Torn leg muscles and dislocated joints made it impossible for her to walk, so she could do little more than lie on the bed of straw that reeked from months of use. Yet one more time, she forced herself to endure the anguish as she shifted again to better her view out the barred window high on the other side of her prison cell. From any angle, she could see only a patch of azure sky and the occasional wisp of cloud; but she was determined to see as much of that sky as possible. Satisfied at last, she stared upward as if she could see beyond the sky, as if she could see home.

A flock of blackbirds glided by, and the young woman gasped with delight and yearning. Joy welled up within her as she realized that before the day was over, she, too, would soar free. Free and secure.

They imprison my body, she thought with triumph, *but they cannot imprison my soul.*

At the thought of her earthly jailers, her mind went to the Holy Scriptures that had sustained her through the months of imprisonment, interrogation, and torture.

"The Lord is my light and my salvation; whom shall I fear? The Lord is the strength of my life; of whom shall I be afraid."[1]

"I am not afraid, dearest Lord," she whispered. "For I know Thou art with me and shall be with me even as I pass through the fire."

A strange euphoria enveloped her, and she shivered again, only this time in anticipation. *Today, I shall be with my Lord*, she thought. *I shall see His beautiful face and hear His sweet voice. Oh, such wondrous joy! My heart can barely endure it. Eternal joy is but hours away. Soon, oh, so very soon, I shall be loosed from these earthly bonds and be with Him forever!*

She closed her eyes as she thought of the haven that awaited her. The pain ebbed away. The dampness ceased to rob her of warmth. The prison sounds faded. A solitary tear coursed down her cheek and was met by upturned lips of joy.

"And now shall mine head be lifted up above mine enemies round about me: therefore will I offer in His tabernacle sacrifices of joy; I will sing, yea, I will sing praises unto the LORD."[2]

As she quietly lay on the prison bed, she pondered her present state and recent suffering. Oddly, it was all so magnificent to her. Why should she, a young woman of no extraordinary means, be counted worthy to gloriously suffer for her Lord in such a manner? What events had brought her to this place?

I do suppose it began when I was first arrested, she answered herself. But no, it had begun long before that. But where and when? Her thoughts drifted into the past. What moment in time forever put her foot on the path that was leading her to this triumphant end?

"When did it all begin, sweet Lord?" she asked, and her mind drifted to a May morning more than fifteen years past...

South Kelsey, England
May 1531

"Anne! Make haste, Anne!" Martha called excitedly. "I can see him coming! Francis is almost here!"

At the sound of her sister's voice, eleven-year-old Anne Askew threw down the needlework she had been working on and hurried to the polished glass for a quick glance. An oval face neatly framed with dark hair and containing large blue eyes stared back at her. Satisfied with her reflection, Anne smiled, then dashed from her bedroom, and ran down the long hall. Gathering her long skirts, she descended the long staircase as quickly as she dared, fearful Francis may arrive before she could reach the courtyard. At the foot of the stairs stood her stepmother, Dame Elizabeth Hansard Askew, a stately and genteel woman. She smiled warmly at Anne, but put out a hand to stop the young girl when she reached the bottom step.

"Anne, you will break your neck in a fall by running down the stairs in such a manner," she said firmly, but gently. "You are no longer a little girl, but a young lady; and young ladies do not race down stairways."

"But Francis is almost here," Anne replied breathlessly. "And I want to be outside before he arrives."

"But Francis would be most grieved if his sister took a tumble down those steps on his account. Now, compose yourself, and conduct yourself as the young lady you are," Elizabeth replied a touch more sternly, for she did not tolerate even small acts of disobedience from either her children or her stepchildren.

Elizabeth was not Anne's natural mother, but she was the only mother the young girl had ever known; and Anne had come to adore her and, more importantly to Elizabeth, respect her. Anne's own mother had died shortly after giving birth to her sixth child, Anne's sister, Jane. Because Anne had been little more than a year old at the time of her mother's death, her memories had long since faded. Now, all she knew of her own mother were from the stories her elder siblings told and the portrait that hung in the gallery. But Anne never felt the loss because her father, Sir William Askew, had married the widowed Elizabeth Hansard late in 1523 when Anne was only three-and-half years old.

The marriage between Dame Elizabeth Hansard and Sir William Askew had been both congenial and profitable for the two parties. Elizabeth's first husband, Sir William Hansard, had died in January of 1523 of the sweating sickness, leaving Elizabeth with a grown son and two teenage daughters. However, tragedy plagued the Hansard family and struck again in April the same year. William, the only son and heir to the Hansard lands and fortune, took ill and succumbed to the same sickness that had taken his father only months before. Grief-stricken, Elizabeth buried him next to his father in the family burial plot. Compounding her grief was the overwhelming sense of vulnerability resulting from the absence of male family members. So when Sir William Askew, a man of considerable wealth himself and well established at king Henry's court, presented himself as suitor for her hand in marriage, she readily agreed.

In marrying, Elizabeth gained the protection and security Sir William afforded, and Sir William gained a mother for his young children and thousands of acres of fair lands—an agreeable exchange for both persons. To the delight and satisfaction of all, a genuine affection grew between the couple and the newly formed family. Elizabeth, though firm in her discipline, soon endeared herself to the young Askew children, and the pain of their loss gave way to the happiness that a secure home brings.

Nearly nine years had passed since Elizabeth had joined the family, and now she stood appraising her maturing stepdaughter with a proud, but critical eye. Of all the Askew children, Anne caused her the greatest concern. She was well gifted to be sure, having not only a pretty face and lively disposition, but a keen intellect as well—too keen in Elizabeth's estimation. And her exuberance and zest for life had, on occasion, evoked sharp words from Elizabeth, who strongly believed that young ladies should be reserved and demur. Anne was neither. Her curly dark hair bounced as she walked, for she rarely moved slowly; and her blue eyes sparked of life and love to all around her. Now Elizabeth saw in those eyes the intense admiration Anne had for her eldest brother, Francis Askew, heir to all the Lincolnshire estates held by his father.

"Come, let us walk out together," Elizabeth said, slipping her arm through Anne's. "Can you believe it, Anne, that Francis has already finished his third year of studies at Cambridge? 'Twill be so good to have him home again even if it is only of short duration."

Anne's eagerness made it difficult for her to slow her step to match the dignified pace of Elizabeth, but not wishing to spoil the excitement of her brother's homecoming, she walked obediently beside the older woman. They crossed the great entry hall and stepped out into the bright sun of the warm spring day. The rich scent of freshly turned fields wafted on a gentle breeze, and Anne inhaled deeply, delighting in the delicious odor. Her father, Sir William, along with Anne's siblings, Edward, Martha, Jane, and Thomas, had already assembled on the green. A good many of the household staff, standing discreetly behind the family, also gathered to greet their returning master. Anne hurried to stand between fifteen-year old Martha and fourteen-year old Edward. Squinting against the blazing light, Anne stared down the long hedge-trimmed road that connected South Kelsey Hall to the outside world.

In the distance, a lone rider had come into view, riding at a leisurely trot toward the family mansion. Even from this distance, Anne knew it was Francis for she could see the young horseman's curly chestnut-colored hair and well-trimmed beard. *How handsome he is!* Anne thought proudly. *But why does he not ride faster?* she added to herself impatiently. As though able to discern his sister's thoughts from afar, Francis suddenly kicked the sides of his steed, urging it into a gallop. Moments later, he bounded from the red stallion and warmly embraced his father. Even after Sir William released Francis, he continued to slap him heartily on the back as Francis turned to kiss Elizabeth. There was no mistaking the pride the father held for his son and the joy at his return.

"Francis, how we thank God for your safe return," Elizabeth said, returning his kiss.

"As I am thankful to find you all well and happy," Francis replied, grinning widely. "As much as I enjoy my studies, I do miss you all terribly. 'Tis very good to be home again."

Anne waited impatiently as the eldest son greeted his parents for she knew her place; but no sooner had he turned from Elizabeth to face his siblings, she flew at him with open arms. He hugged her tightly a moment, then gently pushed her away from him.

"And who can this pretty young lady be who is so open with her affection?" Francis teased, holding her at arm's length to admire her. "I do not remember seeing such a grown lady on my last visit."

Anne laughed in response; but before she could reply, she was pushed aside as Martha and Jane threw their arms around Francis. The sisters' simultaneous lunge caught Francis off-balance, and he nearly toppled to the ground before he regained his footing. Laughing, he returned their embraces and kisses.

"What man ever had such a warm reception? So many pretty ladies! I shall be the envy of every man at court!"

Sir William stepped forward to rescue his son from the enthusiasm of his sisters. "Enough! Enough! Will you injure the poor boy on his first day home?" he exclaimed, though his eyes danced merrily.

"Come, Francis," he continued. "You must be tired from your ride. No doubt, you will want to rest up and then join us for one of Cook's feasts."

Turning momentarily to a male servant, he ordered, "Robert, tend to master Francis' horse. Come now, son. If you tarry much longer, your sisters will have you torn to pieces!"

With his arm draped across his son's shoulders, Sir William escorted Francis into the great hall all the while peppering him with questions concerning his studies and the journey home. Anne followed close behind, anxious to catch every word.

While Francis retired to his bedchambers to freshen up and change clothes, his family busied themselves with menial tasks simply to pass the time until he rejoined them in the large family dining hall. Presently, they were all seated around the massive oak dining table.

"So pray tell us, Francis, what news do you bring from Cambridge?" Sir William asked as soon the blessing had been returned.

"As of late, there has been much news, sir. You remember, of course, Master Thomas Cranmer, under whose teachings I have had the privilege of sitting."

Indeed, Sir William was well acquainted with the Cranmers, though he had little interaction with the actual family as they were of lesser gentry standing. Even so, they were considered decent neighbors, having an estate of their own in south Lincolnshire although moderate in comparison to Sir William's vast holdings. Reports circulated that Thomas Cranmer openly embraced the new Reform theology, which had swept into England more than ten years earlier. Sir William, though not considering himself a Reformist, held sympathies that inclined toward the new ideas; but for the most part, he kept his thoughts confined to his family.

"Although I do not know by what means," Francis continued, "it seems that Master Cranmer has gained favorable attention from king Henry himself. As a result, he was ordered to court to assist His majesty in this matter concerning the Pope. From what I understand, the king has grown quite weary of the length of time 'tis taking for the Pope to consent to his divorce from Queen Catherine, and he is quite anxious to take Lady Anne Boleyn as his wife. Now I have it that His majesty has sent Master Cranmer to Rome to plead the king's case personally before the Pope."

This was news indeed! For Thomas Cranmer to be sent on such a mission clearly demonstrated a high standing with His Grace.

Sir William sighed inwardly, letting his thoughts drift back in time. Years before, he had met the young Spanish queen and had been impressed by her intelligence, but even more so by her gracious demeanor. He could neither understand nor agree with the king's pursuance of a divorce, but wisely he did not voice his opinions openly. He understood the desire, yes, even the king's need for an heir, for he only had to look at his own fine sons and know the blessed security of being assured that his lands were safe for future generations. How much more must the king desire his throne secure! But to callously put away a faithful and pious wife of more than twenty years for the hope of an heir seemed imprudent at best and harsh at worst. But it was not for Sir William to find fault with his sovereign, at least, not outwardly.

"How long has it been since Thomas Cranmer departed?" Sir William asked as he speared another slice of beef from the platter in front of him.

"I do believe he left the end of January, traveling with the Earl of Wiltshire and other members of the embassy to meet with the Pope in Bologna," Francis replied, picking up his wine goblet. He took several gulps, then continued. "From what I have gathered, the earl was not altogether successful and was unable to persuade either the Pope or Charles to change their views on the matter. The earl has since returned to England, but Master Cranmer has traveled on to Rome to press the matter further."

"He is the king's man to be sure," Sir William responded absently, his mind already diverted in other directions.

He glanced down the table at his third son, Edward. Although Edward was only fourteen, Sir William knew the time was right to consider his future. He desired to place Edward in the home of a nobleman who would in time introduce him into the royal court. William's second son, Christopher, had been strategically placed with a noble family not two years before and was doing very well in his learning and advancement. Now it was Edward's turn, and who better than this newly appointed favorite of the king, Thomas Cranmer, to set his son's feet on the path leading to rank and wealth. Yes, he must make inquiries into the matter immediately.

Anne listened to the exchange between her father and Francis with great interest. Although she had just turned eleven, she was an avid reader and eagerly devoured all the books and tracts she could get her hands on. She particularly enjoyed hearing any news of the Reformation movement; and since Francis had begun attending Cambridge and Christopher had been away at Lambeth, the news they brought home was always the latest happenings. Until recent years, her father had been the one who had brought home news of the court; but the last few years saw him more at South Kelsey Hall than Westminster. Now her brothers supplied the family with the intimate details of the royal court and the progress of the Reformation.

"Francis," Anne interjected as the conversation between father and son momentarily lapsed. "What of the Reformers? What news of them?"

Francis smiled at Anne, though he was quick to notice the frown that creased Elizabeth's brow. Of all his sisters, Anne captured his heart the most even though he tried not to show his favoritism. For one so young, she seemed to grasp the impact and importance of this Reformation movement far beyond that of some of his university friends.

Upon arriving at Cambridge, Francis had been quickly swept into the excitement of the new Reform ideas and spent hours with his colleagues debating the writings of Martin Luther and William Tyndale. Many of these debates he carried home with him to share with his family the truth of which he was now convinced. But his arguments found scant fertile soil. His father, though tolerant, saw no real need to change his way of thinking. It was not because he was convinced that the Roman Catholic Church was not in error, but more that he was comfortable with his life and saw little reason to risk all he had accomplished for sake of a principle. In like manner, Elizabeth also preferred to keep these matters private and resisted any attempts by Francis to draw her into such conversation. As for Martha and Jane, they were much more interested in their needlework and poetry than in any spiritual considerations, though they, too, out of respect for their eldest brother listened politely. And Thomas at seven was just too young. But in Edward and Anne, Francis found open hearts and minds. Anne particularly latched onto his words, asking question after question, reading the tracts and books he brought home, and comparing their statements with what she read in the Tyndale's New Testament that her father had secretly secured several years before. Anne, it seemed, had a true heart for God and a thirst to know His truth.

"'Twould seem that the king himself is inclined toward the Reformers," Francis answered with satisfaction. "This matter over his divorce has divided the senate, with those standing for the Pope in open opposition to His Majesty. Although this may serve the Reformers well, no one truly believes that the king is wholly converted to the new way of thinking. At this point, it is more politically expedient for him to agree with the Reformers concerning the authority of the Pope, but he is not yet ready to throw off the other evil practices that corrupt the church."

"Let us not have talk of this now," Sir William interrupted, catching the look of concern in his wife's eyes. "While I do agree that the church has its abuses, you walk on dangerous ground by embracing this New Learning. The Roman Church will not soon, or graciously, release its power to a group it considers a serious threat, and the Pope does regard these Reformists as serious."

9

The young scholar made no reply. His heart and mind were set, but he had neither the desire nor the need to press the issue with his father on his first day home. There would be opportunities later for discussion. Indeed, Francis was grateful to his father for allowing him the freedom to explore these new teachings without fear of condemnation or intolerance. Many of his colleagues at Cambridge did not have such welcome receptions when they journeyed home.

But Francis did not miss the droop in Anne's shoulders when Sir William effectively diverted the conversation. He watched her until she caught his eye. Smiling mischievously, he winked. Anne grinned back. They would talk later, of that she was sure.

The gardens at South Kelsey Hall were a favorite haunt of Anne's, especially in the spring when they delighted her senses with their vivid colors and sweet scents. Along a moss-covered stonewall, a host of fledging primroses, marigolds, columbine, and sweet williams shimmied as the evening May breeze slipped around their leaves. Lying on a blanket spread under a weeping willow, Anne gazed at the bobbing flowers as her mind wandered into a lovely daydream. Dancing, laughing, flirting, Anne was the delight of the court. Eager and handsome young men surrounded her, each declaring his undying love. But she would have none of them, until…

"Anne, where are you?" a familiar male voice teased gently.

Jolted back to the present, she looked up to find Francis grinning down at her.

"By that faraway look in your eyes, you are not at South Kelsey Hall, at least, not in your thoughts," he laughed and settled himself beside her on the blanket. He stretched his long legs out before him and leaned back, propping himself up on one elbow. She rose to a sitting position.

"Someday, I shall be a great lady of the court," she confided. "And I will have a hundred handsome suitors vying for my hand in marriage, but I will hold them all at bay until I meet the perfect one."

"And how will you know when you meet him?"

"Simple, he shall be just like you!" Anne declared. She saw the laughter in his eyes and impulsively bent forward and kissed his forehead. A lock of his dark curly hair tickled her nose, and she giggled.

"I hope for your sake you marry a man far superior to me, but I am honored by your regard." Francis replied and reached behind him. "For now, I will accept your admiration for what it is though I may become quite jealous in years to come when these one hundred suitors come calling."

He grinned and from the waistband at his back he pulled a rather worn booklet.

"'Tis not a new copy, but these are hard to come by so I take what I can get," he said as he handed the book to her. "A belated birthday present."

Anne took the book and turned it around to read its cover: *The Babylonian Captivity*, Martin Luther.

"Oh, Francis! I have wanted so to read this! I have heard you and Christopher talk about it, but I never thought I would have the chance to read it for myself. You are so good to me, dear brother."

"I know you will have it devoured before the sun sets," he teased. "But perhaps 'twill be worth one evening's amusement. In any case, read it and enjoy." Francis hesitated, then added, "It may be best not to show this to the others, except perhaps Edward. Father is tolerant to be sure, but even he has his limits; and I do believe this particular work of Luther's would not be welcome."

Anne nodded in agreement. Certainly, she felt fortunate to have a father who not only allowed his daughters to be well educated, but encouraged their learning as well. Many of his contemporaries held firmly to the belief that young women needed to know little beyond the skills necessary to the running of a household, and even Elizabeth voiced concerns that he was too liberal in his encouragement of his daughters' education; but Sir William believed strongly that women should be well versed in the academic skills in addition to those required to serve as an efficient wife. Because of this, Anne had learned to read not only in English and French, but also in Latin and had become quite proficient in mathematics and sciences. But she understood the concern Francis voiced. Sir William was open to the New Learning in so far as it did not require a change in him, for he had grown too comfortable with his life to risk stepping over the line—and *The Babylonian Captivity* certainly stepped over the line in its devastating attack on all that the Roman Catholic Church held sacred.

"I shan't breathe a word of this to anyone," she promised, gently caressing the worn cover. She smiled at Francis, but her smile quickly turned to puzzlement at the look of concern on her brother's face.

"What is it, Francis? Do you fear I will break my promise?"

"No, dearest. I know I can trust you completely. I, that is…" He fumbled a moment, then went on. "I am concerned about another matter altogether."

He stopped to collect his thoughts. Then taking a deep breath, he plunged ahead. "Anne, you have read all the Reformist literature I have brought home, and I know you think about these things in light of their impact on society and the church, but what of you, dearest? What does it mean to you?"

Anne wasn't sure she understood what he was asking, so she simply looked at him hoping he would explain. Francis obliged.

"Everything that the Reformists teach shall have a great impact on history, but only as it changes individual lives. A person may read all he wishes and gain great knowledge, but if his heart is unaffected, it remains as naught. Truth is not meant for the mind only, but for the heart and soul of a man. And 'tis only in the heart that one can truly lay hold of God's greatest truth—salvation by grace through faith alone."

Francis grasped Anne's small hand. "Anne, do you know this in your heart? Have you trusted in the atoning work of Christ alone for your salvation or do you seek some other means to merit God's favor? These are the questions that must be answered. And you alone before God must answer them."

Anne remained silent. She wanted to answer him, but had no assurance within herself that her words would be true. Up to this point, she had never truly considered her own standing before God; and now she found that she was uncomfortable in doing so. Francis sensed her discomfort, but wisely did not press her further. God must do the work of conviction Himself, and Francis must trust Him to do so. He released Anne's hand. Standing, he smiled down on her, then quietly walked away.

The sun inched its way across the cloudless sky, and the early evening shadows began to lengthen. Still, Anne sat under the willow, gazing out across the rolling hills surrounding South Kelsey Hall. In her mind, she recounted over and over the things she had read about justification through faith, full atonement through the Lord's death on the cross, and the open access every believer has to God. These ideas—so different from what the priests taught—had excited and stimulated her mind as she read them, but she had never seriously considered how they affected her personally. Now, she was forced to examine her own heart. Had she, eleven-year-old Anne Askew, ever taken the step of faith? Had she trusted in Christ alone or did her hopes remain in her own good works? Had she the assurance of salvation upon her death? Anne did not like the answers that swirled in her head. Nor did she like the coldness that gripped her chest as the sun continued its waning journey.

A moment is all that is necessary for a sinner to repent and enter the kingdom of God; and for Anne, this moment would be forever etched in her mind and heart. She did not fully understand all that God had promised, but in that transforming moment, she understood that she wanted all that He freely offered. She also understood that it could be hers only through faith. Clasping her hands together, she bowed her head. Her prayer was simple; her heart sincere. The sun set, but Anne Askew rose up a new creature in Christ.

Chapter II

Summer of 1536

Anne Boleyn was dead—executed by order of the man who broke with Rome to win her hand. Having failed to produce the all-important male heir, the young outspoken queen was discarded like a worn out garment; and a new queen took her place. Jane Seymour now reigned at court, and all England hoped and prayed that this queen would soon give their sovereign the long-awaited son.

Sixteen-year-old Anne Askew prayed as well, but her prayers inclined more toward the salvation of her monarch than for the birth of a son. Through her brothers, she had learned of Hugh Latimer's bold preaching at court and prayed that his words would find their way into the king's heart. But as time passed, Henry VIII displayed more antagonism toward the Reformation than sympathy; and many godly men and women lost their lives rather than renounce their faith.

Yet the Reformists remained hopefully optimistic even though a growing hostility between the evangelicals and those loyal to the Roman Church threatened every English town and shire. The death of queen Anne had encouraged Pope Paul III to believe that reconciliation with England was not only feasible, but also very likely. But Henry had no intention of relinquishing his newly acquired power; and Parliament, wishing to align itself fully with the king, passed a bill proclaiming that heavy penalties would be inflicted on anyone who upheld the authority of the Pope. While those in sympathy with the Reformation were ecstatic over this proclamation, those who held to the authority of the Roman Catholic Church were greatly alarmed.

And as if to further fear and speculation, Thomas Cromwell, acting under the king's orders, sent royal commissioners throughout England to assess the wealth of the Roman Church for purposes of taxation. Having witnessed first hand the luxury in which many monks and priests lived, Henry determined to acquire some of that wealth to replenish the government coffers. To accomplish this end, Cromwell required the local gentry to assess the income of each parish and to make recommendations as to which churches should be shut down and their wealth transferred. This mandate placed the gentry in the very unfavorable position of effecting a policy that was quite unpopular among the people. To make matters worse, as a result of the assessment, monasteries and abbeys in every part of England were seized, their wealth carried off, and their doors closed; and monks and priests found themselves in the desperate circumstance of being turned out with no where to go. Although many were secretly sympathetic to the plight of the monks, both the gentry and the peasantry saw little recourse to help and could only watch and wonder what their king would do next. Tension mounted throughout the country as wild rumors and speculations ran rampant.

By September, tensions in Lincolnshire had risen to fever pitch. In every tavern and wayside inn, heated conversations decried the king's taxation policy and fear spread that every church and abbey within the shire would soon go the way of others and be despoiled. The ones who stood to lose the most, spoke the loudest; and the people responded to their parish priests first with sympathy, then in outright indignation. Encouraged by the response, the priests continued to incite the people against the crown, and a peasant solidarity began to form. From village to village, frightened and angry people came together to voice their fears and take their stand.

The hour was late on October 2 when Sir William entered the front room of South Kelsey Hall and tossed his rain-drenched cloak to a servant. He stomped his feet to shake the remaining droplets from his clothing then strode across the hall and into the downstairs parlor to warm his tall, stalwart frame in front of the roaring fireplace. Elizabeth, who always waited up for her husband's return, looked up from her needlework when he entered, but said nothing, preferring instead for him to initiate the conversation.

Much to his distaste, Sir William Askew found himself among the unfortunate gentry who were tasked with assessing the churches in Lincolnshire. The job had been unsettling at best and downright disagreeable at worst. Sir William did not wish to make recommendations to Cromwell concerning the local churches even if he did agree that excesses were common. But he had known and lived among these people all his life; they were not faceless masses in opposition to the king, they were his neighbors. And now, he realized that their pent up anger was beginning to fester.

"There has been some trouble in Louth," he began, trying to maintain a casual air. When Elizabeth did not respond, he continued. "From what I have gathered, the people have armed themselves and taken the king's commissioner prisoner. They have also imprisoned all his aides and publicly burned the king's injunctions as a show of their displeasure over the tax."

Elizabeth rose and went to stand beside her husband, consternation in her eyes. When he saw her fear, he smiled wanly and patted her arm.

"No need to be alarmed, my dear. I am sure such a reprehensible offense will soon be contained and forgotten, and things are relatively quiet here."

"But I have heard rumors of such talk here as well, and there are many in Lindsey County who resent his Majesty's invasion of the churches. Do you think they will remain passive when they hear of this uprising in Louth?"

"I would hardly call it an uprising, Elizabeth. They have demonstrated their grievances to be sure, but 'tis a small matter that the king will soon put to right. 'Tis very likely, 'twill go no farther then Louth, and it certainly will not come this far north." Sir William said, hoping silently that his words of comfort to Elizabeth would prove true.

"In light of these events, will you still meet with the other commissioners at Caistor to collect the tax?" she asked.

"Of course. I see no reason to allow the insanity of some to govern the actions of all. But I have sent messages to the others

suggesting that it might be prudent to meet earlier than originally planned. I have also suggested a meeting place outside of
Caistor."

Seeing new alarm in his wife's eyes, he quickly added, "'Tis
merely a precautionary measure, my dear. Once we assess the
situation, we will know better how to proceed; but I have seen no
indication that anyone in the neighboring wapentakes are
inclined to rebellion."

He smiled again to reassure her, but saw it had no effect. Elizabeth Askew had suffered the loss of one husband, and her anxious heart feared the loss of another. She slept very little that
night.

October 3, 1536

Anne awoke early the next morning, as was her custom, to
read her Bible and to pray. Preferring the morning light for reading as opposed to candlelight, she enjoyed sitting in her bedroom
window seat that overlooked the front lawn and the long drive
of the great manor that stretched away from the house toward
the town. Because her bedroom faced east, she would oftentimes
gaze serenely toward the rising sun as it glided over the horizon,
dispersing the night's shadows and coloring the Lincolnshire
countryside in hues of soft pink and orange.

But this morning, no soft colors arose to greet her. Instead, a
dark, dreary fog shrouded the land, refusing to relinquish its
hold. Even the sun's brilliance could not pierce it through, and
Anne was forced to light a candle. She sighed as she peered
through the leaded-glass pane. Feeling the chill autumn air
seeping through the window's frame, she gathered her woolen
wrap more snugly about her and settled herself comfortably on
the cushions beneath the window. Opening her Bible, she began
to read, but a movement from below distracted her.

She leaned forward for a better look. From her vantage point,
she saw Robert, a servant from the stables, leading her father's
large black gelding to the front lawn. Then she saw her father

emerge from the house, Elizabeth close behind. The couple stood a moment, exchanging quiet words; then, in an unusual display of affection, Elizabeth reached up and wrapped her arms around Sir William's neck. They embraced, and it seemed to Anne that they clung to each other longer than what society would deem appropriate. Then disengaging himself, Sir William quickly turned, mounted his horse, and galloped off into the morning mist. Elizabeth watched him disappear into the haze, but still she stood staring into the bleak fog. Finally, she turned and reentered the house.

For reasons she could not explain, the scene she witnessed below her window unsettled Anne's heart. She did not know where her father was off to so early, but it was clear from the look on Elizabeth's face that her stepmother did not want him to go. In vain, Anne sought to dismiss the anxious feelings and return to her reading, but feelings of foreboding invaded her heart and would not relent.

"Gracious Lord, help me," she whispered. Even before the prayer was off her tongue, a verse sprang to mind.

Be anxious for nothing; but in everything by prayer and supplication with thanksgiving let your requests be made known unto God. And the peace of God, which passes all understanding, shall keep your hearts and minds through Christ Jesus.[3]

Anne slipped off the cushions, knelt beside the window, and prayed the first of many earnest prayers that she would offer up on her father's behalf over the next ten days.

The morning mist still clung to the Lincolnshire countryside when Sir William along with Thomas Moigne, his stepson-in-law, arrived at the appointed meeting place. In a meadow below the west side of Caistor Hill, Thomas Heneage of Hainton and Sir Edward Madison, a remarkably feisty 82-year old, met them as they rode up. The new arrivals dismounted, shook hands, and exchanged pleasantries as they awaited the remaining commissioners. The pounding of horses' hooves heralded their arrival, but several moments passed before the shadowy figures of Lord Burgh, William Dalyson, William Booth, Thomas Partington, and Sir Robert Tyrrwhit emerged from the dense fog, followed by a number of servants. The newcomers appeared anxious; and their uneasiness, like the mist and dampness, settled over the entire group. As their horses cropped the grass, the gentlemen of Lindsey County huddled together to hear the latest news.

"The reports of looting and violence are unfounded," Thomas Heneage began. He had ridden up from Hainton, only a few miles from the center of the disturbance. "However, I did hear they have chosen a man by the name of Nicholas Melton to lead the rabble. To what end, I do not know."

Lord Burgh, a heavy-set, red-faced man spoke. "What is happening in Louth is not our concern at this moment, but rather what is happening in Caistor. What news of there?"

"As of last evening all was quiet, but Lord Burgh is right," Sir William replied. "We should send several men into Caistor to find out what is happening this morning, if indeed, there is anything."

The others agreed, and four servants were dispatched to gather what news they could. The men who remained behind exchanged little conversation as they awaited the return of the messengers. The mist hung on, draping the huddled forms in disquietude. Each hoped for the best, but secretly feared the worst. At the sound of approaching horses' hooves, the men arose and stood expectantly. The servants had returned.

"What news, man?" Sir Edward demanded as one servant hastily dismounted.

Nicholas, a slightly built, slender man in the service of Lord Burgh, hurried forward. Dropping to one knee, he announced, "Milords, all is quiet. We were able to find and meet with the wapentake representatives. Even now, they await your coming to render their taxes as they have been so ordered."

A simultaneous sigh of relief escaped from the commissioners. Hastening to their own horses, they mounted and turned north to ride toward Caistor as the mist finally began to dissipate. But as they reached the top of Caistor Hill, a lone rider galloped toward them from the south, intercepting their path. It was obvious that horse and rider had ridden hard, for the horse was greatly lathered. The disheveled man reined in his steed as he came along side the group. Thomas Heneage immediately recognized him as a servant from his own household.

"Arthur! What is it, man?" he asked, sidling up to the servant's horse. The man seemed ready to topple to the ground, and Thomas quickly reached out a hand to steady him.

"Milord, they are coming this way! Thousands of them!" he answered breathlessly, grasping the outstretched arm that steadied him.

"Who is coming?" demanded Sir William.

"Farmers, peasants, priests... all of them from Louth. They are marching to Caistor across the wolds. Even now, they are only a few miles behind me!"

Instinctively, each man glanced toward the southeast as though he expected to see the great horde appear at that very moment on a distant hill. Then, a startled cry from Nicholas made the gentlemen glance backwards toward the town. Immediately, they realized that their most pressing worry lay in quite another direction. Nicholas, noticing first the flurry of activity, called it to the others' attention. As the fog dispersed, the town of Caistor became clearly visible from the top of Caistor Hill. Word of the marching rebels must have reached the townspeople as well for they poured forth onto a grassy knoll on the southern side of the town to welcome the Louth dissenters.

Alarmed at the sight of the people rallying, the gentlemen exchanged anxious glances and began to debate amongst themselves their best course of action.

"We must leave now!" Sir Robert insisted. "What can we do against so many?"

"Sir Robert is right," Thomas Partington concurred. "We must return to our homes immediately."

Others nodded in agreement, but Sir William hesitated. He hated the idea of being frightened off by mere commoners, no matter how large their number. But just as he was about to speak, William Dalyson spoke out.

"Gentlemen, if we retreat without so much as addressing the people of Caistor, 'twould appear as though we support, even encourage this rebellion. 'Twould serve us better to ride on to Caistor and persuade the people to disperse before the rebels from Louth arrive."

"But as they know we are coming to collect the tax," Sir Robert interrupted, "we will not be a welcomed party."

"Perhaps 'tis as you say, but if we tell them that we have decided to postpone the collection of the tax for the time being until we have had further opportunity to examine their grievances, they may listen," Dalyson countered.

"Maybe they will and maybe they will not, but I, for one, am not inclined to place myself in the midst of an angry mob," Sir Robert retorted.

Sir William could remain quiet no longer. "My friends," he interjected. "We are men of valor and have a sacred duty to our king. We must show these commoners that our authority cannot be undermined so easily; otherwise, all is lost before it is even begun."

A murmur of assent rippled through the group, but still no one moved. Finally, William Dalyson offered a solution. "Let us send a servant back to Caistor and have him summon the town leaders to us. We can speak to them here where we have a good view of the surrounding countryside. In doing so, we protect ourselves and fulfill our duty."

Everyone agreed that this was the best suggestion, and the hapless Nicholas was once again dispatched to the town. To shield themselves from view, the men turned their horses and descended the southern slope of the hill a short distance. From this position, they could still survey the distant hills, but they themselves were not as vulnerable. They once again dismounted and began their impatient wait, casting anxious glances across the southern heath, fearing the imminent arrival of the Louth mob.

Three-quarters of an hour passed before Nicholas finally returned—alone. The men descended on him, demanding to know where the townsmen were.

"Milords," he pleaded. "By my faith, I argued with them for nigh onto a half hour that they must come out to meet you, but they would not. They said if milords have something to say, then you must come to them."

Such effrontery incensed the gentlemen, and several muttered oaths under their breath; but their anger soon gave way to concern when Thomas Moigne made apparent to the unsettled commissioners the greater dilemma they each faced. Only two options lay before them: they could either ride into Caistor to perform their appointed duty and risk their safety in the hands of an unpredictable crowd, or they could make a hasty retreat to their homes and expose themselves as cowards. Neither option was appealing, and the debate was rekindled.

Heated words flew between them, and they were not even close to a consensus when horsemen appeared at the top of Caistor Hill, effectively ceasing their discussion. The startled gentlemen turned to face the one hundred horsemen from Caistor as they descended the hill toward them. The commissioners eyed them warily, searching for signs of hostility. Somber faces stared back at them. When the group drew near, a burly, dark-haired man with a scraggly beard dismounted and approached.

"Milords," he said, bowing low before them. "I am your most humble servant, George Hudswell, as well as the appointed leader of these worthy men." He waved his hand, indicating the men on horseback behind him. "We beg your lordships' pardon as we have realized that we were too hasty in our decision to disregard a meeting between us and your esteemed persons."

Encouraged by these words, Thomas Moigne stepped forward.

"Neither I nor these kindly gentlemen desire trouble," he declared. "We are here only as servants of our most gracious king to carry out his majesty's orders. However, we do not lack compassion for the grievances you may have concerning this subsidy. Therefore, we have chosen to postpone collection of the tax until such time as we can ascertain the validity of your concerns."

A murmur of approval arose from the Caistor men, and they nodded to each other in agreement.

Emboldened by the response, Thomas continued talking as quickly as the words would tumble out. "Notwithstanding, in light of your king's most gracious and favorable goodness, it has been reported to us that a number of people from Louth have unlawfully assembled themselves together; to what end, we do not know. But we can assure each man here that the rumors to which you have given ear are unfounded. There are to be no harsh taxes levied; and, even that which has been required of your parish, you will be given the opportunity to appeal. As to your fear that your churches will be destroyed or seized, you may be assured that His Grace would not approve such an offensive act. As he is the Supreme Head of the Church, would he then on his honor see that the same Church be destroyed? I do implore you, friends, disperse yourselves so that you will not come under the king's displeasure!"

As Thomas spoke, the other commissioners watched in hope for signs that his words were being well received. Indeed, the grave demeanor of the Caistor men seemed softened; and after only a few moments of whispered exchanges, George Hudswell spoke.

"Very well, we accept your words in good faith." The other men nodded in agreement and turned their horses back toward town. Visibly relieved, the commissioners mounted their own horses.

Suddenly, the clanging of church bells from Caistor shattered the air! As though summoned by the ringing bells, more horsemen appeared at the top of Caistor Hill. The commissioners froze. Even from a distance, the gentlemen realized these new arrivals had to be from Louth, and the pealing church bells were urging the people to join the rebellion. Leaving the Lindsey men behind, the townsmen urged their horses up the hill to meet the Louth delegation. For the gentlemen, momentary alarm gave way to frantic plans as each man leapt into his saddle. William Dalyson was dispatched to find Lord Hussey, the Lord Lieutenant, and beseech his help. A meeting place was decided. Spurs were set to horses, and the commissioners fled in every direction.

Sir William sped westward toward the strong refuge of South Kelsey Hall. Following close behind him rode Sir Edward, William Booth, and a large number of servants. Even Nicholas had abandoned his master, Lord Burgh, preferring to take his chances with Sir William's group.

From their vantage point on Caistor Hill, the Louth leaders watched with contempt the fleeing commissioners. A pale-faced man sporting a scraggly beard spat out orders, and horsemen charged forward. Sir William's party was by far the largest, so it was after them that the greatest number of rebels gave chase.

Sir William never glanced behind, but kept his eyes firmly fixed on the road that led to South Kelsey Hall—and Elizabeth. He did not see the Louth horsemen fast approaching from the rear, nor did he see the furtive hand signals that passed between riders, but he did see the chestnut gelding that suddenly cut across his path, forcing him to abruptly rein in his horse to avoid colliding with the reckless rider. He yanked the reins to the left to charge around the man, only to be blocked by another rider. Angered and momentarily confused, Sir William turned his horse back. The sight that confronted him sickened him. Their own servants surrounded the commissioners' horses, forcing them to a halt. Nicholas, chafed by the unsavory tasks he had that morning been forced to carry out and emboldened by the rebels' strength, had incited the others to surrender the lords into the hands of the Louth guard. Despairing, Sir William saw there was no recourse but to wait for the rebel guard to approach.

Chapter III

Nicholas smiled triumphantly as the commissioners under guard were escorted back to Caistor Hill. Surely, he would be rewarded for his part in the capture of the august Sir William. By the time the group reached the top of the hill, the entire Louth procession had arrived; and men from Caistor and the surrounding countryside had added to their already massive number. They swarmed over the land, chanting slogans and encouraging each other in their unified cause. The men on the top of Caistor Hill numbered approximately two hundred, the elite of the rebel throng. As the lords approached, shouts and cheers erupted. The jubilant rebels parted and shoved forward two other very frightened men—Sir Robert and Thomas Partington, also thwarted in their attempt to flee.

"But what of the others? Where is Lord Burgh?" demanded a man standing guard over Sir Robert and Thomas with nothing more than a stout walking stick.

Angry voices echoed the question and clamored for an answer. Fists raised, the unruly crowd pressed in, demanding to know why all the gentlemen had not been brought back. How could they be allowed to escape? The sudden change in the mob's demeanor terrified the gentlemen, but by sheer force of will, they managed to maintain their outward composure.

Weeks of fiery rhetoric and pent up frustration had stripped the otherwise peaceable individuals of reasonable emotions. Now, pressed by their fear and unified under what they deemed a just cause, the crowd fomented rebellion. An accusing voice rose above the din and a finger pointed to the captured horsemen.

"That one! He is a servant of Lord Burgh! He helped him escape!" All eyes turned toward a startled Nicholas.

Hungry for first blood, they surged forward as one unyielding force. Terrified by the sea of bloodthirsty faces, Nicholas reined his horse to turn, but the rebels swarmed around him. Clinging with all his strength to his horse's mane, Nicholas shouted his innocence, but his cries were drowned in the raucous fray. Several large hands grabbed his clothing and arm and yanked him from his perch. He sank helplessly to the ground. A momentary opening in the crowd exposed the little man, eyes wide with terror, pleading for his life; then just as quickly, the gap closed. The enraged mob descended on its chosen victim. Shrieks, dull thuds, then silence.

Their wrath expended, the crowd fell back. Nicholas' lifeless form lay huddled in fetal position at his accusers' feet. His mouth gaped in a silent scream; his lifeless eyes frozen in terror. Blood trickled from his ear and nose. The rebels stared stupidly at the bludgeoned body as if they were wondering from where he had come and what he was doing lying on the ground. But there was no sign of remorse, no condemnation. Then, without uttering a word, two men bent down, picked up the broken body of the little man, and carried him off. The others stepped aside to make way, but none spoke, none felt shame.

Sir William, horrified by the brutality, stared numbly. *Is this to be the fate of each of us?* he thought. *Has every man gone mad?* His numbness gave way to anger, and he turned abruptly to William Morland, a dispossessed monk and the appointed spokesman for the Louth rebels.

"What do want of us?" he demanded.

William Morland trembled inwardly when he saw the angry flash in Sir William's eyes. Unaccustomed to speaking to such a revered man, he was quite uncomfortable at being cast in the role of rebel spokesman. Mustering what little courage he had, he addressed the stately figure before him with all the respect deserving the man's title.

"Milord, before we present our requests, we must first be assured of your fidelity. Each of you must be sworn before this assembly."

A Bible appeared, and a priest stepped forward. Surrounded by such a crowd, the gentlemen, though angered by the request, had little recourse but to swear an oath of allegiance to God, the king, and the commoners. Swearing allegiance to God and king did not trouble Sir William, but he hesitated on the word *commoners*. Fortunately, his hesitation went unnoticed; and when all had been sworn, William Morland unrolled a parchment and proceeded to list the demands of the Louth commoners. Clearing his throat, the monk began reading in a loud voice so that as many as possible could hear.

>*"We, the true and faithful servants of His Most Esteemed Majesty, Henry VIII, grant that the king might enjoy the title of Supreme Head of the English Church and that the Church shall remain severed from the Holy Church of Rome, but His Majesty must promise not to seize or despoil any more of the religious houses.*

>*"We grant that the king might have the tax voted in by Parliament and may collect the ecclesiastical revenues rightly due him, but he must not tax the people further.*

>*"Furthermore, the king must renounce and hand over to the commoners, his evil and heretical advisers, namely Thomas Cromwell; Thomas Cranmer; John Longland, Bishop of Lincoln; John Hilsey, Bishop of Rochester; Thomas Goodrich, Bishop of Ely; Hugh Latimer, Bishop of Worcester; and John Browne, Bishop of Dublin."*

When he had finished, Morland rolled up the parchment and handed it to a tall, surly man beside him now identified as Nicholas Melton, the rebel leader nicknamed "Captain Cobbler." Once again, the monk addressed Sir William.

"As you can see, milord, our demands are simple." He smiled. "We seek only that which is honorable and just."

Sir William might have agreed with him were it not for the last demand. He recognized the names of the "heretical advisers," several of whom were leaders in the Reform movement as well as being his friends. With the image of Nicholas' broken and bleeding body still fresh in his mind, he trembled to think what the fate of these men would be if the rebels' last demand were met; and his anger burned more deeply at the idea that this rabble had the audacity to make demands of the king. Yet, whatever he felt inwardly, he was wise enough not to betray it outwardly.

"Those are your demands," he responded. "Pray, what have they to do with us?"

"Surely, you must realize that his Grace, the king, would never entertain a petition from lowly men such as ourselves although we are as loyal as any of his subjects. Therefore, we require you and these other gentlemen to present them to his Majesty on our behalf."

"Us?" Sir Robert exploded. "You want *us* to present these treasonous demands to the king?"

"You have sworn allegiance to the commoners!" Morland shot back. "You either stand with us or die."

Sir Robert started to reply, but Sir William interrupted. "Allow us a moment of privacy, sir," he said to Morland as he pulled Sir Robert back from the confrontation. Wrapping his arm about Sir Robert's shoulder, Sir William directed the man several paces away from rebel mob. Sir Edward, Thomas, and William Booth joined the two men, heads and voices lowered.

"'Twill serve no purpose to defy them!" Sir William hissed. "We are only five against thousands. Time is our only hope. Perhaps Dalyson or Moigne got through. We may even hope that Lord Burgh was able to send a message on our behalf. If we are patient, the king will come to our aid; or this rabble will disperse when hunger and discord have their way with them."

The others agreed, although Sir Robert did so reluctantly. As they turned again to face their captors, Morland stepped toward them.

"We have decided to return to Louth," Morland informed them, "and make our headquarters there. You gentlemen will kindly accompany us to a place we have made ready for you."

The gentlemen could only oblige, though inwardly they chafed at the servile civility. Mounting their horses, the party set off toward Louth. As the October sun passed its zenith, lengthening shadows stretched across the landscape, appearing to Sir William as grasping fingers, reaching out to seize him and hold him against his will.

As they rode, Sir William thought of Elizabeth and his children. Would he ever see them again? A sharp pain stabbed at his heart as he remembered the anxious face of Elizabeth at their parting. Then one by one, the images of his offspring paraded through his mind's eyes: Francis, a strong, resolute young man; Christopher, earnest and intelligent; Martha, quiet and reserved; Edward, serious and determined; Jane, whimsical and shy; Thomas, his youngest and his only child by Elizabeth; and Anne... his beautiful Anne, headstrong, vivacious, witty, and more intelligent than any woman ought to be! Despite the wearisome journey on which he now found himself, a smile played at his lips as he recalled the lively, and sometimes heated, discussions he had with his Anne. Indeed, she was strong in her religious convictions, much like Francis, but obstinate as well, refusing to give ground on any of her opinions. Yet, whatever annoyance she may provoke in him, she need only flash her winsome smile and all his irritation would immediately dissolve so that he quite forgot what caused the irritation in the first place.

Thinking of her tenacious faith, Sir William whispered to himself, "Pray for me now, Anne dearest."

Anne stared out the same window from which she had watched her father disappear into the early morning mist so many long hours ago. Now, a sickle moon bathed her face in its pale light as her eyes searched the hills, but her father did not return. Francis had sent out messengers to try and determine the fate of his father and the men with him, but no news had come back. Elizabeth, inconsolable, hid herself behind her bedchamber door.

A quiet knock at the door distracted Anne from her vigil. "Yes?" she answered.

Jane's head peeped around the doorframe. "May I come in?" she asked timidly.

"Of course, dearest. You are always welcome."

The door flew open and Jane ran across the room and sank down at Anne's feet. Suddenly, sobs burst forth from the young girl, and she buried her face in Anne's soft woolen skirt.

"Oh, dearest, you mustn't cry so!" Anne said, bending her head toward the one in her lap. She gently stroked the honey-colored hair. "Father will be home before you know it."

"I... I cannot help it, Anne," Jane choked out the words. "I... am not as strong as you. I greatly fear for Father. What... what if we never see him again?" She turned her tear-streaked face up toward her elder sister, seeking the strength she lacked.

Seeing the genuine fear in Jane's eyes broke Anne's heart. She wanted to assure her that all would be well, but she could not make promises of a future she could neither foresee nor control. Instead, she just continued stroking her hair and replied, "God will take care of him, sweet one. We must trust Him to do so."

Jane laid her head back on Anne's lap. She did not have the faith of her sister, but was comforted in knowing that Anne's faith was strong enough for the both of them. For her part, Anne prayed that she would hold true to the counsel she had just given.

By the time the rebels reached Louth, the day's events had taken their toll. Weary to the bone, the gentlemen longed for nothing more than a hearty meal, a glass of very old wine, and a comfortable bed. The first two were served promptly upon their arrival at the home of Guy Kyme, a wealthy local merchant who felt extremely honored to host the esteemed party. But as for the comfort of a bed, that they were to be denied until they had attended to a matter deemed urgent by William Morland and Captain Cobbler. At the insistence of their captors, the gentlemen were tasked with composing a letter to the king that outlined the rebels' demands. All protests from the weary gentlemen fell on deaf ears; and parchment, quill, and ink were produced. Resigned, the men set to the task with little enthusiasm. Perhaps due to the lateness of the hour or their strong natures, several hours passed and many drafts were written and discarded before a final letter agreeable to all was signed. It read thus:

> *If it please your Highness, those whose names are signed below wish to make known unto your Grace the events that have transpired this third day of October as we, under the direction of your most gracious commission to collect the subsidy granted by Act of Parliament, assembled together at the town of Caistor within your county of Lincoln to accomplish the same. There were assembled at the time of our coming no less than two thousand of your true and faithful subjects. Their reason for gathering, as they affirmed unto us, was to make known unto you that all the jewels and goods from their churches have been taken from them and brought to your Grace's council and also that they, your loving and faithful subjects, have been charged with new taxes, which they in their extreme poverty are unable to bear. Concerning these matters, they did swear us first to be true to your Grace and to bear with them in maintaining the commonwealth. Thus, they have conveyed us from Caistor unto the town of Louth, twelve miles distance, where we yet remain until they know further of your gracious pleasure. We humbly beseech your Grace to be gracious both to them and to us and send us your gracious letter of general pardon; otherwise, we shall be in grave danger of never again seeing your Grace or our own homes. We beseech you to give credence to the bearer of this letter who has witnessed these things and can attest to their veracity. Furthermore, your devoted subjects desire us to write to your Grace that they be yours – bodies, land, and goods – at all times wherein your Grace shall command for the defense of your person and realm.*

> *Robert Tyrrwhit   WilliamAskew*
> *Edward Madison   Thomas Partington*

Sir William handed the letter to Morland, who read it and handed it on to Captain Cobbler. Satisfied, the captain turned to a nearby guard.

"Bring John Heneage here," he barked to the man, who immediately scurried from the room. Within a few minutes, he reappeared, shoving a disheveled and angry man before him. The man's hands were tightly bound in front of him, and his face showed several days' growth of beard. He scowled at Captain Cobbler when he entered the room, but said nothing. The rebel leader took notice of the scowl, but his newly acquired power gave him a confidence he would not have dared display previously before a commissioner of the king.

"Untie him," the captain said. The guard drew a knife and sliced through the tightly knotted rope. Without thinking, John rubbed his wrists where the rope had chafed him, but kept his unrelenting glare fastened on the cocky leader.

Unperturbed by the obvious disdain, the captain continued, his voice heavy with sarcasm. "Milord, may I have the honor of introducing some of your fellow commissioners? Sir Robert Tyrrwhit, Sir William Askew, Sir Edward Madison, Thomas Partington, and William Booth. Gentlemen, John Heneage."

Obviously, John Heneage had not been accorded the same preferential treatment the newly arrived commissioners had been. His once fine clothes were torn and spattered with mud, and his haggard face spoke of little sleep. Still, he carried himself as a gentleman and bowed low before the lords presented to him.

"I am honored, milords. I only wish our meeting could have been under more agreeable circumstances."

"And I truly wish there was time to become better acquainted," Captain Cobbler mocked, enjoying the control he held over his captives. "But you were not brought here to socialize. Rather, you were brought here to do my bidding."

The impudence of this man! Sir William thought hotly. *I only hope I live to see him hanged for this!*

"You will ride tonight for London to deliver this letter to the king," the captain remarked casually, handing the rolled up parchment to John. "And to make sure you fulfill your duty faithfully, I am sending Sir Edward with you."

The startled gentlemen rose in simultaneous protests. In immediate response, the guards stepped forward, their hands gripping their swords. Sir Edward alone remained seated, too stunned to rise.

"Are you mad!" Sir Robert cried, his eyes glaring in hatred. "None of us has the strength to make the ride to London tonight, but this man least of all. He has passed his 80th year!"

Captain Cobbler was unconcerned. Rather, his hardened face appeared somewhat amused by the whole affair. "For your own well being, you had best pray that he does make it. Master Heneage may be one of the king's commissioners, but Sir Edward has the title that will afford him access to the king."

"If that is what you want, send me," Sir William proposed. "I have served many years in His Majesty's court; and my son, Christopher, is a Gentleman of the Privy Chamber. I shall have the king's ear."

"'Tis as you say, Sir William, which is why it is more important that you remain here. I daresay your good standing with the king will work to our favor. I could believe that he would not wish to lose so loyal a subject."

Then you do not know the king well, Sir William thought sadly. He had been at court long enough to understand that the king may regard a man highly one day and cast him out the next. Cardinal Wolsey, among others, had been proof of that. The king used men—and women—to his advantage. When they no longer served his purposes, they were removed. And the king's conscience was never bothered.

The others again raised their voices in protest, but by now, Captain Cobbler had tired of the discussion. His patience had worn thin.

"Enough of this!" he snapped. "My mind is set. Either Sir Edward goes, or you shall each die this very night!" He then dismissed them as though they were subordinates and ushered John and Sir Edward toward waiting horses.

Through an open window, Sir William looked on as Sir Edward mounted. Although the man had to be exhausted, he still sat tall and dignified in the saddle. Sir William's admiration toward his old friend deepened as he watched them ride away. *Truly, a worthy gentlemen*, he thought.

Early Evening, October 4, 1536

The lone rider sped northward in the evening twilight, the sun making its final descent below the hills. The pounding of his horse's hooves reverberated, and he glanced nervously behind him as the comfort of daylight ebbed away. The urgency of his mission and the promise that just a few more miles lay between him and safety enabled him to stay his course; but as he approached a copse, an acute sense of danger gripped his heart. He urged his horse to quicken its pace.

Then in the gathering dusk, he saw them, shadowy figures of horsemen emerging from behind the trees. Sudden panic jolted through him, and he yanked the bit to the left to head his horse off the road across a clearing. But the unknown horsemen anticipated his move and spurred their horses to quickly intercept.

They numbered close to thirty and were part of the rebellion, of that he was sure. Their rough clothing and rougher demeanor identified them. He tried in vain to still the pounding of his own heart as they encircled him. Hoping to sound braver than he felt, he glared at the man directly in front of him and demanded, "What right have you to stop me? I have no business with you!"

"Your livery tells us otherwise," the man responded coolly. "You are in the service of Lord Hussey. We want any letters you may be carrying."

"I have no letters," he asserted.

"I do not believe you, sir, for you would not be riding so hard this late in the evening unless you were on urgent business. Therefore, I ask you again. Give me the letters, or else we will be forced to hang you on this very spot." As if to give credence to his statement, he retrieved a rope from his satchel.

The servant of Lord Hussey paled. With trembling fingers, he reached inside a leather pouch and pulled out two letters. He handed them to the ringleader.

The last rays of the evening sun spilling over the horizon provided just enough light to read the letters' contents. Both were addressed to Sir William Askew, South Kelsey Hall. The leader broke the first seal and unfolded the missive. It was from Lord Hussey himself, offering his men's assistance in crushing the revolt. The second, in like manner, was an offer of support from the mayor of Lincoln.

Enraged at this apparent duplicity of Sir William, the rebel leader barked out his orders. Two men were to take the trembling servant back to Caistor. Two others he dispatched to gather reinforcements. The rest would ride with him. Then breathing threats, he turned his horse northward and raced toward South Kelsey Hall.

Chapter IV

Anne sat on the window seat in her bedroom, gazing out over the hills as the last of the evening's light faded into dusk and hoping fervently that tomorrow would see her father's safe return to South Kelsey Hall. Though careful to hide her anxiety from her family, before God she confessed the fearful thoughts that kept tumbling through her mind; fears that stemmed not only from the fact that her father's life may be in grave danger, but more so that his mortal soul may be in greater peril. She had oftentimes enjoyed lively discussions with her father concerning her beliefs, but she had never come away from them with an assurance that he had truly come to faith. The thought that he might perish for all eternity was more than her heart could bear; and so now, with head bowed and eyes closed, she earnestly interceded for him as she had never done before.

Rumblings, distant and faint, intruded on the evening quiet. Yet so deep in prayer was Anne that she did not hear the first thundering echoes reverberating from the surrounding hills. Even as the rumblings increased in strength, her mind did not comprehend their warning. *A storm must be moving in*, she thought absently. But, no, this was not the sound of thunder... She glanced up from prayer, momentarily perplexed by the interruption.

As she watched, tiny flickering lights materialized on the graying twilight's horizon. Rising from the hills, bobbing heads emerged and grew larger, forming bodies and finally becoming distinguishable as a band of horsemen, thundering toward South Kelsey Hall. Anne pushed opened her window, leaned out, and strained to see whether her father was among them. But the lead rider was not her father, nor were those following him her father's men. Terror suddenly clutched Anne's heart, and she leapt from the window seat.

"Francis!" she cried, racing down the hallways toward her brother's bedchamber. Just as she reached his room, his door flung open and Francis emerged, buttoning his doublet.

"I have seen them, too, Anne," he said, brushing past her. She turned to follow and quickened her pace to match his long strides.

"Do you know who they are?" she asked.

"No, I could not recognize them at this distance, but I do not believe they are intent on paying a social visit."

Elizabeth, in her evening wrap, stood anxiously at her bedchamber door as Francis and Anne approached. She held a single candlestick in her trembling hand, and the flame flickered wildly from the tremors.

"What is it, Francis? I heard horses and Anne calling. Has your father returned?" she asked, her voice hopeful, her eyes fearful.

"I do not believe so, but I will find out. You stay here with Anne. Keep the others upstairs as well." Francis tried to sound calm, but his stomach churned within him.

Suddenly, thirteen-year-old Thomas bounded from his room, his untucked shirt billowing around his waist. "Riders are coming," he exclaimed. "Has Father come home?"

Francis caught the young curly-haired boy by the shoulders before he could dart past them down the stairway. "No, he is not home. Now, go back to your room and properly dress yourself. Then stay up here with Mother."

"But I want to see what is happening," he protested.

"Thomas," Elizabeth spoke sharply, startling the boy. "Do as your brother tells you."

Her tone and expression warned Thomas that it was best not to disobey, and reluctantly he returned to his room. By this time, Martha and Jane, having heard the voices in the hallway, had wandered from the upstairs drawing room to find out what all the commotion was about. Martha, who had in recent months lost both weight and color, looked even paler in the evening twilight. Anne instinctively wrapped a protective arm around her waist, drawing a weak smile of appreciation from Martha in response. Jane pressed in close to Elizabeth, and they stood silent as Francis rapidly descended the stairs.

A sudden thunderous pounding at the door reverberated though the hall. Anne tightened her hold on Martha whom she feared would collapse with fright. A servant scurried to open the large oak doors, but Francis stepped up first. Mustering his courage, he opened the door just far enough to see out. Only one large man stood on the portal, but more than twenty-five armed men sat astride horses on the green, the dancing light from their torches casting hellish shadows across their sober faces. Francis stiffened.

"What is the meaning of this?" he demanded. "How dare you disturb our family at such an hour!"

The rebel leader was unconcerned with social amenities. "Where is Sir William?" he asked brusquely. "Our business is with him."

Francis hesitated. Should he reveal his father's absence or have the man standing before him believe that Sir William was indeed in residence? Francis chose to stall.

"And what business may that be?"

"That is not your concern! We will speak to Sir William only!"

"You are not the sort of man who can make demands of my father!" Francis replied hotly. "Now be off with you!" He pressed his weight against the door to close it, but a stout club thrust forward jammed it open.

"We *will* speak to Sir William," the man stated again.

"My husband is not home."

Francis started at the soft voice behind him. Elizabeth, clutching her wrap tightly to her, stood calmly in the entranceway. Anne, Martha, and Jane had also descended and positioned themselves at the foot of the stairs. Behind them, a smaller figure crouched, his eager face peering between his sisters' skirts in his determination not to miss a thing.

"Mother, go back upstairs!" Francis pleaded.

The rebel leader, taking advantage of Francis' momentary distraction, heaved his weight against the door, shoving it open, and strode into the great hall. Several scowling men immediately followed, clattering into the hall and flashing swords and scythes to convince the hapless family that they would be wise not to resist.

"Where is he?" the man demanded.

"What do you want with him?" Elizabeth asked. Her voice quavered slightly, but her face, though drained of color, was nonetheless resolute.

"He has conspired against us! He must answer to the people he betrays!"

"My husband answers only to his sovereign, the king. That alone is his duty."

"'Twould appear, milady, that his *duty* also includes inciting the gentry to crush the common man who by his labors pays for your life of ease!" the man hissed, holding out the intercepted letters in his fist. Angry choruses behind the man echoed his sentiments.

Fearing the hostile mood of the men before him, Francis moved quickly to stand at Elizabeth's side. At the same moment, a small figure darted down the stairs past Anne and took up a defensive posture on Elizabeth's other side. Young Thomas glared defiantly at the man who towered over him.

"You have no right to speak to my mother that way! My father will have you beaten!"

For a moment, the taller man stared incredulously at the diminutive figure, then he bent down until his portly face was only inches from Thomas'. A strong smell of soured ale hung on his breath. Thomas wrinkled his nose and turned his face away.

"And just who is going to carry out this beating?" he sneered. "Your servants perhaps? Now that would be difficult because from what I can see, 'twould seem as though even your own servants have taken up sides with us." Casting an upward glance at Francis, he smiled sardonically.

If the man had punched him, his fist would not have had as forceful an impact on Francis as these words; and for the first time, Francis anxiously scanned the faces in the mob. Clustered in the back as though trying to hide behind the rebels stood Robert, who tended the stables; his son, James; and three under gardeners. Francis knew full well that they had not ridden in with the group, so they must have given their allegiance to the rebels upon their arrival. Robert had been with the family for more than twenty years and been treated fairly. How could he now so easily take up arms against them? Catching Francis' eye, Robert quickly averted his glance. Francis' heart sank within him.

But Elizabeth was not going to allow this man to cower her. Though terrified, her anger at the man's obnoxious disrespect bolstered her courage to speak out. Wrapping protective arms around Thomas' shoulders, she pulled him back against her.

"I have already told you. My husband is not here. I pray you, leave us in peace!"

A strained silence hung momentarily in the room. The tall man straightened. His hardened eyes stared into Elizabeth's fearful ones, then slowly moved to scrutinize the young women at the stairs and the haughty young man who had opened the door to him. A callous smile played at the corner of his lips. When he spoke, the words came quietly but firmly.

"So be it. Since Sir William is not here, 'twould seem we must go to him. But we shall not go empty-handed. We will need insurance so that when we at last meet with Sir William, he will be persuaded to listen to our demands."

He turned to the men directly behind him. "Take those two," he ordered, indicating Francis and Thomas. Four men immediately moved forward.

"No!" Elizabeth screamed, clutching Thomas all the closer. But the men paid no heed and roughly moved to shove her aside. Unwilling to let these crass men take her son, she clung tightly to Thomas, twisting her body around to act as a shield for the boy.

"Out of the way, woman!" one of the men demanded, brandishing a knife. His hand flew up. A body dove forward. A glint of silver flashed. Blood splattered, and Francis crumpled to his knees. Anne shrieked and charged forward to her brother's side.

"Enough!" the leader yelled and yanked the offender back. "'Twill do us no good to have dead hostages!"

Anne bent to examine her brother's wound. The sleeve of his silk shirt and woolen doublet oozed red, but Francis had been successful in deflecting the knife enough so that the wound was not serious. Elizabeth, eyes wide in terror, had never let go of Thomas, who now squirmed from his mother's grasp. Crouching beside Francis, he, too, examined the wound, his eyes now wide with fear.

"Please," Elizabeth pleaded, her eyes filling with tears. "I beg you, leave us be. We have nothing to do with your grievances. Why must you hurt us?"

"We have no wish to harm you, milady," the man replied a little less harshly. "But we *shall* take your sons with us. They will assure us that Sir William will rightly choose to whom he owes allegiance when the time comes."

Seeing a frightened servant huddled in a doorway, he barked. "Get bandages for this man's arm. Quick, woman! We haven't all day!" The woman immediately scuttled off.

As soon as the wound was dressed, Thomas and Francis were herded outside. Darkness had fully descended, broken only by the circle of wavering torchlights. Elizabeth's pleadings and crying were ignored, and she could only watch helplessly as her sons were forced to mount two horses that had been led up from the Askew stables. Thomas, no longer defiant, tried to put on a brave face for his mother, but the yellow-orange light dancing across his face clearly reflected the fear in his eyes. Francis also feared, not as much for his own life as for the safety of his mother and sisters, left alone now without a male family member to watch over them. There was a time when he could have trusted them to the care of faithful servants, but now he wondered whether the remaining servants held any loyalty to the family. As the group rode off, Francis prayed silently that God would deliver them all from the hands of these fearsome men.

Anne, too, prayed as she watched the night's blackness swallow her brothers into its stronghold. At the rim of the reach of the flickering torchlights, grotesque shadows wavered, and Anne could almost imagine demons dancing in the darkness. *Surely, the*

Antichrist has come among us, she thought in great alarm as the rebels, arrogant and sneering, led their prizes away.

The rebels of Caistor were in an uproar. Rumors had been circulating for hours of large armies marching toward Louth and Caistor to put down the rebellion. Disorganized and alarmed, the commoners were desperate for good leadership; but because few were trained or experienced in military maneuvering, the rebellion showed signs of foundering. When the party from South Kelsey arrived, many of the commoners were ready to take action – any action. Seething over the reports of Sir William's apparent treachery, they demanded that the young men be slain on the spot.

Hearing the unruly crowd's demands, Thomas struggled to hold back terrified tears, yet the terror he felt showed clearly in his eyes as he and Francis were dragged from their horses and their hands bound with ropes. Rough hands then shoved them across a small green into a tavern where they were thrown into a dark corner while their fate was decided. A burley farmer, who grasped a pitchfork and reeked of sweat and cow manure, stood guard.

"They are the sons of a traitor! The very same man who would see your own children go hungry so that he can live his life of ease!" cried out a red-bearded man dressed in monk's garb. "They do not deserve to live!"

Rallying cries of assent rang out, and several men surged forward. Thomas and Francis shrank back against the stone wall, cowering from the mob that pressed toward them. But the grim-faced farmer who stood guard raised his pitchfork and planted his feet firmly between his charges and the angry men, daring any to pass him. In the same instant, the rebel leader who had brought them in leapt atop a wooden table.

"Friends!" he yelled, his stentorian voice carrying clearly over the din. "Friends, listen to me!

The angry voices grudgingly subsided.

"What good will it do us to kill these two lads? Will Sir William render aid to those who have murdered his sons? I beseech you, good men. Keep these two alive, and we will have the support of Sir William. Kill them, and he will do all in his power to see us each hanged!"

Frustrated murmurs rippled through the group. Reluctantly, the Caistor rebels accepted the wisdom of the words, and their desire for blood was temporarily averted. But their agitation remained. These men, convinced of the harsh injustices dealt them, were thirsty for vengeance, impatient for action. Moreover, fearing that at any moment a great army would swarm over them, they possessed a compelling urgency to act.

Understanding their mood, another man spoke out. "I have heard reports that Thomas Moigne is lodged at Willingham. We can send out a party to ride over there first thing tomorrow morning and bring him back. He will be a great asset to us."

Appeased by this suggestion, the mob disbanded, leaving two very relieved though quite shaken young men still under guard of the bulky figure. The corner into which they had been shoved was not only dark, but damp and cold as well; and the tavern stank from the lingering odor of unwashed bodies and spilled ale. Denied the opportunity to eat his supper and combined with the putrid odors that assaulted him, Francis' head began to throb and his stomach churn. He leaned against the cold stone wall and closed his eyes. Thomas' small quivering voice aroused him again.

"Francis, do you think they will change their minds?" he whispered.

"No. That man was well said. If they kill us, Father will exact his revenge. We are of far more value to them alive. Now, try and get some rest. I do believe we will be needing our strength."

Assured by his brother's words, Thomas emitted a sigh of relief and scooted a little closer for warmth. Francis gave him a reassuring smile and once again closed his eyes.

October 5, 1536

Having neither exercise nor much freedom to change positions during their first night of captivity, the brothers' muscles were quite cramped when Francis and Thomas were aroused from their sleep before dawn the next morning. Stumbling badly as they were led to their horses, the two provided their captors with much amusement.

"These 'gentlemen' can't even walk!" one man derided.

"Did you not like our gracious accommodations?" another mocked.

Francis refrained from a tart reply. A small wiry man, who took great pleasure in prodding the brothers toward the waiting horses, had replaced their burley guard. When one of them stumbled, he jeered and struck out with his walking stick that doubled as his weapon. Francis held his anger when jabbed unmercifully from behind; but when the little man whacked Thomas on the back of his legs and sent the boy sprawling, Francis erupted. He lunged backwards, hurling his body against the slight frame. Caught off guard, the man had no time to react and both tumbled to the ground. Landing right beside his tormenter, Francis kicked and pummeled the man with all his strength. The little man began screeching, but the crowd surrounding them only whooped in laughter as he struggled to free himself from flailing arms and legs.

Finally, he rolled free and scrambled to his feet. Enraged, he swung the club over his head and brought it down full force. Francis lurched to the left, and the club slammed the earth beside his ear. Onlookers crowded around, urging the little man on. The club shot up again. Fearing no escape, Francis instinctively doubled up his body, wrapped his arms around his head, and waited for the blow. But it never came. A huge figure barreling into the crowd yanked the club from the little man and shoved him aside. Then a pair of rough hands grabbed Francis by his doublet and jerked him to his feet. He stood face to face with the South Kelsey ringleader.

"I have saved your hide twice now," the man growled. "I shan't do it again."

Francis felt no gratitude. Had this man not taken them captive, his life would never have been endangered. Without replying, he turned and mounted his horse. Thomas rode beside him.

"Did they hurt you, Francis?" he whispered.

Francis only shook his head.

The party of fifty men rode swiftly to the home of Thomas Moigne. Forcing their way into his home, they quickly found their intended victim, made him swear allegiance on his own Bible, and ordered him to ride with them to Louth. Francis was amazed at their easy apprehension of Moigne and wondered why he had remained at Willingham when surely he must have known how dangerous such a decision would be, but he learned en route that Thomas' wife was gravely ill and the poor man was loathed to leave her in such a state.

The riders made good time, arriving in Louth by midmorning. The rebels gathering at Louth had also heard rumors of large armies on their way and were anxious to organize themselves into an army. While the leaders met, the newly arrived captives were ushered into the room where the other gentlemen were still being held. When Francis and young Thomas entered, Sir William gasped in horror, then rushed across the room and tightly embraced them. The sons, just as relieved to find their father unharmed, returned his embrace fully. When they stepped back from each other, Sir William noticed Francis' torn and bloody sleeve. He looked at his son for an explanation.

Francis then recounted the events that had led to their capture as the gentlemen listened quietly to the grim account. Sir William anguished over the knowledge that his wife and daughters were left unprotected; and along with Francis, he fervently hoped that the servants remaining at South Kelsey Hall would prove faithful. The gentlemen fell silent, each occupied with his own thoughts of family.

Suddenly, the door flew open and William Morland charged in, a fistful of letters held tightly in his hand. His face flushed, he strode across the room directly toward Sir William. Slamming the letters down on the table before him, he demanded, "What means of treachery is this? At the first opportunity, you play the traitor!"

Stunned, Sir William had no reply. He picked up the first letter and saw it was addressed to him from Lord Hussey. The second letter likewise was to him from the mayor of Lincoln. Sir William read their contents, and though inwardly alarmed, he summoned his courage, determined not to show his captors any trace of fear.

"How can you accuse me of being a traitor? I had no part in this."

"They write to *you* pledging *you* their support, and *you* claim to have no part in this! You think me a fool? Why would they do so unless you had written requesting as much?"

"Pray tell me, sir, when could I have written to them to request such assistance? I had no knowledge of the widespread extent of this uprising before I left my home, so I had no reason to think I needed assistance. And," he added sarcastically, "as I have been your guest for the last two days, I have had little opportunity to write anyone, except his grace, the king, and that only under your direction."

"Lord Burgh was with you at Caistor. Perhaps you instructed him to send for help from Lord Hussey."

"If Lord Burgh sent word to Lord Hussey, he acted of his own accord. I cannot be held accountable for another man's actions."

"But I do hold you accountable!" Morland knew he was losing the argument, which only fueled his anger. Turning to the sentry, he snapped, "Take these men outside! Leave these two," he said, indicating Francis and Thomas. Thomas, not wishing to be parted from his father again so soon, clung to his father's arm.

Sir William smiled reassuringly to his son. "'Tis best you stay with Francis," he said, gently disengaging his arm.

Under guard, the gentlemen were herded outside. Morland conferred several minutes with several of the Louth leaders, including Captain Cobbler. The captain then turned to one of the guards standing nearby.

"You, take twelve men and ride to Sleaford. Find out exactly what the Lord Lieutenant is doing. Report back here as soon as you discover anything!"

The man immediately hurried off to gather his riders. A few minutes later, the scouting party mounted and rode toward Sleaford. Morland also rode off, but in the direction of Horncastle to get the latest news of the events unfolding there. As soon as both were gone, Captain Cobbler turned his attention once more to the gentlemen.

"Now is the time to prove whether your oath of allegiance was sincere," he said. "We need to organize these men into military units of which each one of you gentlemen will take charge of one. You shall also send for weapons to arm them." He paused, then continued with a half laugh. "Now, you understand why we sent Sir Edward to London. We hardly thought him capable of leading armed men!"

"If we do as you ask, we would be taking up arms against the king! And I, for one, have no intention of committing treason. Surely, even you are wise enough to know that the king does not look kindly upon such offences." Sir William protested.

"You swore allegiance to the commoners!"

"We first swore allegiance to the king!"

"If you would rather die, I can arrange that."

"To die for one's king is an honorable death." Sir Robert replied, though his voice quavered slightly.

Captain Cobbler studied the men before him. Each was unyielding and headstrong. After a long moment, he turned and whispered instructions to a guard standing nearby. The man left but returned only moments later with several armed men escorting Francis and young Thomas.

"Yes, your own deaths would be honorable," the captain smiled sardonically. "But tell me, Sir William, would the death of your sons be just as 'honorable'?"

Sir William paled. He gazed into the faces of his sons: Francis, brave, but ashen; Thomas, eyes reflecting unconcealed terror. Sir William's eyes shifted back to the hard, unyielding face of the rebel leader. Certainly, this man would suffer no compunction in murdering his sons on the spot. With heavy heart, he knew that this time the captain had won.

"I shall lead your men," he said, his voice barely audible. "But bring no harm to my sons."

Captain Cobbler jerked his head, indicating to the guards to take the two young men back to their holding area. Then he turned to Sir William, and a cold, predatory smile spread across his face.

"A wise decision, Sir William. And lest the rest of you think your families safe, 'twould be easy enough to give orders to these same men to ride to your homes and seek out your families. 'Tis up to you. I await your decisions."

With the greatest reluctance, the others agreed, knowing as Sir William did that this man would not hesitate to carry out his threats. But in agreeing to help, they also knew that their own position had now become quite precarious. If the rebellion failed, of which they felt certain it eventually would, they could all face charges of treason – charges that would certainly end with their executions. But the safety of those they loved was paramount to them; thus, having no other recourse, they spent the better part of the afternoon dividing the rebels into military units and trying to establish some semblance of order among the rabble. The task proved to be quite difficult as most of those gathered were peasants, monks, or farmers who had no military experience. The few who had spent time in the king's army had done so as mere foot soldiers and had no experience in leadership, so the gentlemen were forced to train as they went along. To make matters worse, most of the rebels were highly suspicious of the gentlemen's loyalty and were not inclined to take orders from them. Only under threats from the rebel leaders did the horde finally submit to their appointed gentlemen commanders.

The sun was sinking low in the western sky when Morland returned from Horncastle. He rode in quickly, dismounted his horse, passed the reins to a waiting farmer, and hurried toward the church where the leaders had set up headquarters. The gentlemen as well as rebels leaders gathered to hear what news he brought.

"I bring good tidings!" he began, grinning widely. "Horncastle is ours!"

Cheers went up from all but the forlorn gentlemen. Morland turned a gloating and accusing eye on them, then continued.

"The Horncastle gentlemen possess a much greater understanding of the people's grievances and have joined wholeheartedly in the people's rebellion. Sir Edward Dymock, a righteous and devout man of the true Church of Rome, has taken charge and organized our brethren very well. He also has the support of several other gentlemen, among them his own father, Sir Robert, and Sir John Coppledyke. 'Twould seem there was some resistance from Sir William Sandon, but he, too, has been made to see the rightness of our cause."

"What about the Bishop's chancellor, Raynes? Has he sworn allegiance to our cause?" someone in the crowd wanted to know. Chancellor Raynes had been one of the first commissioners ordered to Louth to read the king's injunctions to the people; but upon hearing of the uprising, he had diverted his travels and taken refuge in Bolingbroke just south of Horncastle. For these reasons, the people of Louth held nothing but disdain toward this cowardly messenger of the king. Still, Morland hesitated before answering.

"Chancellor Raynes was sworn to the cause, but..." He stopped, unsure of how much he should say in front of the Lindsey gentlemen.

"Well, go on! But what?" a man's voice urged.

"Chancellor Raynes is dead," Morland stated matter of factly. He then hurried on in his explanation. "But he was a traitor to our cause and deserved to die!"

"How did he die?" Sir William asked quietly, eyeing the man directly.

Morland averted his gaze and answered weakly, "By the will of the people."

The still-fresh images of the brutal death he had witnessed just hours before invaded his mind, causing Morland's stomach to churn. The unfortunate Chancellor Raynes, though sick and weak, had been forced to ride to Horncastle to face Sir Edward

Dymock. Upon his arrival, and to Morland's horror, the unrestrained angry mob had dragged Raynes from his horse and literally torn him limb from limb—and all this under the approving eye of Dymock, a ruthless and fearsome man.

Morland forced the grisly images from his mind, determined not to appear weak before these men. Wishing to change the mood settling over the group, he pulled a parchment from a small pouch slung around his neck and held it aloft.

"I have here articles of grievances that Sir Edward and the other gentlemen of Horncastle have drawn up to present to the king," he shouted in triumph. "These articles affirm our own grievances and add to them others that are just and good. Every hour, we grow in strength and number! Tomorrow, we march to Lincoln where we will join our brethren and soon know the sweet taste of victory!"

Another cheer erupted. Then someone cried out, "Not tomorrow! Tonight we must march!"

Thunderous cheers shook the building, and the gentlemen feared it might fall about their heads. Yet they feared even more that if they joined in leading the men on their march to Lincoln, their own fate as traitors would be sealed. Above the din, Thomas Moigne struggled to be heard. He jumped atop a wooden table and shouted out with all his strength, but the crowd could not be quieted. The gentlemen were forced outside to the waiting contingents of men.

By now, the sun had disappeared below the horizon, and campfires had sprung up, small flickering lights dotting the black countryside. Jubilation over the news Morland brought and the desire to be on the move sent the camp into feverish activity. Men scurried back and forth, trying to organize the large horde into columns for marching, but cross signals, inexperience, and miscommunication proved their endeavors worthless, and the camp dissolved into mass confusion. In exasperation, they finally ordered the Lindsey gentlemen to take charge. Sir William took advantage of the moment.

"'Twould be folly to march to Lincoln tonight. The fenlands are difficult enough to traverse in daylight. At night, 'tis nigh impossible! And the roads cannot contain such numbers. Please, be reasonable and wait 'til morning," he urged.

"Moreover," Thomas Moigne added, "these men have been drilling all day. They have not the strength for such a march. Surely, a good night's rest is deserved."

Morland and Captain Cobbler wanted to disagree. The pervading mood throughout the camp told them that their men were anxious to be on the move, but the logic of the gentlemen was irrefutable. The fenlands were dangerous to cross at night; and the men, though newly energized, would soon be drained of strength after such an undertaking and of little use if confronted by the king's army. With reluctance, they ordered the camp to stay the night. Disgruntled conversations snaked through the crowd, and angry voices accused the gentlemen of playing them false; but in the end, the multitude settled down to await the march the next morning.

Emotionally drained, the weary gentlemen longed to see the end to this interminable day. After a light supper with little conversation, they trudged off to the bedchambers assigned them. Sir William had to carry his young son Thomas to their room as the poor lad could not even stay awake through the meal; his eyes heavy, he slumped in his place at the table. Francis, too, quickly fell off to sleep, exhausted by the day's events. In envy, Sir William listened to their steady breathing; for even though his whole body yearned for sleep, hours passed before he could quiet his anxious heart enough to allow sleep to come. Yet even when his body finally succumbed, foreboding, unsettling dreams that seemed more real than imagined robbed him of the rest that once had come so easily.

Chapter V

October 6, 1536

Christopher Askew sat astride his chestnut mare, straining forward in his saddle to survey the countryside stretched out below him. Though the reports he had received had been alarming, the region he now surveyed appeared deceptively calm. But if the reports given to him were true, and he believed they were, then somewhere out across these vast gray wetlands was an army thirty thousand strong and gaining in strength. Somewhere, too, were his father and brothers.

His orders from Cromwell had been clear. Ride to Spalding, a town at the southern-most tip of Lincolnshire, and determine whether the uprising had spread that far. But as he peered across the land to the north, he desperately wanted to continue on to South Kelsey to assure himself that his stepmother and sisters fared well. Words from a letter he had received only the day before from Elizabeth replayed themselves in his mind and tugged at his heart. Frightened words, lonely words, words pleading for his help and his return. But Cromwell, forbidding him to venture any further north than Spalding, even now awaited his return with news of the region. Sighing deeply, he turned his horse southward and began his journey back to London.

The news he brought Cromwell was not good. Though the uprising had not yet reached the region of Spalding, he knew that a very real possibility existed that it would.

"The commoners about Stamford, Spalding, and Peterborough have no desire to rise up against the rebels as they fear universal reprisals from His Grace should the rebellion fail, so they feel they have no choice but to support the cause," Christopher reported to the dour-faced man sitting before him. "They also have heard that they will be required to pay a third of all their goods to the king, and even be sworn as to the truth of their worth. And if they swear falsely, they shall lose everything."

"And what of Lord Hussey?" Cromwell asked, being certain neither to confirm nor deny before Christopher the veracity of these rumors.

"From what I could ascertain, Lord Hussey's situation in Sleaford is hopeless. He is hemmed in on all sides and lacks any support from his tenants. 'Tis only a matter of time before he, too, is taken captive."

Cromwell slammed his fist against the desk. "Foolish man! Had he moved forward when he had the opportunity, he could have put down this rebellion! If he survives at the hands of the rebels, he will surely face the wrath of the king."

Christopher wisely did not reply as Cromwell studied the young man before him.

"What news of your father?"

"None, sir."

Cromwell sighed. "Well, I hope for the sake of your family that Sir William remembers where his loyalties lie," he said as way of dismissal.

"Of that, my lord, I have no fear," the son replied coolly, bowing at the waist. He then turned and walked from the room.

October 8, 1536

The march to Lincoln had been riddled with strife. Not only did the rebel leaders argue with the Lindsey gentlemen, but they also argued amongst themselves regarding the best course of action. The magnitude of their undertaking was beginning to take its toll, and tempers flared quickly. Adding to their problems was the acute tension that permeated throughout the ranks of commoners as well, who knew that their lives as well as their families were in grave danger should the rebellion fail. But as the rebellion reached its eighth day, resolutions were not forth-coming, and rumors of the king's great army caused many to cast doubts concerning the path they had chosen. As a means to alleviate the state of tension, the leaders allowed, even encouraged, looting of Lincoln's finer buildings and homes. The gentlemen could only look on in disgust.

Once in Lincoln, Sir William, his sons, and the other gentlemen took up residence in the cathedral that occupied a steep hill overlooking the town. From this vantage point, the men could keep an eye on the camp of the rebels below as well as enjoy some much needed privacy. During the two days since their march from Louth, reports had poured in of support from counties as far away as Yorkshire and Holland. Once again, hopes among the commoners soared, and the rebels became anxious to engage the king's men.

Then on the afternoon of October 8, Sir Edward Dymock led his southern host triumphantly into Lincoln. As they marched, they waved banners and shouted victory slogans. Sir Edward, a tall, lanky man with a thin face, dark eyes, and neatly trimmed black beard, rode at their head, acknowledging and reveling in the cheers ascending around him. From his proud manner, one might conclude that he alone had masterminded the entire endeavor. For his part, he was not quick to disagree with such an assessment. Indeed, in his mind, he was the one who had turned the rabble into an army, and the promised power that would be his upon success was intoxicating. To Sir Edward, the cause was already won—but he had not yet met up with the gentlemen from Lindsey.

Sir Edward strode into the cathedral chapter house where the Lindsey gentlemen awaited him, his footsteps echoing on the stone floor. Following close behind him came Sir John Coppledyke, Thomas Littlebury, and Nicholas Sanderson. The briefest of introductions and barest of civilities were exchanged. The coolness of their reception did not escape Sir Edward, and inwardly he seethed at the affront; but outwardly, he smiled most pleasantly, even arrogantly, confident in his imagined success.

"I am honored to finally make your acquaintances," Sir Edward said, nodding his head toward Sir William and his colleagues. "Such esteemed gentlemen are well known throughout Lincolnshire."

"Dispense with the flattering words, Sir Edward." Sir William could barely contain his anger. "We have heard of your traitorous and brutal acts, especially your part in the murder of Chancellor Raynes!"

"Chancellor Raynes was a cowardly old man who deserved to die!" Sir Edward shot back.

"Because he was loyal to the king?"

"Because he was loyal to no one! At the first opportunity, he abandoned the king's cause and swore allegiance to ours. But the commoners knew him for the serpent he was, and he died accordingly."

"When you are threatened with death, I rather suspect your loyalties, too, will lie in another bed," Sir William remarked, not realizing how prophetic his words would turn out to be.

"I have no fear with regards to my loyalties. I have aligned myself with those whose cause is just and good. The king has overstepped his rights as monarch, and the good people of Lincolnshire shall have no peace until these unjust acts are righted. Think not that we shall suffer loss. Indeed, we shall be victorious, and the king will know what it is to suffer great loss!"

"And just how do you propose to effect this 'great loss'?" Sir Robert asked, somewhat sarcastically.

"By marching on the king's army and destroying it!"

Stunned silence enveloped the room momentarily. Then Sir William exploded. "Advance on the king's army? Have you gone quite mad? Do you think such treason shall go unpunished! If so, then you attribute more grace to his majesty than he himself would own. And what liberty do you claim to advance on the king's army before even knowing the king's mind in this matter? We have not yet received the king's replies to know his intentions or his pleasure."

"His pleasure? Nay, rather his anger! The king has had more than enough time to answer the demands sent to him. He plays for time to gain the strength he needs to crush us. But if we move first, we shall crush him!"

"If you advance without knowing the king's mind, then you sign your own death warrant!" Sir William warned. "And... you advance without my assistance."

"And without mine," Sir Robert echoed. Each Lindsey gentlemen quickly chimed in his resolution to remain behind as well.

Sir Edward went purple with rage and responded through clenched teeth. "So be it! We can advance without your help. I have men of my own ready to lead this army, with me at its head."

"It takes more men than you have to command a host numbering more than forty thousand, especially men not trained for battle. The ranks will not hold, and the king's army will decimate you." Thomas Moigne replied evenly.

Sir Edward again started to speak, but Sir John stepped forward, laid hold of his arm, and pulled him away from the heated discussion. Near the small wooden entrance of the chapter house, he and the other Dymock supporters held a tense, whispered conference of their own. For several minutes, the Lindsey gentlemen waited. Then Sir John turned to face them.

"We give the king until Wednesday to respond. If a reply is not forthcoming, we shall advance – with or without you."

Once again the Lindsey gentlemen had successfully stalled for time.

October 10, 1536

The days of idleness began to have the effect the Lindsey gentlemen had hoped. The commoners, weary of inactivity, grew increasingly agitated and fought frequently amongst themselves. And, as time passed without the order to advance being issued, their suspicions of the gentlemen's loyalty escalated. Much to his dismay, even Sir Edward's allegiance was called into question, and he had considerable difficulty persuading the angry mob that the delays were necessary and that his only desire was to see the commoners' demands met. Though it galled him deeply, he found himself relying heavily on the persuasive qualities of Sir William and the other gentlemen from Lindsey to keep the unpredictable horde at bay.

As rumors continued to circulate of the king's great army mustering at Nottingham, many commoners, now certain that defeat was inevitable, slipped away during the night to families or hiding places. The gentlemen also desired nothing more than to be rid of the whole matter and be back on their own estates, but they were too closely guarded to be given an opportunity to leave.

Finally, at midday on October 10, a courier from Charles Brandon, Duke of Suffolk, rode into Lincoln carrying letters to the gentlemen from the king himself. Angry rebels immediately surrounded the hapless courier; and had it not been for the missives he carried, he most likely would have been dragged from his horse and killed on the spot. Instead, he was quickly escorted to the chapter house where the gentlemen continued in conference. News of the courier's arrival flashed through the camp, and an anxious crowd of rebels jammed the chapter house to hear king's reply.

Morland, himself, took the letters from the courier and thrust them into the hands of Thomas Moigne, demanding that he read them aloud. Thomas, his face pale, unrolled the parchment handed to him. The crowd pressed forward. Several men clambered atop the stone ledge directly behind him to peer over his shoulder as he read. Clearing his throat, Thomas began to read.

> *To all true subjects of His Grace residing in the northern province of Lincolnshire: With regards to the choosing of councilors, I have never read, heard, nor known that a Prince's councilors and prelates should be appointed by rude and ignorant common people; nor that such people possessed the ability to discern and choose suitable councilors for a Prince. How presumptuous then are you, the rude commoners of one shire, and that one being the most brute and beastly of the whole realm, to find fault with your Prince on the election of his councilors. Rather, contrary to God's law and man's law, you take upon yourselves to rule your Prince, whom you are bound by all laws to obey and serve with your lives, lands, and goods. You have behaved as traitors and rebels, and not as the true subjects you have named yourself.*

Thomas' voice quavered. He sensed the anger sweeping through the assembly and felt on his neck the hot breath of the commoners behind him. Glancing at Sir William, who nodded slightly, he hurried on.

> As to the suppression of the religious houses and monasteries, know the charge that I lay against you and all subjects who be of like mind by demonstrating such unkindness and unnatural thinking. You would rather that those pledged to poverty enjoy such possessions, profits, and wealth as these religious houses acquire so that they may continue in their life of ease rather than that We, your natural Prince, Sovereign Lord, and king should rightly possess, who has spent six times as much of his own resources in your defenses.

> Furthermore, in regards to the subsidy, which you demand of Us that you be released, do you think that We be so fainthearted that you of one shire could compel Us by your insurrections and rebellions to repeal the same? Or do you think that any man will take you as true subjects those who contrive to compel your Sovereign king in such manner?

> And thus, We pray unto Almighty God to give you grace to do your duties and to give yourselves in service toward Us, as true and faithful subjects. Return to your homes and choose from amongst yourselves 100 of your leaders to be delivered into the hands of our Lord Lieutenant to be tried according to our will and pleasure for the transgressions committed against Us. Let not your obstinacy or willfulness against your king expose your lives, wives, children, lands, goods, and possessions to the wrath of God, but also utter ruin by force and violence of the sword.

As Thomas' voice died away, the man beside him snatch the letter from his hands. Brandishing it aloft, he cried out, "What say you, good men, to this your king's reply? Is it not clear that his grace means to abolish Christianity and that soon you shall find yourselves under the sword of the Turks! But whoever sheds his blood with us shall inherit eternal glory!"

The whole room exploded in a thunderous uproar as angry shouts reverberated off the vaulted ceiling. Cries of treason against the gentlemen erupted on all sides, and several rebels drew their swords, demanding their immediate death. For a terrifying moment, it seemed as though the leaders were bent on allowing the mob to have its way. In a desperate act, Sir Edward leapt atop the stone ledge, crying out to the unruly crowd.

"Good men, listen to me! I beg you, listen!"

Several minutes passed before the angry men could be quieted enough to hear him out.

"Do you think the king will deal more kindly with you if you kill any of us? And if we be dead, who then is able to lead you in your cause? What man among you has the military knowledge sufficient to lead so great an army against the king's?"

"We can lead ourselves! I say, kill these men! They have played us false from the beginning!" shouted a gruff voice from the back of the crowd. The voice belonged to a large dark-haired man named Humphrey, known for his volatile temper. He stood defiantly, his sword poised. The crowd erupted again.

Fortunately for the gentlemen, Morland, Captain Cobbler, and several other leaders understood the wisdom of Sir Edward's words. Morland stepped up beside him and begged to be heard.

"Friends, please! I commend your zeal, but if we are to be victorious, we need these men awhile longer. More than ever, we must be unified in our effort. We cannot risk arousing the king's anger further." He then turned to a group of twenty men standing nearby who he knew would obey his orders. "Remove those men from this meeting."

Immediately, the men began to push their way through the crowded room, grabbing and shoving each dissident bent on violence toward the entranceway. Though tempers flared and a few scuffles ensued, within several minutes, the troublemakers had been herded out of the chapter house into the cloister. Order was finally restored, and the gentlemen all breathed a little easier.

As the door of the chapter house closed, shutting out the troublemakers, the large dark-haired man cursed and threw his sword to the ground.

"Cowards! All of them! Ne'er a one of them has the courage to stand up to those traitorous gentlemen, let alone the king!" He clenched his fist, then eyed his comrades. "But we understand what is at stake, do we not, fellows?"

"What be ye thinkin', Humphrey?" asked a smaller man, who noted the malicious glint that appeared in the larger man's eyes. The others gathered in close around him.

"I'd be thinkin' 'tis up to us to rid ourselves of these traitorous creatures. What say ye? Are you with me?" he asked, eyeing each man before him. Each nodded in turn.

"Then draw your swords, friends, and follow me. We shall wait on the cathedral steps until the meeting has broken up. When the traitors emerge, we shall deal with them as they deserve."

Grinning and confident, the would-be assassins sauntered around to the west façade of the cathedral. Taking up positions on either side, they waited. Above them, the statues of the saints peered intently down at them as if imploring them to abandon their murderous plan, but the men took no notice. Their eyes were fixed on the massive cathedral door, waiting for it to open, waiting for it to send forth their prey.

Chapter VI

Eight days had passed since Sir William Askew's early morning rendezvous with the other Lindsay commissioners, yet no word had come to South Kelsey Hall concerning the whereabouts or safety of the Askew men. Rumors abounded, but none that could be substantiated. Although Elizabeth had sent out numerous messengers, most did not return; and she could only guess that they had joined the ranks of the rebels. Those that did return had little to report because they refused to venture too close to any place where the rebels and reliable news were to be found for fear of being taken captive as the young Askew sons had been. Even a letter from Christopher supplied no news of their fate. So the Askew women waited.

From morning 'til evening, Elizabeth remained cloistered in her bedchamber, coming out only when the promising sound of horse's hooves pounded up the long driveway. Martha, Anne, and Jane took turns sitting with their stepmother, trying to offer whatever hope or consolation they could invent. But the terror that had gripped the household the day the rebels had descended upon it continued to lay hold its icy grasp; and so the days passed in desperate silence as Elizabeth stared out her bedroom window, watching everything, seeing nothing.

The October days had grown unusually chilly, but still Anne chose to spend much of her time walking the garden paths surrounding the great house. The multitude of flowers had long since disappeared, and most of the trees were barren; but Anne still found solace in this garden. It was in this garden that she first surrendered her heart and life to her Lord, and it was here that she came to seek Him in prayer and meditation for the strength she needed whenever she felt weak. The last eight days had brought her to these gardens often.

She walked the garden paths now in spite of the bitter weather. Like a mischievous sprite, a brisk wind from the south whipped at Anne's dark green velvet cloak causing it to billow up around her. She snatched the lining of the cloak and pulled it snugly around her slender body to fortify herself from the biting cold. Although the sky was gray and the air frigid, Anne had no desire to return to the house—a house, oppressive and taunting in its memories, that afforded no comfort within its walls. So Anne sought the grandeur of the open skies and far horizons for relief; but, today, these did little to quell the growing anxiety. Her heart and mind were deeply troubled and agitated, and she feared her mood would further disturb her mother and sisters. For eight long days she had spent endless hours in prayer, begging God for the safe return of her father and brothers, but it seemed her prayers went unheard. She sensed her young and untried faith was faltering and, perhaps, giving way completely, and she was greatly alarmed. Desperate, she sought the garden trails and walked aimlessly, crying out to God for relief.

"Oh gracious Father, never have I known such fear! My own dear father and brothers may well be dead and then what is to become of us! Mother could not stand so great a loss. And Martha. Dear, sweet Martha, she is so frail! How could she survive such sorrow? I have struggled with all that is within me to be strong for them, dear Lord, but my own heart is failing me…and failing Thee."

Her voice trailed off. She stopped walking and gazed out across the vast Askew lands. In a moment of realization she knew that it was not for her mother and sisters that she feared, but rather, for her own loss. Tears burned in her eyes and spilled down onto her cheeks.

"How can I bear to lose Father and Thomas? And my dearest Francis? Francis, who is my confidante and spiritual counselor, how could I ever live without him?"

Suddenly, the tears gave way to choking sobs. Anne crumpled to the ground and buried her face in her hands. A wave of fear washed over her; and the young woman, unable to stifle the sobs, huddled on the narrow path, her shoulders shuddering under the weight of her emotions. Nothing in her brief life had prepared her for such fear, and its magnitude overwhelmed her, paralyzing her to her very core.

"My God, my God, help me!" she gasped.

Though the flood of tears gradually subsided, Anne's heart and mind remained numb. Fear clung to her as tenaciously as dead leaves cling to their branches, and despair mocked her fledgling faith. Hunched over, eyes and heart cast down, she was only vaguely aware of the cold October wind. She felt so very tired and oh, so alone.

Yet, the wind continued its unrelenting attack on the lone figure, yanking free tendrils of hair from under her headdress and whipping them about her face. Anne paid no attention. She waited silently, anxiously, yearning for relief. Her heart pleading, her mind questioning.

"Gracious Father, speak, lest my heart fail Thee completely."

With a heart full of turmoil, her wait continued. New tears misted her eyes as tumultuous feelings of abandonment invaded her soul.

Be still, and know that I am God.[4]

Dragging in a ragged breath, Anne sought to stifle her tears and calm her heart. Then softly, almost beyond perception, came the beloved Voice she was learning to listen for and trust: His Voice calling to her remembrance His words.

Whom have I in heaven but Thee? And there is none upon earth that I desire beside Thee. My flesh and my heart fail, but God is the strength of my heart and my portion forever.[5]

The words tumbled over and over in her mind, slowly penetrating the numbing pain. Understanding began to lay hold, and her heart yielded to the revelation.

'Whom have I in heaven but Thee?' God is all I have, all I need. He must be my first, my only love, she realized.

'My flesh and my heart fail.' Tis vain to trust in Father or Francis or even my own heart, for surely each will fail.

'God is the strength of my heart and my portion forever.' He alone must be my sufficiency in everything; He, alone, my soul's satisfaction.

As these thoughts took hold, a deeper understanding, frightening yet compelling, pressed in upon her. She struggled to resist, wanting to flee the terrifying thoughts that brought painful awareness to her heart. She knew what He was asking of her, but it seemed too much. She hadn't the strength. She could not yield them up, yet neither could she fight against Him. Slowly she realized she had to let them go; had to surrender all those whom she held dear.

Even if Thou takest these precious ones from me, Thou must be enough, she conceded. *I must trust Thee no matter what the cost.*

Anne's head dropped again to her chest. Her tears once more flowed, but these were the freeing tears of surrender. In the quiet of the moment, she came to understand that He was all she needed even if she lost everyone and everything she loved.

Why art thou cast down, O my soul? And why art thou disquieted within me? Hope thou in God, for I shall yet praise Him, who is the health of my countenance, and my God.[6]

"Forgive me, dearest Lord, for not hoping in Thee alone, for not making Thee 'the health of my countenance.' I do surrender all to Thee and beseech Thee to guard their lives. But whether Thou deems it right to return my father or brothers to our safe keeping or take them to be with Thee, I trust that Thou shall be to me 'the strength of my heart and my portion forever.'"

For the first time in eight days, Anne's heart knew peace.

In the chapter house, the king's reply was read a second time, this time by a parson who took great pains to read the letter slowly and not gloss over the angry words the king had written. The reaction of the commoners was mixed. Many were angry, others frightened, still others were simply stunned by the king's apparent disregard for their plight. Thinking it best to give them all time to digest what they heard, the rebel leaders dismissed the commoners; and the meeting broke up. The massive oak doors at the front of the cathedral were pushed open, and the crowd spilled out. So agitated and absorbed in conversation were they that no one took notice of the men who stood to the side with drawn swords held close to their thighs. No one, except one.

Alfred had been faithful in his service to Sir John Coppledyke
for more than fifteen years. He had found this uprising quite
disturbing but was even more disturbed that his master had chosen to align himself on the side of the commoners. He didn't
trust this common rabble and wondered more than once why his
master did. Now, as he filed out of the meeting and heard the
angry conversations brewing on all sides, his distress only
increased. His eyes continually darted from face to face, looking
for signs of violence about to erupt. As he emerged from the
cathedral, a glint of silver off to one side caught his attention. A
drawn sword! Alarmed, he recognized its owner's face as being
the same troublemaker who had been loudest in his demands for
blood. Discreetly, for fear of detection, Alfred glanced about
him. Several others who had been forced from the meeting as
well stood poised with swords drawn, and Alfred realized in
horror that they were waiting with deadly intent for the gentlemen to emerge.

He turned and hurried back into the cathedral, weaving his
way as quickly as possible through the flow of commoners trying to exit. Breaking free from the crowd, he hastened down the
corridor to the chapter house, his footsteps echoing off the
vaulted ceiling. As he entered the smaller room, he spied Sir
John still in conversation with several of the other gentlemen. Sir
John saw his servant reenter the chapter house, and one look at
his face told him that something was terribly amiss. He excused
himself from the group and went to hear what Alfred had to say.
Moments later, he hurried over to where the rest of the gentlemen stood.

"My friends," Sir John interrupted. "'Tis dangerous for us to
remain here. Even now, several men await outside the cathedral
with swords drawn. 'Twould seem their intent is to kill us as we
leave."

"I should have expected as much," Sir William said. "Our
efforts to delay their cause have shortened many tempers. They
want blood and will be satisfied with nothing less."

Young Thomas edged closer to his father. Since his abduction,
his life had been threatened many times; and each new threat
sent renewed terror coursing through his body and mind. Sir
William wrapped a protective arm around the trembling boy's
shoulders and smiled reassuringly at him.

"There is a south exit to the cathedral that we can take that will give us access to the chancellor's house. We should be safe enough there, but we must move quickly before the crowd disperses from the sanctuary. As long as commoners remain within, our assassins will not come looking for us," Thomas Moigne suggested.

The others agreed. Gathering up their few belongings, they quickly left the chapter house and headed into the cathedral. A large group of commoners still made their way out of western doors and paid no attention to the men who moved swiftly and quietly through the far end of the cathedral toward the shrine of St. Hugh and the southern entrance. Under the saint's vacant gaze, the gentlemen exited the cathedral. Quickening their step, the gentlemen hastened across the green and entered the chancellor's house. When all were safely inside, they locked and bolted the heavy doors. Only then did they allow themselves to breathe easier.

Outside the west doors of the cathedral, the armed men waited impatiently as the crowd thinned. Where were the gentlemen? Why did they delay in coming out? When the last of the commoners had dispersed, the men rushed through the doors. Charging through the cathedral like hounds in pursuit of their prey, they quickly came to the chapter house and burst through the door. Empty. Humphrey cursed, enraged that once again he had been denied his prize.

"John, Richard, search the cloister," he barked. "The rest of you, search the chapel and the choir. They have to be here."

The men fanned out, only to return several minutes later to report that the gentlemen were not to be found in the cathedral. Breathing threats, Humphrey stormed from the room bent on finding the rebel leaders whom he was convinced had helped the gentlemen escape. Charging through the camp, he spied William Morland conferring with several other men. He stalked up to him.

"Where are they?" he demanded.

Morland, clearly annoyed at the rude interruption, glanced at the man.

"Even if I knew to whom you refer, I have no time to answer your trivial questions," he snapped and returned to his conversation.

But Humphrey was not easily put off.

"How long will you protect those traitorous gentlemen?"

Morland turned slowly and glared at the surly man.

"If I have 'protected' anyone, it has been to keep your worthless hide from hanging!" he growled. "Look around you, man! Every day our ranks dwindle as more and more desert our cause. 'Twould serve you better to stay your sword and your thirst for vengeance and put your mind to determining a course of action that may yet succeed! Otherwise, we will all hang!"

Morland again turned his back, and the look he gave as he turned away warned the man not to press him further. But Humphrey had no intention of pursuing the conversation. The shock at the priest's words forced him to look about the camp in astonishment. Their number was indeed diminishing. All around him swarmed confused and frightened men. Sheathing his sword, Humphrey headed for his own tent.

"Humphrey, what do we do now?" one his companions asked.

"Go home," Humphrey answered as he strode off.

Sir William studied the men before him as each contemplated what their next move should be. How odd that a few brief hours can make such a difference, he thought. This morning, they had vehemently opposed each other, with Sir Edward still in full support of the rebellion. Now, with the mounting fear and confusion wrought by the king's reply, it was apparent that the rebellion was on the verge of collapse; and to save themselves, the gentlemen were now forced to ally themselves and work toward a common goal.

This latest turn of events brought to the forefront only two objectives: stay alive and obtain a pardon. Sir Edward in particular, so confident of victory only days before, now realized that the cause he hoped would bring him glory was irretrievably lost and that his life was in the greatest peril for having taken such an aggressive stand against the king. Without the aide of the other gentlemen or some quick scheming, he would surely face execution for his part in the rebellion. Sir William didn't know whether to pity him or expose him.

'Tis best to let Providence have his way with him, he thought. *I must look to my own safety and that of my sons.*

The threat of execution hung heavily on each of the men for they knew full well that the king would not be looking for justice as much as for examples. Their only hope was to beseech the Duke of Suffolk to intercede on their behalf before the king. Gathering parchment and quill, they quickly composed a letter and dispatched it to the Duke who still held the king's forces at Stamford. Then, as they had done so many times over the past eight days, they settled down to wait.

October 11, 1536

The rebel leaders were frantic. Though they tried to arouse zeal for the cause, the number of peasants and farmers who slipped away during the night escalated. Hunger and fear drove the commoners away, and many of the lesser gentry deserted to take up arms for the king, hoping in that way to expiate their sin against the king.

The gentlemen took advantage of this exodus and declared that they would not move until they had a reply to their request for pardon from the king. Without the leadership of the gentlemen, the rebels realized that their final hope for victory had vanished. Their host dwindled further.

On the evening of October 11, Thomas Miller, the Lancaster Herald, arrived with a proclamation from Lord Stewart of Talbot. His arrival brought increased apprehension, and the remaining rebels eyed him warily as he rode into the camp. The rebel leaders immediately demanded to know what news he brought, but he refused to speak to anyone but the captive gentlemen. Reluctantly, they led him to the chancellor's home where the sequestered gentlemen welcomed him eagerly.

Finally, they were able to obtain first-hand news of the king's army and its movements. When they learned of the small number of men the king had actually been able to gather, they were stunned; and Sir William trembled when he thought of what might have been. Had the rebel leaders known they outnumbered the royal forces by more than five to one, they would have eagerly pressed their advantage; and the rebellion would surely have succeeded. Sir Edward, realizing this as well, seethed inwardly, thinking that had he moved when he deemed opportune, he could have easily brought victory to the commoners and glory to himself. Now, he wondered if he would even escape with his life.

October 12, 1536

The sun climbed steadily over the town of Lincoln as the remaining host of commoners obediently trudged up the steep hill toward the cathedral. Acting under the authority given him by Lord Stewart, Thomas Miller ordered that all must come forward to hear the proclamation. Numbering less than half their original strength, the rebels were acutely aware of the seriousness of their circumstances; and many wanted nothing more than to see this rebellion done with. The sullen crowd, knowing full well that defeat was at hand, filled the cathedral cloister to hear the message the herald brought with him. A large table was dragged from the chapter house, and Thomas climbed atop so that all who gathered would be sure to hear him. Unfolding the parchment, he began to read in a loud and commanding voice.

> *To all true and loyal subjects of His Majesty: you are hereby ordered to lay down your arms and disperse yourselves immediately, each one of you to your own home to await the king's pleasure concerning your most treasonous and treacherous acts against His Grace and His sovereign realm. If any man among you continues in this place, it shall be understood that he furthers the cause of rebellion against His Grace and will be dealt with as befitting a common traitor.*

As he finished and folded the letter, a hush fell over the sullen rebels as the realization sank in that all was truly lost. Their glorious and exulted cause had indeed ended, not in the victory of which they had been so certain, but in shame and guilt. Now, there was nothing left to do but pursue every means possible to save their own necks. A few of the leaders tried once more to incite the crowd with angry and valiant rhetoric, but their words died quickly as they watched the commoners, tired and resigned, file out of the cloister and head home. The rebellion was over.

Relief swept over the gentlemen albeit short-lived as they became only too conscious of the fact that they, too, had to convince the king that their roles in the rebellion had been coerced and that, under the most difficult of circumstances, they had acted honorably and loyally. Once again, they secured parchment and quill and wrote out a formal request for clemency, citing in detail the events that had transpired and their efforts to thwart the rebellion at every opportunity. They also inquired as to whether they should await the Duke of Suffolk in Lincoln or come to Stamford with armed men. When the letter was complete, Sir Edward stood up.

"I feel 'tis my duty to take the letter to the Duke," he announced, hoping his display of humility would soften some of the bitter feelings he knew that many of them harbored toward him.

All in the room understood well that his part in the rebellion would be difficult to explain and that his need to seek the king's mercy was by far the greatest. Therefore, they agreed to his carrying the letter, though some begrudgingly.

Sir Edward wasted no time in departing, and accompanied by his father and brother, set out for Stamford. Knowing that a reply would not be forthcoming for at least a day, the gentlemen passed the time writing letters to all whom they believed could serve them in their quest for pardon. Sir William, who still had many friends at court, would do the same. But for him, a more pressing letter had to be sent. Taking parchment and quill in hand, he began to write in his bold script. *My dearest Elizabeth...*

When Anne heard the voice of a servant announcing the impending arrival of riders to South Kelsey Hall, she did not move from where she sat on the window seat in the west library. Too many times over the last ten days, messengers had returned to the Askew estate with nothing to report, and she felt sure that this time would be no different.

Since her garden revelation two days earlier when the Lord had shown her that He must be her sufficiency, she had spent much time to herself. She discovered that *knowing* that God must be everything and *living* that way were not the same thing, and she struggled with aligning her feelings with her faith. Therefore, to strengthen her resolve, she secluded herself in the library where she could study her Bible with little worry of being interrupted. Since Jane and Martha were not avid readers, preferring music and needlework to books, Anne felt secure in her hiding place.

She had found a passage in Philippians that was of great encouragement and was diligently trying to commit it to memory when the door of the library burst open. Jane flew in and ran to Anne's side.

"Anne, come quickly! Oh, you must come!" Jane cried breathlessly, tugging on Anne's arm with one hand and grabbing the Bible from her with the other.

"Jane, what is wrong? Pray, tell me, what is the matter?" Anne asked, seeing the excitement on her sister's face.

"You shall see for yourself, but hurry now. Make haste!"

Alarmed, Anne was up and racing out of the library with Jane close on her heels. They headed for the great entry hall. As they entered, Elizabeth and Martha were descending the grand staircase more rapidly than Anne would have thought possible. Elizabeth did not pause when she reached the hall, but ran to the massive front doors. She pulled on them with all her strength, and the doors swung open. The women poured out into the afternoon sunlight.

Anne's alarm gave way to exultant joy as she immediately recognized the two riders galloping toward the house. Moments later, Francis and Thomas bounded from their mounts and were immediately enveloped in the ecstatic embraces of mother and sisters. Tears streamed down Elizabeth's worn face as she held

Thomas close to her, afraid that if she let him go, he would vanish from her sight. Thomas squirmed in her possessive grip; and finally, she relinquished her claim but kept her eyes steadfastly on his face.

Then a shadow fell across her brow. She turned anxiously toward Francis, her immediate joy swept away as she feared for the fate of the one who had not returned.

"But what of your father? Why has he not come?" she asked, though she was unsure as to whether she wanted to hear the answer.

Francis grasped her trembling hands in his young, strong ones and smiled.

"He is well, Mother. He sends you a letter by me. The rebels have dispersed, but he felt he needed to stay on in Lincoln to await word from the Duke of Suffolk concerning the king's pleasure."

Elizabeth felt her knees give way as overwhelming relief swept through her. Francis grabbed her about the waist and laughed.

"Now, you must not swoon before me! Father would be quite disapproving," he teased. "But enough of these tears and kisses. I am famished, and a man needs more than affection to keep his strength up—even though the affection be from such lovely women!"

Thomas gleefully echoed his brother's sentiment though he was eager to tell his family of his harrowing experience.

"Yes, yes, of course you are hungry and no doubt exhausted. We can hear of your tale as you dine," Elizabeth said, still trying to calm her trembling hands. She once again wrapped a protective arm around Thomas' shoulder as they turned toward the house.

Anne hung back, still too overcome with emotion to trust herself to normal conversation. Francis, realizing she was not accompanying them, turned to face her, puzzlement in his eyes. But as he gazed into her face, he understood. He stepped toward her and again took her in his arms. The gratitude that she felt as she laid her head against his chest brought renewed tears.

"I prayed every day for you, dearest," she whispered hoarsely.

"I know. I felt the strength of your prayers on my behalf."

"I also learned that I had to surrender you completely into God's hand. Yet, I feared He would try my faith by taking you away forever. Now, here you are returned to us!" she smiled up at him through glistening tears. "God is so good, Francis."

"He is good, indeed."

Five days later, a bone-weary and emotionally exhausted Sir William returned home, thankful that the rebellion had come to an end with so little bloodshed. However, it soon became apparent that the bloodshed was just beginning. King Henry, incensed that his subjects would take up arms against him and determined that such an outrage should not happen again, made it quite clear that he expected retribution to be exacted quickly if not judiciously. Henry cared little who bore the brunt of his anger as long as someone was made to pay. Therefore, in apprehending and punishing offenders, it was expediency and not justice that prevailed.

Many of the more visible rebel leaders, among them Captain Cobbler, were immediately arrested and hanged. Others were rounded up more slowly and imprisoned throughout the long winter months to await trial in the spring. Of the one hundred and forty that were originally apprehended, only one hundred survived the harsh prison conditions in the Lincoln castle dungeons. These went on trial in the spring of 1537; and not surprisingly, each was found guilty. Their lands and goods were confiscated, yet only thirty-six were sentenced to hang. William Morland was one of the thirty-six.

In Sir William's estimation, the most notable examples of justice gone awry were played out among the gentry. Sir Edward Dymock, doing all within his power to avert personal calamity, betrayed a man of lesser gentry standing and saw to it that he was executed. In doing so, he convinced those looking for scapegoats that he was above reproach. Along with his father and Sir John Coppledyke, he managed to retain his favor with the king and live out his life in comfort.

Thomas Moigne was not so fortunate. He was arrested that same October and brought to trial in early March the following year. Being a lawyer, he defended himself both eloquently and skillfully, but to no avail. In truth, his judgment had been decided long before the trial began, making the ritualistic trial a mere formality. On March 7, much to horror of the Askew family, Thomas Moigne was hanged, drawn, and quartered in the Lincoln square.

However, the king could little afford to decimate the ranks of gentry through which his government wielded its power; therefore, most of the upper class gentry escaped both prison and execution. Still, many fell under a cloud of suspicion that remained with them all of their lives. Sir William was one such gentleman. Though he tried to persuade otherwise, his actions in the rebellion were interpreted as wanting in their support of the king, and Henry's displeasure became evident. Sir William never regained the favor of the king and was thus barred from ever appearing at court. With the loss of the king's favor, there came the inevitable loss of personal fortune; and for the first time, Sir William found himself worrying over whether his sons would be secure in their future.

For Anne, she remembered those uncertain October days as a turning point in her young life. Her own convictions grew stronger as she became more deeply convinced that Martin Luther's teachings were indeed of God. She saw the uprising as a deadly threat against God's true servants, and she determined that she would give her life to fight against the darkness of false religion. God had been gracious in sparing her family, but she understood that the day may come when she would once again face the possible loss of those things she held most dear. Yet, even so, God's promise that He would be "the strength of her heart" encouraged her. And she knew when the time came, He would be enough.

Chapter VII

Spring 1538

Elizabeth stormed into the study where Sir William sat reading and slammed the door behind her as she entered. Sir William, looking tired and much older, glanced up as she strode toward him, fire in her eyes. His shoulders sagged and he sighed inwardly, knowing instinctively what was coming.

"You must speak to Anne," she began hotly. "I am at my wits' end. No matter what I say to her, she quotes scripture to me! What impertinence! That she should instruct me on matters of religion! And if that weren't enough, she takes the servants away from their duties to read the Bible to them! When I scold her, she simply says 'tis her 'Christian obligation' to share the gospel with the less fortunate. What is to become of such an unruly child!"

Elizabeth paced back and forth in front of her husband, clasping and unclasping her hands as she spoke. She was obviously exasperated and her exasperation boiled within her, causing her to lash out on a frequent basis, though it provided little relief for her overwrought emotional state and only intensified tension in the Askew manor.

It hadn't always been so. Indeed, not so long ago her calm composure had been a source of strength to her husband and children. Then October 1536 happened. From that point on, Dame Elizabeth Askew was a changed woman. The Lincolnshire rebellion had had a profound impact on all the family, but Elizabeth had weathered it worst of all. The emotional nightmare she endured those ten days and the resulting loss of family fortune and their good standing at court bred fear and shame in her heart along with a bitterness toward all religious thought – Catholic and Reform. She blamed both for her presently reduced state, and she wanted nothing more to do with either one. Now, to her utter dismay, she found that in her own household, a religious zealot resided; and this fact was more than she could handle. The affectionate relationship she had once enjoyed with her stepdaughter had deteriorated into a match of wills, and too often Elizabeth felt herself on the losing side. She stopped abruptly, directly in front of Sir William.

"She has even begun taking excursions into the village to convert the commoners! William, this must stop!"

Sir William sighed again, being sure this time that his wife standing before him took notice. He laid his book on the end table beside his chair and rubbed one hand over his eyes as he composed his thoughts. It was bad enough that he had to defend himself before other local gentry who, for reasons he never understood, had fared much better since the rebellion than he; but now, he found himself continually interceding between wife and daughter. A most repugnant task.

He particularly found it difficult to take a definitive stand on either side, though he understood perfectly Elizabeth's complaint. As mistress of South Kelsey Hall, Elizabeth deserved to be treated with respect and to have her words obeyed even when they crossed his daughter's convictions. But he also understood and secretly admired Anne's ardor. Aside from the most fundamental rituals of which she was expected to take part, Elizabeth had rejected religion in her life; but Sir William found himself leaning more and more toward Reformist theology, though he still kept his beliefs private. His daughter, however, undeterred, availed herself of every opportunity to speak of her beliefs, convinced that she must do all within her power to see her family, friends, and, for that matter, anyone who happened across her path won to the true faith.

Anne—strong-willed, dogmatic, and possessing the zeal and hubris that often accompanies youth—was not easily discouraged – or disciplined. She endured each scolding or whipping with an air of sublime resignation, believing that in doing so, she was entering into the sufferings of Christ. How could a father stand against such thinking! Not once in disciplining her had he heard her utter an unkind word against him or Elizabeth; rather, she was pointed in letting them know that she felt no resentment at all and that she eagerly forgave every act. This generosity only galled Elizabeth all the more, and the gap between the two widened.

Sir William sighed again.

"I will speak to her once more, my dear, but she is not easily denied."

"A good thrashing may help her see her place."

"Thrashings have not accomplished that as of yet. I rather doubt that another one would," he responded, loathed to carry out such a harsh treatment. "Send her in, and I will try again to make her understand."

But even as he spoke, he knew full well that Anne would be trying just as hard to make him see the errors of his ways, and too often, her arguments were uncomfortably sound. He dreaded this.

Elizabeth strode from the room, her long silk skirts swishing angrily as she left. A few minutes later, Anne quietly entered the study. She knew what was coming, but if she felt any anxiety, she did not display it. Rather, her entire demeanor was calm, almost complacent. *Most irritating*, thought Sir William. She stopped obediently before her father, smiled pleasantly at him, and waited for him to speak. Sir William drew a deep breath.

"Anne, your mother has informed me of certain behavior that she finds unacceptable. She tells me that you take the servants away from their duties by reading the Bible to them and that you continue to do so even though she has spoken against such conduct on numerous occasions." Sir William hoped his words sounded sterner than he felt.

"I take them away from nothing. Is it impossible for one to work and listen at the same time? When Cook is plucking a pheasant, is the task so difficult that it takes her every bit of concentration to perform it? Or when Isabel is on her hands and knees scrubbing the floors, are her ears also required to produce a clean floor?"

"Of course not, but 'tis a distraction nonetheless." Sir William answered weakly.

"Are not their immortal souls more important?" Anne continued. "What cheer have they in this life, confined as they are to a life of servitude? Would you wish that after a dreary life of hard labor, they enter eternity without the hope of salvation, forever languishing in the horrors of hell?"

This was not going well for Sir William. He switched approaches.

"Your conduct is grievous to your mother," he countered.

"'Tis more grievous to the heart of our Lord for souls to be eternally lost."

Sir William was beginning to appreciate more the feelings Elizabeth expressed. How was it that he could easily out argue most of his peers, but his own daughter left him flustered and on the defensive. Exasperated, he rose from his chair and towered over his petite daughter.

"I shall not speak of this to you again, Anne. You do not see Francis behaving in such a manner though, I daresay, his passions equal yours. Leave the saving of souls to the parish priests, and tend to matters more appropriate for a young woman. You shall refrain from these Bible readings while the servants are at their duties, and you shall give Elizabeth the respect she is due," he ordered.

"In what way have I been disrespectful to Elizabeth?" Anne asked, refusing to be intimidated by her father's stalwart frame. She stared up at him, her gaze unwavering.

"She tells me that you have taken it upon yourself to instruct her in the way of religion. This will not do, daughter, as I rather think 'tis not the place of the child to instruct the parent."

"I do not instruct, Father; rather, I reply to her accusations with the revealed word of God whereby I live. She wishes to know why I act as I do. I simply tell her what God tells me. If that is instruction, then I do it because I cannot do otherwise."

Sir William's patience had worn thin.

"Then kindly refrain from explaining your actions and keep your tongue still! Why must you make this so difficult?" he thundered.

Anne did not reply. Her eyes clouded over; and for the first time since entering the room, she looked away from her father. Sir William could not read her face, but he immediately felt remorse at his harsh words. He hated these confrontations with his daughter, especially since nothing was ever resolved by them. He turned away from her and dropped into his chair, careful to keep his eyes diverted. Silence hung heavily between them. Finally, Anne spoke.

"'Tis only my love for you and Mother that compels me to speak," she said quietly. "If I have offended, then I beg you to understand that I do so out of an earnest desire to see you both secure in the grace of our Lord. You forbid me to speak; the Lord forbids me to be silent. To whom do I owe the greater allegiance?"

Anne waited, but her father did not respond. He stared wearily at the blackened stone fireplace where a dwindling fire crackled only a few feet from his chair. He was tired and hadn't the strength to enter into a theological debate with Anne. He also knew his threats would be dismissed and she would continue as she had, willing in time to submit to the inevitable whipping. Taking his silence as a dismissal, Anne slipped from the room. Relieved to find that Elizabeth had not waited outside the study for the outcome of the conversation, she hurried down the hall toward the stairs that led to the back entrance. The gardens beckoned.

Spring was just beginning to make its presence known in Lincolnshire. Tiny pale-green buds appeared on the trees, and newly awakened flowers stretched their stems through the rich, moist earth to laze in the sun's warming rays.

Anne inhaled deeply, reveling in the delicious smell of new life springing up on every side. Rain the night before had left the air fresh and exhilarating, and the young woman savored every sweet scent that wafted on the cool breeze. The cloudless azure sky and soft green grass provided a welcome relief from the oppressive rooms, and rules, of South Kelsey Hall. Anne could not understand Elizabeth's anger or objections to her Bible readings, but with such delights surrounding her, she could not hold onto the sadness and frustration that drove her to the gardens. Choosing her favorite path, she strolled along, quietly singing a psalm of praise—totally unaware of the solitary figure who solemnly watched her from his study window.

January 1539

Thomas Kyme was not a handsome man, at least not in Anne's eyes. With his short, stocky build, reddish hair, and wispy goatee, he reminded Anne of a faun she had once seen in a classical painting. He even swaggered as she imagined a faun would. Yet she could forgive him his appearance for she understood that a person's physical traits were not his own to choose. She could even overlook that as a farmer, he lacked the education she so dearly prized. For indeed, the twenty-four-year-old Thomas knew little beyond the skills necessary to raising his crop and negotiating a fair price for it at market. All this, she could, though only by supreme effort, forgive. What she could not forgive, however, was his complete lack of imagination and his boorish contempt for any idea that did not agree with his own. But worst of all, he was a staunch Catholic.

Anne thought of all these things as she watched Martha being fitted for her wedding gown. The shimmering white silk underskirt overlaid with the green- and gold-embroidered brocade bodice and gown was striking; though, as Anne sadly observed, Martha's sallow complexion did little to enhance the gown's beauty. Anne knitted her brow in a worried frown as she contemplated her sister's upcoming marriage. What shame that Martha should be shackled to a man who lacked so many attributes that Anne considered vital in a man.

When Sir William began to take thought of a possible husband for his eldest daughter, it never occurred to him to consult Martha's feelings on the matter, nor did he consider the sons of his close friends or acquaintances as viable contenders, many of whom had suffered similar financial downturns as a result of the uprising. No, he determined that only a man of considerable wealth would suffice for his frail daughter. He found such a man in Thomas Kyme. Although a farmer, Thomas was quite well to do as his father owned thousands of acres of good farming land throughout the county – rich, fertile land proven in its ability to produce abundantly. Long months of negotiations between the Askews and the Kymes had finally culminated in the betrothal of Martha to Thomas. Sir William and Elizabeth considered the agreement a fine match for both families, and, for once, Anne was careful to keep her thoughts to herself. She pitied Martha, but if her sister was content with the proposal, then Anne was determined to be happy for her.

Whatever Anne's opinions might be, the rest of the family seemed quite enthused about the match, Martha not least of all. And if the twenty-two-year-old woman had any misgivings about marrying Thomas, she, too, kept them to herself. When Anne casually mentioned one afternoon what she believed to be the shortcomings in her soon-to-be brother-in-law, Martha was quick to chide her for such unkindness.

"Anne, you allow for no differences in temperament. Thomas may not be as well educated, but he is hardworking and honest. I believe those are qualities for which a wife should be grateful."

Anne was grateful—grateful that Martha would become Thomas Kyme's wife and not she. But perhaps Thomas suited Martha, for she was quiet, reserved, and delicate – all qualities Thomas was not but expected in a wife. She would dutifully keep his home and bear his children, and he would be undisputed lord of his manor. Although he did find it rather disagreeable that Martha was so well educated, he graciously conceded that as long as she remembered her place, he would not make it a point of contention. He also made it clear that no daughter of his would be granted the same privilege.

"What think you, Anne, do you like it? Do you think Thomas will like it?" Martha asked, interrupting Anne's thoughts. Anne looked up to see Martha posed before the long polished glass, admiring her reflection in the shimmering gown.

Anne smiled.

"Of course, dearest. How could he do otherwise? You and the gown are beautiful."

Martha crossed the room, her skirts softly rustling as she walked, and settled on the bench beside Anne.

"I know what you think of Thomas. But 'tis truly a good match, and I believe I shall be very happy."

"I pray with all my heart that you shall be, although I shall certainly miss your companionship. Whatever shall I do without my dearest Martha?" Anne reached toward her sister and gave her a hug.

Martha smiled and started to reply, but a coughing spasm suddenly overtook her. Anne quickly wrapped an arm around her sister's thin shoulders as the young woman shuddered from the uncontrollable attack. Finally, the hacking subsided, but Martha, pale and trembling, leaned into Anne for support. Anne continued to hold her. After several minutes, Martha sat up straight, her feeble strength regained. She smiled wanly at Anne who could not conceal her worry. These spasms had become more frequent in the last few days, and Anne was greatly alarmed.

"You needn't fret over me," Martha offered weakly. "I am fine."

"You are not fine! You are tired, and you must rest. Come, let me help you out of your gown and into your nightclothes," Anne said, encircling her arm around the other's waist and helping her to her feet.

"'Tis too early for bed," Martha protested, "and I do not wish to miss supper."

"I will see that a tray is brought to your room. Now, I will brook no argument. You must take care of yourself, dearest. I daresay, Thomas would not wish to take on such a sickly wife." Anne laughed, but the sadness in Martha's eyes brought instant remorse for her callous statement.

"I am quite sickly, aren't I? Thomas may decide 'tis not such a good match after all."

"He will do no such thing. You will be well in no time if you would simply take care of yourself. Now, enough of this. Come and lie down."

Realizing she hadn't the strength to resist her sister's strong will, Martha allowed Anne to help her out of the heavy gown and skirts and direct her to the soft feather bed that occupied the greater part of the room. Anne tucked the woolen blankets and coverlet snugly around Martha, who smiled up at her and then almost immediately drifted off to sleep.

Anne stood by her bedside a moment, looking down at the slender body barely outlined beneath the heavy bedding. Martha had grown much weaker over the past few weeks, and her figure was more like that of a young girl than an adult woman. Anne worried so for her. Dark circles under Martha's eyes had become a permanent feature of the fragile face, a face already sunken and hollow. Still, Anne refused to believe that anything was seriously wrong. Martha only needed to rest.

Offering up a quick prayer, Anne leaned down and gently kissed her sister's forehead.

"Rest well, dearest. Your groom awaits."

And so wedding plans progressed. The date was set for the first Saturday in April, providing sufficient time for the banns to be published and for the Askew manor to be made ready. From the early morning hours until nigh unto midnight, the servants of South Kelsey Hall worked feverishly to prepare the large house for the upcoming event. All the silver had to be polished, the floors and walls scrubbed, the tapestries beaten and aired, the guests rooms made ready. Cook was in a frenzy as she considered the amount of food that must be prepared for the large number of expected house guests; and the kitchen servants dreaded the coming weeks as they knew that as the day of the wedding approached, Cook would unmercifully push them to their limit and beyond to ensure that nothing was overlooked.

English winters were generally mild in the midlands, but February 1539 seemed determined to outdo itself in the overbearing amount of cold, wet weather it forced upon the hapless Lincolnshire residents. Icy blasts from the north dumped freezing rain and snow on the countryside, shrouding the county in a blanket of silver and white. Unaccustomed to such weather, gentry and commoner alike struggled to stay warm as the bitter wind pierced through windows and doors. Although the servants of South Kelsey Hall kept every fireplace ablaze with a crackling fire, the house refused to relinquish its damp, chill air; and everyone bundled up in as many woolen garments as possible to overcome the unmerciful cold.

Martha, too, struggled to stay warm, wrapping herself in a heavy woolen blanket and sitting as close as she dared to the roaring fire in the front parlor. Still, she felt chilled. Undeterred, she bent over her needlework, her nimble fingers expertly plying the needle and thread through the linen cloth. The emerging floral pattern was almost halfway finished, and she was determined to have it complete before her wedding day, notwithstanding how she felt physically.

From across the room, Elizabeth quietly watched her, worry lines creasing her face. Martha's coughing spasms had become more frequent and more severe with the passing weeks, and she seemed to be shrinking before their very eyes. *And this savage cold only worsens Martha's condition,* Elizabeth thought as she wished fervently for spring and the warmer days that it promised.

Freezing rain pelted the windows, and the wind sighed through the cracks around the window frames making them shudder and wheeze. Annoyed by the sound, Elizabeth arose to see whether she could fasten the window more securely and reduce the chilling draft. As she vainly tried to tighten the latch, a thump from behind startled her. She turned toward the sound and gasped! Martha's slim body lay crumpled on the floor, her outstretched hand only inches from the flickering flames.

"William! Francis!" Elizabeth screamed as she raced to her stepdaughter's side. She yanked the white hand away from the flames and gently turned the young woman over.

Heavy footsteps pounded the hardwood floors, and Francis burst into the room to find Elizabeth crouched on the floor, cradling the limp body of Martha in her arms. As he reached them, Anne and several household servants appeared simultaneously at the doorway. One look and Anne was across the room, kneeling with Francis and Elizabeth beside the unconscious young woman. Francis slipped his arms under Martha and lifted her to his chest, surprised at how little she weighed. Clutching her tightly, he stood and hurried from the room, Elizabeth and Anne following in close procession. In the hallway they met Sir William, leaning heavily on canes for support and looking toward Elizabeth for an explanation as to what the commotion was all about. But seeing his eldest daughter's limp form in the arms of his son answered his unasked questions. He understood immediately. As Francis bounded up the steps with his precious bundle, Sir William barked orders to the servants. Then, on the arms of a strong manservant, Sir William hobbled up the stairs as quickly as his weakened legs would take him. The servants scurried in every direction to do their master's bidding, frightened that their young mistress suddenly seemed so gravely ill. Martha was well respected and loved among the servants, and each wanted nothing more than to see her strong and healthy once more.

Hearing the frantic cries and seeing Francis carrying Martha, an upstairs servant ran ahead and had Martha's bed turned down ready to receive her. Francis gently lowered Martha to the bed, then placed his hand to her cheek. Her face was flushed and hot. Francis called for a basin of cool water and herbal remedies to be brought immediately, and another servant ran from the room. As one of Martha's personal attendants came around to disrobe her, Anne immediately stepped forward to assist. Even Elizabeth condescended to the task normally considered fit only for personal attendants.

Realizing they were in the way, Francis and Sir William reluctantly backed from the room, leaving the women to tend Martha. As they exited, they almost collided with a servant who had gathered the required home remedies and was hurrying to the bedside. They stepped aside and let the servant enter, then slowly and quietly headed for the stairs.

"Perhaps we should send for Stephen Peerson," Francis suggested, extending his arm to support his father as they began the slow descent down the stairs. Stephen Peerson was considered to be the local physician though his training was somewhat questionable.

"I rather doubt that Peerson could do any more than Elizabeth or the servants. No, 'tis best to let our women nurse her."

At the bottom of the stairs stood Jane, face white and frightened. In her hand, she held the needlework on which Martha had been working. As Sir William reached her, he steadied himself on his canes and then placed a reassuring hand on her shoulder. But no words of comfort came to mind to allay his youngest daughter's fears.

"Please tell me, is she grievously sick? She will recover, will she not?" Jane asked, her eyes searching the faces of the two men for assurance.

Sir William sighed, then mustered a slight smile.

"'Tis too early to know, child. We can only wait and pray."

"But God would not take Martha from us, would He? Surely, He knows how much we love her."

Sir William looked at Francis. The same question hung heavily in his mind, and he waited to hear how his son would answer. Francis stared into the earnest face looking up at him. He wanted to reassure his youngest sister as well as his father, but he had realized some time ago that Martha's condition was deteriorating at a rapid pace. Though wedding plans had blissfully continued, he had secretly doubted that a wedding would ever take place for Martha. Now, he was sure it would not. But as neither his father nor Jane had yet professed true faith, he worried that this situation could drive them away from God rather than draw them near. Finally, he spoke.

"I doubt not that God knows our hearts and our love for Martha, but her life belongs to Him. He gave her life; 'tis His sovereign right to take it from her if He so chooses. But rather than turn bitter over what we may lose, we should be thankful for what we have had. He may yet spare her life, but even if He does not; He is worthy of our devotion."

That was not the answer Sir William wished to hear, and he turned back toward the stairs.

"I shall be in my study," he simply said and with the help of his manservant, trudged back to the second floor.

In the upstairs bedchamber, the women huddled around Martha, each doing her part to soothe and care for the seriously ill woman. Martha's heavy woolen gown and stockings had been removed, and she lay in her night clothes under as many wool blankets as could be found. Yet, still her tiny frame shivered, and she murmured against the chills that set her body trembling. Though she had regained consciousness, she appeared confused and kept mumbling unintelligible phrases. Anne bent close to her sister's face.

"Be still, dearest," she quietly urged. "You need to rest."

But if Martha heard or understood, she made no indication and continued her secret monologue. Anne dipped a cloth into the water basin and placed the cool rag on Martha's forehead. At its touch, Martha jerked her head to the side and moaned.

For long hours, the women remained close to the sick bed, rendering what little comfort they knew how. Martha slipped in and out of sleep, but never became fully alert. On regular intervals, Francis and Sir William quietly appeared in the room to make inquiries as to her condition and each time went away heavy hearted as the news never changed. Jane also joined the women in Martha's bedchamber, but she sat away from the bed at the window seat, refusing to gaze upon her eldest sister's emaciated form. She wanted to be near, but her young heart refused to deal with the frightening idea that she could possibly lose one she loved so dearly. As the day crept toward night, the women decided it was best to take turns sitting with Martha so that the others could get some much needed rest. Elizabeth insisted on the first watch, so Anne and Jane quietly withdrew from the room. As she closed the door behind her, Anne paused as she saw Elizabeth reach for Martha's hand. A pang of jealousy bit at her heart and she couldn't help but wonder if Elizabeth would feel such tenderness were she the one lying in the bed. Wishing to separate herself from the painful scene, Anne quickly pulled the door closed and headed for her room.

It was well after midnight when Anne returned to take her watch at Martha's bedside. She cracked the door open and peered in. A burnt-orange glow from the dying fire cast long quivering shadows around the room. Elizabeth sat in the exact spot she had been when Anne had left her, still clasping Martha's white hand in her own. She made no indication that she was even aware that Anne had entered. Anne slipped up beside her and placed a timid hand on her shoulder.

"Mother, you must go and rest. You have been sitting here for hours. I will stay with her now," Anne whispered.

For a long moment, Elizabeth did not move; then slowly she turned toward Anne and looked at her as though she were seeing through her to another time, another sickbed. Her eyes were strangely vacant and her voice distant.

"I have kept a vigil beside many a loved one, each time hoping, praying that God would have pity on my heart. Yet, even so, I have lost a husband,… son,… two small babes. I prayed earnestly that God would spare them; yet He would not." She stopped and looked again at Martha. "Nor will He this time, though I have begged Him once again."

She returned her gaze to Anne, her eyes now clearly focused and snapping with anger. When she spoke, her voice was low and filled with a venom that Anne had never heard from her lips.

"How is it you can be so devoted to such a ruthless God?"

The question did not want a response. Elizabeth rose slowly until her eyes were level with Anne's. Bitterness, anger, pity stared out from her eyes. Anne could not speak.

"You are a fool, child," she said almost imperceptibly. Then Elizabeth, shoulders sagging, turned and left, leaving Anne alone with her sister and her God.

Anne slid onto the stool where Elizabeth had sat. Elizabeth's words resounded in her ears, stinging her heart. Why could she not think of a reply? Martha *was* dying and God could save her, but even Anne knew in her heart that He would not. What then was the purpose in all this? She remembered again how God had taught her that He must be enough; and she tried to pray, but the words sounded hollow to her ears. How could He be enough when she felt so much pain? Yet He promised He would be.... Questions without answers tumbled in her mind, a mind already wearied by the day's events. Unable to cope with the mounting fear, she forced the questions from her mind and simply sat and gazed at Martha's diminutive form. Occasionally, she bathed the hot forehead with the cool cloth, but mostly she did as Elizabeth had done and held Martha's limp hand in her own.

The hours dragged on. The house grew eerily still. Anne's head began to droop.

"Anne?"

The voice was so soft and weak, Anne was certain that she had dreamt it. But then...

"Anne,... dearest."

Anne jolted awake. She leaned forward, clutched Martha's hand to her, and was surprised to feel the pressure on her hand returned. Martha was fully awake and staring intently at her.

"Yes, dearest. I am right here. What is it you need?"

"I... am... afraid, Anne. I...I know that I am dying, but I am afraid..."

"I am right here beside you, my love. I promise I will stay with you as long as you need me."

Martha took a deep, gasping breath, trying to muster the last of her strength.

"You... have always... been so strong. I confess... I have often been jealous, ...but now I am... thankful for your strength."

Anne leaned closer, wanting to hear every word.

"God is my strength, dearest, just as He is yours."

Martha stared up at the ceiling. A small tear slipped from the corner of her eye and lost itself in her tangled hair.

"I...fear...I do not... know His strength. Tell me again, Anne,... tell me how I can be certain that I am eternally secure."

"'Tis faith in our dear Lord Jesus alone that makes us worthy. He has paid the full price. We are merely recipients of His wondrous grace." Anne whispered, trying hard to hold back her own tears.

"'Tis faith?...but...I have... sinned... so grievously."

"Confess your sins, Martha. Trust in His blood to take you safely home."

Martha's eyes closed, but her lips moved in a whispered prayer heard only by God. Then she was still. Anne's heart pounded as she leaned in closer.

"Dearest! Can you hear me?" Anne demanded in a hoarse whisper. Martha's eyes fluttered opened, and Anne saw a sparkle in them that she had never witnessed before.

"'Tis true, Anne. He... has heard... He... has forgiven." Her voice was barely audible, but she smiled weakly and a new light radiated from her face. "I... am... not...afraid... anymore."

Anne bent her head and kissed the hand she held. Tears wet her cheeks, but her heart nearly burst with joy as she praised God for the wondrous grace He even now showed her beloved sister.

"How... beautiful... they are,... Anne," Martha said, her voice barely a whisper.

Confused, Anne glanced around.

"Who, Martha? No one is here save us."

But Martha did not answer. Her eyes filled with wonder stared transfixed, seeing beyond Anne's ability to see as her life hovered between two worlds. Then, she exhaled one long shuddering breath and lay forever still.

"Martha?"

But Anne knew there would be no response.

What strange emotions engulfed her. Overwhelming grief; utter joy. Martha was gone; her earthly life snuffed out. Yet, Martha *was* alive. Martha *was* home.

Chapter VIII

The gray skies drizzled cold rain and sleet over the black-clad mourners; yet they stood resolutely, refusing to allow the wet droplets to force them from their place. They stood close to each other, but felt strangely alone. They faced the same loss, but no one's pain was equal. The voice of the priest droned on, speaking words of comfort, speaking words of emptiness. Each mourner heard what he believed was said; one was encouraged, another, desperately forlorn.

As the oblong box was being lowered into the ground, Anne glanced at the chiseled faces of her family as they gazed on. Sir William, supported by his manservant and his canes, stoically maintained his privacy, refusing to show outwardly any pain he had to be feeling inwardly. As if taking her cue from her husband, Elizabeth, in like manner, displayed a face devoid of emotion, though her eyes hinted at her heart's pain. Jane, leaning heavily against Christopher, had not stopped crying since the news had been broken to her. Thomas felt confused and awkward, not wanting to betray his budding manhood with tears, but not knowing how to deal with such invasive grief. Francis, Christopher, and Edward outwardly displayed countenances of strength, but Anne could well guess what they, too, must be feeling. Still, they ignored their own grief and willingly offered themselves as instruments of comfort to whomever seemed in need of it.

Anne needed it. She clung tightly to Francis' arm, relieved that the strength that held her up came from a source without herself. The last several days had tumbled together into indistinct activity as wedding plans abruptly ended and funeral arrangements solemnly began. Her memories of the hours immediately following Martha's death were more like a dream than reality.

Indeed, her first clear recollection was of Francis gently trying to disengage her hand from that of her dead sister's, hours after Martha's spirit had departed. She did not remember how she passed those hours, but she did remember the wash of conflicting emotions that followed and the game of tug-of-war played out within her, pulling her from despair to joy and back again. The joy and despair she understood and accepted, but the emotion that surprised her every time she looked into the serene face of her dead sister was envy—envy that Martha now knew an existence that she could not even imagine. In the final few seconds of her life, Martha was given her first glimpse into eternity, that glorious realm that existed beyond mortal comprehension. What had she seen in those last moments? What was she experiencing now? Why had Anne's eyes been blinded to that vision? At eighteen, Anne was full of life's wonders and joy; but now, much to her disconcertment, she felt envy toward a sister dead at age twenty-two.

The last words of the priest died out. The paid mourners filed quietly away. A few friends and acquaintances lingered, offering jaded phrases of comfort and stiff embraces. Anne accepted their embraces, but took no joy in them. She longed to be away from this place, from these people. She wanted to be alone. No, that was not true; she wanted to be with Martha.

She felt Francis gently urging her forward, and she allowed him to lead her back to the waiting carriage. The driver lightly flapped the reins and clucked to the horses, and the carriage lurched forward. As it pulled away, Anne leaned forward and looked through the carriage window to the open pit in the churchyard. Two men, totally disconnected from the import of their task, shoveled the mound of soggy dirt back into the opening.

She is not there, Anne reminded herself as she watched them. *They do not cover Martha; 'tis merely a box. Martha is somewhere beyond, somewhere wondrous.*

"Do not watch, dearest," Francis spoke lowly to Anne. "'Twill only make it harder."

Obediently, she turned away. As the carriage headed back to South Kelsey Hall, Anne began to wonder what life would now be like without Martha. Though she had not been Anne's closest confidante—that position Francis solidly held—Martha by her quiet and gentle spirit had been a good companion and devoted sister. In her presence, Anne was content to be herself without fear of criticism, Martha may not have understood Anne's passions, but she accepted them—and her. Anne knew she would dearly miss her.

At South Kelsey Hall, carriages lined the driveway as family and friends alighted. But the thought of spending the remainder of the day listening to their solemn prattle was more than Anne could bear; and at the first opportunity, she slipped away to her room, the rain prohibiting a much longed-for escape to the gardens. Instead, she sat in the window seat and stared upward. Perhaps if she stared hard enough, the heavens would reveal themselves. But for all her staring, the gray skies stubbornly refused to oblige her, and she finally resigned herself to tracing the paths of the raindrops as they hit the pane and wiggled their way to the window sill.

A light tap on the door; Anne did not answer. Perhaps the person would assume she was resting and leave her alone. The knock came again, more persistent. Then the door opened slightly, and Francis peered in. Unconcerned with the lack of welcome, Francis entered the room and walked to where Anne sat, still staring at the rain. He carried a pewter goblet and a plate covered over with a linen cloth. He placed both on a small table next to the wall, then sat down opposite her. He said nothing, but gently took her hand, grasping her slender fingers in his larger ones.

How she came to be in his arms crying uncontrollably she never quite remembered. All she knew was he was there, offering his strength—a strength she needed. All the while she cried, he never spoke, but stroked her hair gently, reassuringly. When the tears finally subsided, Anne straightened and smiled thankfully at him. He smiled back and handed her his handkerchief to wipe her eyes and nose.

"I brought a plate of food and some cider," he said, indicating his offerings. "I knew we would not be seeing you downstairs again today. I thought, too, you should be warned. Elizabeth is disturbed at your disappearance, thinking you rude to our guests."

Anne didn't care. She was sure that a scolding would be forthcoming, but that mattered little. She had endured too many of Elizabeth's tongue lashings to be bothered by them, but she was angry that Elizabeth seemed more concerned with decorum then Anne's need to handle her grief in her own way.

"She is probably more disturbed that it was Martha who died instead of me," Anne retorted.

Francis could not conceal his shock at Anne's words.

"Anne, what a ghastly thing to say! Elizabeth loves you as her own daughter. You must have more charity toward her for she bears her grief in solitude, having not the comfort of God to sustain her."

Anne was instantly sorry for her rash statement, but her bitter feelings remained. And whatever Francis may say, she believed in her heart that Elizabeth had since long lost any true affection for her. Still, she could forgive her, knowing, as did Francis, that Elizabeth had all but forsaken any remnant of faith she may have once possessed. Losing a loved one was painful enough; Anne could not imagine how difficult it must be to face such sorrow with only her own strength to carry her through.

Francis leaned forward and gently kissed her forehead.

"Try and eat something, dearest. You need to keep up your strength."

He rose, smiled down at her, then left.

Anne did not care to eat, and she cared even less about keeping up her strength. She continued to sit and stare into the nothingness outside her window pane. At the sound of footsteps in the hall, she held her breath, expecting Elizabeth to barge into her room with a tirade of angry words, but Elizabeth did not come. Hours passed undisturbed, and finally the weariness of the day's events caught up with her. Summoning her maid to assist her, she undressed and crawled between the sheets of the feather bed. The plate of food lay untouched where Francis had set it.

Where grief has captured the heart, time is the only champion able to set it free. And so, as days flowed into weeks, the Askew household slowly adjusted to life without Martha. Christopher and Edward returned to Westminster where the former served as a gentleman of the privy chamber and the latter in the royal service under Thomas Cranmer. Though gradual in degree, conversations around the dinner table once more became animated, and daily activities resumed. For her part, Anne found solace in her continual efforts to share her faith with those around her. Unconcerned with Elizabeth's disapproval, she continued reading the Bible to the servants. However, with some urging from Francis, she decided that discretion was the wiser alternative and carefully avoided her reading when Elizabeth was anywhere near. She also resumed her trips to town where she met with a small group of townswomen who enjoyed her discourses on the Bible. It appeared that life was settling back into a comfortable routine.

Then the letter came.

When her maid, Joane, informed her that a letter had arrived for her father from the Kyme family, Anne paid little heed. The Kymes had not been in attendance at either Martha's funeral or burial, which only solidified Anne's opinion of the family as a whole. She did not take into consideration that at that time of year the distance between the Kyme's estate in Friskney and South Kelsey Hall would make such a journey quite hazardous. She only knew they had not bothered to come, and she was not obliged to make excuses for them. Secretly, she rejoiced that Martha had been spared the fate of marriage to Thomas.

"'Tis probably a letter of condolences, nothing more. Though you would think instead of a letter, a man about to be married would have attended the funeral of his intended bride," Anne scoffed.

"Perhaps, he was too brokenhearted," Joane suggested, wishing to think the best of him.

"Nay, rather, he was too busy mourning his losses."

Indeed, Martha's dowry to Thomas would have been quite substantial, and the young man could not hope to fare so well with another family. Anne was not a romantic and knew that financial considerations played a large part in deciding marriages, but she hoped fervently that when it came time for her to marry, her father would at least consider her feelings.

For close to an hour after the letter came, Sir William and Elizabeth remained closeted in his study, and the household servants began to whisper their imaginings as to the letter's contents. Even Anne's curiosity was aroused, but she refused to give the matter little more than a passing thought. A rap on Anne's door sounded and at Anne's response, a servant entered.

"Your father wishes to see you in his study, milady," the servant announced as she bobbed a curtsy. An unsettling feeling crept into Anne's heart.

"Tell him I shall join him presently, Amy."

She put down her book and glanced at the polished glass. At eighteen, Anne was considered quite a comely young woman. Her features were even, her blue eyes large, her dark hair shiny. The reflection in the glass pleased her, but she quickly reminded herself that vanity was a sin that must be forsworn. She hurried from the room as if she believed that she could out run the prideful thoughts.

When she arrived at her father's study, she paused a moment to gain her composure. She then strode in, holding her chin high. Elizabeth was still there, looking quite pleased and rather triumphant. Suddenly, Anne's unsettled feeling ballooned into trepidation, but she was determined to remain calm.

Her father sat in his chair, his ever-present canes propped against it. The past year had seen a terrible decline in Sir William's health, and walking had become an ever increasingly difficult task. But however his body may be in decline, his mind was sharp as ever; and no one questioned who ruled at South Kelsey Hall. It grieved Anne to see her once stalwart father diminishing before her very eyes; but, as with Martha, his waning health spawned renewed interest in spiritual matters and Anne sensed a change in his heart. But today, he merely looked older and more tired.

"Come in, daughter," he said and waved her toward a seat opposite him. He held a creased parchment in his hand.

Anne moved across the room to stand in front of him, but chose not to sit. She waited quietly for him to speak and hoped that her face did not betray her anxiety.

"I have received a letter from Thomas Kyme, offering his deepest condolences." He stopped, half expecting Anne to say something. She did not. "Although he is as grieved as we are at the death of Martha, he is willing to proceed with a marriage."

Anne's heart began to pound in her chest.

"He has asked whether I would consider giving another daughter to him in marriage."

She felt the color drain from her face.

"More specifically, he has asked for your hand in marriage, and..."

"No!" The word exploded from her lips before Anne even realized it. The thought of being joined in marriage to that odious man was beyond her comprehension.

"Anne," her father looked at her gravely. "Your mother and I have discussed it, and we believe 'tis the best suitable alternative, both for Thomas... and for you. Thomas will be able to provide amply for you and..."

"I will not marry him, father!" Anne replied hotly. "He is a heretic!"

Elizabeth stepped forward sharply; and for a moment, Anne thought she might strike her. But she did not raise her hand; she simply glared at her.

"'Tis not for you to decide whom you shall marry. As to his being a heretic, he may be well to think the same of you! But as your beliefs are of little consequence to him, then you should demonstrate as much charity and accept his. He may be the only man willing to put up with your wild and unruly spirit!"

Anne sensed that her anger would only exasperate the situation—a situation going much against her. In a moment of desperation, she flung herself at her father's feet. Grasping his gnarled hands in hers, she searched his face for some hint of sympathy.

"Father, please, I beg you. Do not do this horrid thing. I cannot,...I shall not marry him! If he wants a wife, what of Jane? She is but one year younger and would be much more..."

"Anne, compose yourself! Your behavior is unbecoming. 'Tis not Jane for whom he asks, but you. And… I am inclined to agree with Elizabeth that his serious temperament may well be suited to your oft times spirited one." Sir William spoke harshly, but inwardly he ached. The sight of Anne before him on her knees begging forced him to consider things he did not wish to admit. In all honesty, he rather doubted the match was well suited, but Elizabeth had convinced him that only a man of strong temperament, as Thomas undoubtedly was, would prove a worthy match for his high-spirited daughter. Elizabeth had further convinced him that even though Anne opposed the match now, in time, she would come to respect and, perhaps, even love this young farmer. And Sir William hoped fervently with all his heart this would prove true.

But Anne was not about to sacrifice herself on the marriage altar to prove Elizabeth's theory. She pulled back and rose to her feet. Regaining her composure, she stated evenly, her voice measured.

"Say what you will. I shall not marry Thomas Kyme."

"Perhaps a willow branch will make you see the folly of your ways!" Elizabeth snapped.

"I would sooner submit to the sting of a willow branch that lasts but a moment than the horror of marriage to a man who would only make my life miserable," Anne retorted.

"Daughter, you are too harsh in your opinion of Master Kyme. He is an honest man, and I rather think he will treat you with kindness if given the chance. As to his beliefs, do you find fault with a man who fears God?"

"I find fault with his papist loyalties! Can a man who believes that the word of mere mortals stands above the word of the immortal Creator truly be God-fearing?"

Elizabeth, fearful at the direction of the conversation and knowing all too well from personal experience how difficult it was to debate Anne in matters of religion, interrupted.

"That is quite enough! The matter has been decided, and if you were a grateful child, you would be thanking us for such an agreeable match. But you are not grateful, and you act most unkindly toward your father, whose only concern is your best interests."

Anne searched her father's face once more, hoping yet to see some sign that he may relent. But his face seemed set and his heart unwavering. Straightening her shoulders, Anne stared defiantly.

"Do with me as you will, but I will not marry Thomas Kyme," she reaffirmed, then turned and walked from the study, leaving behind an irate stepmother and despairing father.

Elizabeth watched her go, her anger barely contained. The impertinence of the girl! She needed, indeed deserved, a good thrashing, but she knew Sir William would not agree to that. He had insisted that thrashings stop several years earlier when he came to the conclusion that they were accomplishing nothing. Elizabeth did not share this sentiment. In her frustration, she turned on her husband.

"Do you see what your enlightened thinking has begotten? Had she been brought up to learn the ways of a household instead of being allowed to pour over foolish books, this would not have happened! Since we cannot force her to marry, how do you propose to make her obey?"

"We must give her some time. She may not find the match so disagreeable after she has had time to think on it," Sir William replied. "And there is one other persuasion we have not tried."

For a fleeting moment, Anne considered running away; but she soon banished the thought as she realized she had no idea as to where she would go or how she would survive once she got there. And despite Elizabeth's harsh words, Anne would sooner endure those than consent to life as Thomas Kyme's wife. Her mind drifted to Martha, and her heart yearned again to be with her in that glorious beyond— that eternal place of refuge. But even as she thought of Martha, she was surprised to discover an anger brewing within toward her departed sister. If Martha hadn't died, none of this would be happening. Martha had been content to marry Thomas. Why did she have to die and pass this horrid man on to her? No, this could not be happening.

Anne sat before the fireplace in her bedchamber, her hands clasped in her lap. As she stared into the flames that licked the blackened logs, she tried to pray; but the words would not form. The heat of the fire warmed her face, but failed to touch her heart, which felt as cold as the late frost that laced her windowpanes. Every time she recalled the scene in the study, she shuddered. She was now completely convinced that Elizabeth only meant to be rid of her—that she understood. But how could her own father be so unfeeling toward her. Did he truly believe that Thomas was a good match for her? Did he understand her so little?

Well, she would simply refuse. Though she had heard of situations where parents had forced daughters to marry against their wills, they were the exception. And she could not bring herself to believe her father was of such a mind. No, she would wait. When he realized that she was determined in this matter, he would relent. He must relent. She hoped with all her heart he could relent.

An uneasy truce quietly formed among the Askew family members. Over the next few days, Anne was careful to say nothing more to her parents concerning the matter, and surprisingly, they said nothing to her. Indeed, though somewhat strained, conversation continued much as before, even if the topics were carefully neutral in content. Still, Anne could sense Elizabeth's anger toward her, even though it went unspoken. But Anne could endure the anger if it meant her life could continue as it had.

After several days, Anne was beginning to believe her father had abandoned his hope of persuading her to agree to the match; and Anne breathed a little easier. Twice, she had seen her father and Francis walking the Askew grounds, deep in conversation; and she trusted Francis to come to her aid and persuade her father that such a match was completely unsuitable. Still, she kept up her guard by maintaining a distance from the family, not wishing to give opportunity for another confrontation. She was reading in the library when she heard footsteps approaching. She tensed. The door opened, and Francis came in. Anne exhaled a visible sigh of relief.

"From the look on your face, you would think I were the executioner come for you," Francis teased.

"Perhaps an executioner would be a welcome sight."

"I rather doubt you really believe that, but you have been keeping your distance. Has your family become so repulsive to you that you prefer the life of a recluse?"

Anne reached out a hand to Francis, and as he grasped it, she replied, "You could never be anything but dear to me. If I have been distant, it is because of my fear. Surely, you know what Father intends."

Francis nodded, but said nothing.

"Francis, how could he ask me to marry such a man? How could he think that I would find happiness joined to a heretic!"

Still Francis did not respond. Anne pressed forward. "You do not agree with him, do you? Francis, please! Speak your mind to me!"

Francis looked steadily at Anne and sighed. Anne saw everything as black and white; and her mind once set was nearly impossible to persuade otherwise. But he knew he had to try. Drawing a deep breath, he said, "The Holy Scriptures admonishes children to obey their parents and to honor your father and mother."

Anne was stunned. She had been sure that in Francis she had an ally, but these were not the words she had expected from him, nor the ones she wished to hear. She jerked her hand from his and turned her face away, refusing to return his gaze.

"Would you have me forced into a loveless marriage?"

"Would you have me speak less than the Word of God to you?"

"He is a heretic!"

"He is a man whose eyes have not yet been open, but that is not to say that they cannot be. Perhaps, you are the very one whom God will use to bring light to his soul. You, by your witness and testimony, may be the one who will break through to his darkened heart."

Silence hung between them.

"Anne," Francis continued, "does not God have the right to choose your path? And does He not give parents the right, yea, even the responsibility to guide their children as they deem best? How do you know for certain that God is *not* leading you to marry Thomas when your own mother and father are convinced otherwise?"

Indeed, she did not know. Her prayers during the last few days had been few and rather blunted. At that moment, she realized—though unwilling to admit it to Francis—that she had not wanted to seek God's will in the matter for fear that it would conflict with her own. A great heaviness settled over her. She trusted Francis and knew he was a man who sought God. Could he possibly be wrong in this? Would he give her counsel contrary to the Word of God? Was God truly asking her to become wife to Thomas Kyme, a heretic? Could she possibly be the one who would bring him to the truth?

These troubling questions swirled in her mind, and she did not answer Francis. Nor did she even notice when Francis rose and left her alone again.

"Honor thy father and thy mother[7]..."

She knew this verse well and had even been comforted by it when faced with Elizabeth's harsh punishment. But now it stood as an enemy before her, taunting her and forcing her to walk a path she did not wish to walk. Everything inside her told her this marriage was wrong; but she could not believe that her beloved Francis, gently opening God's Word to her and encouraging her to submit herself to it, would or could lead her astray.

"I will not... I cannot..." she argued within herself, struggling to hold onto her own way.

"Children, obey your parents in the Lord, for this is right[8]..."

"Lord, how can I?" she whispered.

Silence.

Anne felt her heart breaking within her. To obey God meant she must obey her parents even if it meant marrying a man she could barely tolerate. Tears stung her eyes and spilled down over her cheeks. For several minutes, the library was filled with the desperate sobs of a broken young woman. But when the tears had completed their work, Anne felt a renewed strength and resolve. She wiped her face, straightened her spine, and went in search of her father.

Chapter IX

April 1539

In the years that followed, the only vivid recollection Anne had of her wedding day was the memory of the knot in her stomach that refused to be relieved. Though she prayed and fasted, she found no peace in the days leading up to her marriage to Thomas Kyme; and as she stood beside him before the church altar, her lips mindlessly repeated the vows but her heart was numb, refusing to accept the new life into which she was entering.

The feasting afterwards remained little more than a bad dream in Anne's memories. She heard the jovial banter and singing that surrounded her, but she was merely a spectator, a silent fixture around which life whirled but did not touch. Gaiety and celebration filled South Kelsey Hall, but Anne could not join in. Nor could one other, who looked on with sober face. Sitting off to one side, Francis, too, watched but took no pleasure in the festivities. At one point, he caught her eye and gave her a wistful smile, but it did little to lift Anne's spirit.

But if Anne's mood was downcast, Elizabeth's mood was overly joyous as she laughed and smiled, playing the role of the proud mother to the fullest. However, in Anne's mind, the gleam in Elizabeth's eye was not joy for her stepdaughter, but triumph at having at last won. Anne received Elizabeth's embrace stiffly, but the older woman took no offense, attributing it to the nervousness of a new bride.

Indeed, Anne was nervous. In fact, she was terrified; and when she first glimpsed her new husband coming toward her in his nightshirt, her terror gave way to choking sobs and pleadings that he would not touch her. Though disappointed and more than a little disgruntled, Thomas gave into his young wife on their first night together, believing it was her virgin modesty that produced such an emotional reaction. He was soon slumbering deeply, but Anne lay awake long into the wee morning hours, clutching the side of the bed, fearing to even breathe lest she wake him and he decide to take what was rightfully his.

Unlike Anne's heart, the April sun was warm and cheerful three days later as the carriage carrying the newly wed couple pulled away from South Kelsey Hall to begin its journey to Friskney nearly fifty miles south. As the carriage jolted down the long tree-lined drive, Anne summoned every ounce of her will power to restrain herself from leaping from the carriage and racing back to the mansion that had been her home, her refuge, for eighteen years. Beside Anne sat her maid, Joane, who like her mistress, dreaded leaving behind a life she held dear for an uncertain future. Across from her sat Thomas, a look of smug satisfaction on his face at having finally succeeded in consummating the marriage the night before. Anne refused to think on the horror of the experience, but stared resolutely out the window as South Kelsey Hall shrank from view.

Never had she felt so alone or so vulnerable, and the only solace Anne could muster was in her belief that she was a divine instrument of God to bring the true gospel to Thomas and the village people of Friskney. But already, she was missing Francis and Jane; and the ache in heart that had begun the day she agreed to marry only intensified with each mile that put Anne further from her beloved family and home.

The trip to Friskney was uneventful, though tiring. What should have been a six-hour journey turned into ten as the roads, muddied from the spring thaw and rains, twice mired the carriage in their well-worn ruts. When the weary travelers finally arrived at the Kyme estate in Friskney, Anne was totally exhausted. Every bone in her body felt bruised from the constant jostling, and her head pounded. Yet, for these pains she was thankful as it gave her a good excuse to retire to bed before Thomas finished hearing from a servant the news of the happenings since his departure. With the help of Joane, she undressed quickly and slipped between the cool sheets. But though she ached for sleep, it would not come. When she heard the door creak open, she closed her eyes and lay still, hoping her feigned sleep would be convincing to Thomas. It was, and soon Thomas was sleeping, his rhythmic breathing the only sound Anne could discern in the darkness. Her exhaustion finally took hold, and sleep came soon after to Anne as well; but even after she had drifted off, she slept fitfully, dreaming of the home she had lost.

Before Anne even awoke the next morning, Thomas was up and gone, a pleasant surprise to her when she finally did stir. She stretched and pulled herself to a sitting position, then reached for her wrap at the foot of the bed. She had slept longer than she had intended, due to the fatigue from the previous day's journey; and she could tell by the sun that the morning was already late.

She glanced around. Having been too tired to take notice of the bedchamber she had been led to the night before, she now studied her surroundings. The room was much smaller than what she had had at South Kelsey; but then, the entire house was considerably less grand than that to which she had been accustomed. The fire in the fireplace had long since died down, leaving only embers that smoldered but provided no warmth. Still, the room was clean and the furnishings adequate. In one corner, she saw Thomas' nightshirt draped over a straight-backed chair and a pair of dress boots propped beside an armoire. Suddenly, it dawned on her that this was Thomas' room. Though her trunks lay in the opposite corner, she was the stranger here; and this room belonged to another, albeit the "other" was her husband. The thought then struck her that as mistress of the house, she might, no, she *must* have a bedchamber of her own.

With this new thought, she eagerly rose from the bed, cracked opened the door, and called for Joane. The young woman scurried to her mistress' side to help her dress. Impatiently, Anne waited as Joane laced up the back of her gown, a dark blue gown made of finely woven wool. As Joane plaited Anne's long hair to fit under her headdress, another servant brought a tray of bread, cheese, and dried fruit. Anne did not feel like eating, but did so when Joane expressed concern that she was not looking well and needed to rebuild her strength after her tiring journey. Finally, fully dressed and her stomach unwilling to hold another bite, Anne escaped to explore her new home.

The house was little less than half the size of South Kelsey Hall, but still, by local standards, quite impressive. Constructed in the timber-framed style, the house boasted a large downstairs hall with a massive stone hearth occupying almost the entire north end of the room. A long oak table with benches on either side and an armchair at either end occupied most of the space at the south end of the room while two great chairs faced the fireplace. Along the west wall sat a huge oak sideboard, behind which hung an ornate tapestry depicting the return of a successful hunting party. A smaller parlor, a cross-passage, and a kitchen, which adjoined the hall on the east side, were all that comprised the first level. Upstairs were four bedchambers, one of which Anne quickly claimed as her own. In choosing a room, Anne preferred privacy to comfort and chose the one furthest from Thomas' room. Though it was quite small by Anne's accustomed standards, she was pleased with it nonetheless as its primary window faced east and the rising sun. She would not oversleep again.

When she called for a servant to move her trunks into the smaller room, she was met with resistance.

"Master Kyme will not be likin' ye takin' yer things to another room. He gave orders that yer trunk be moved to his room."

"I will deal with Master Kyme. Now, move those trunks immediately, or I shall have you beaten!" Anne snapped. She had never in her life struck a servant, but felt compelled to establish her authority as mistress from the start. Reluctantly, the servant obeyed, casting a wary glance in her direction as he hefted the smaller trunk to his shoulder.

Once Anne was confident that Joane was able to unpack her gowns and arrange her room without her supervision, she ventured outside. Stepping through the outer door into the mid-morning sun, Anne gasped. Her heart sank as she surveyed the dreary landscape that stretched out before her. No gently rolling hills or wooded slopes that she had loved in South Kelsey greeted her, nor were there any finely manicured gardens to which she could flee for comfort. Instead, in every direction, vast acres of fen and dikes melted away toward the horizon. The marshy bogs, which provided such fertile soil for crops when drained, provided no attraction to the eyes. And no matter which way she turned, the endless grey land, which even the sun's piercing rays could not brighten, lay before her. Loneliness and despair clutched her heart.

Anne continued to stare at the distant horizon though the servants paid no mind as they scuttled about busying themselves with the never-ending chores that kept the farmhouse in good running order. Indeed, they appeared oblivious to their new mistress, who seemed bolted to where she stood. If they saw the pain etched in her face, they gave no indication of it. If even one felt any pity on the forlorn young woman, that pity was buried in the urgency to complete the task at hand, lest the master's anger be riled.

Anne never saw Thomas approach.

"'Tis not the same as South Kelsey, but the land is fair and it produces a good crop."

Anne jumped at the sound of his voice. This amused Thomas and he chuckled. "Did I wake you then?" His tone became more serious. "Well, 'tis time you were awake. The day's half gone! I won't be havin' a lazy wife."

Anne turned to face him, drew a deep breath, and met his eyes. "I have had my things moved into another bedchamber. I believe 'twill serve us both well to maintain our privacy."

All traces of amusement vanished from his face. "'Twill not serve at all!" he snapped. "As my wife, you shall share my bed!"

Servants paused momentarily in their duties and glanced sideways at the young couple. Anne pretended not notice.

"I will not, sir. As your wife, I cannot keep you from my bed, but I can keep my bed from your room," Anne replied firmly.

Thomas was stunned. He knew that, unlike the gentle and docile Martha, Anne was quite headstrong, but he did not expect to confront her strong will so early in their marriage. Still, he was unwilling to give in without a fight.

"'Tis unnatural! A man and wife become one flesh and should bed together."

"'Tis not uncommon for husbands and wives to have separate bedchambers. I have been told by my brothers, who reside at the court, that the king himself always maintained private apartments separate from the queen. If the king has it so, do you suppose yourself better than he?"

Flustered at her boldness, Thomas could think of no answer; so Anne took advantage of the moment and turned back to the house. "I believe the midday meal is nigh ready. You must wash up before sitting at the table with me," Anne called to him over her shoulder before disappearing into the cross-passage.

For the first time since Martha's death, Thomas began to wonder what he had agreed to in marrying the younger Askew daughter.

Summer 1539

If the land was unfriendly, its inhabitants were more so. The taciturn peasants who survived off the unforgiving land eyed the new mistress of Kyme Manor with fear and suspicion. She was not one of them. They had been born and raised on this harsh land, they spent their days in back-breaking labor to scratch their meager existence from the earth until their bodies gave out, and then they were buried beneath it. They had little experience with a gentlewoman of Anne's status. In their minds, she was as far removed from their world as was the king and his court; thus, she was viewed as an outsider, a stranger from a great family, about whom they knew little and cared less to know.

For Anne, this new environment only accentuated her misery. Far from the cultured and sophisticated world that she had known, this world was one of peasantry and illiteracy. The conversation of her neighbors centered on their fields and livestock, and they cared not a whit for intellectual discussions of world affairs. Wherever Anne went during her first few weeks at Friskney, she could sense the stares of the local villagers and tenant farmers. Whispered conversations ceased abruptly whenever she came into earshot, though Anne could well imagine what was being said. She was an object of curiosity, an oddity; but even worse, it was whispered, she was a heretic. For in this strongly Catholic part of the country, Anne openly espoused the

Reform theology. Appalling stories circulated that she actually possessed and read from her own English Bible and that she refused to take part in the weekly mass. This last tidbit, the locals learned not from observation, but from servants' gossip.

Being a wealthy landowner, Thomas did not attend mass with the local peasantry at the Friskney parish, preferring instead to have the vicar perform the solemn rites privately for him and his household in the Kyme parlor. However, it quickly became somewhat of an embarrassment to Thomas when Anne refused to participate in these services. Despite his pleading and threatening, Anne remained adamant. She would not involve herself in superstitious rituals, she declared, no matter how much Thomas ranted.

"You defy the church? The holy priests? You, a mere woman, think you know more than they?" Thomas stared incredulously at the young woman who sat defiantly at the opposite end of the long oak table. He had begun to dread the evening meal at Kyme manor, for Anne invariably turned the conversation to matters of religion.

"I know what the Holy Scriptures teaches, and God's word stands above the traditions of men. I cannot, in good faith, betray what God Himself has declared to be the truth."

"Aye, and did not Christ Himself say, 'This is My body…this is My blood?' Did He not declare that when we eat the bread and drink the wine, we eat and drink His own body and blood?"

"In giving forth the bread and wine," Anne responded as though she were speaking to a child, "our dear Lord intended it as an outward sign of His most precious gift—the giving of Himself for our healing and salvation. The bread and the wine He left to us only as a reminder of His broken body and shed blood that we should ever be thankful, not that we should make such common elements holy unto themselves!"

"But He also said, 'I am the bread of life,'" Thomas asserted, his face reddening.

"And did He not in like manner say, 'I am the door… I am the vine?' But do you believe He actually was a door or a vine? Indeed, if that be so, should you not pay homage to the door of the church and kiss the 'holy' vine that grows up beside it? For if it is as you say, they are as much the embodiment of Christ as the host or the wine!"

Thomas slammed his fist down on the table, causing the plates and utensils to rattle nervously. "Enough! I will not be taught by you! You are my wife, not my priest!"

"And as your wife and God's servant, I am obligated to speak the truth to you."

"Truth? Whose truth? You think that the heretical writings of Luther and Tyndale contain truth! Indeed, they are most grievously deceived, and they have deceived you as well! But," his tone softened only slightly, "you are a woman whose mind is weak and susceptible to such things, so it is understandable." Then he quickly regained his authoritative posture. "But I will not have you instructing me in my own house!"

Frustrated, Thomas rose abruptly and strode from the room.

"Then I will go to those outside your house," Anne responded—after Thomas was out of hearing range. She dismissed Thomas' assessment of Luther and Tyndale, knowing full well that Thomas had never read any of their writings as he barely read at all. She had tried in vain to impart the truth to him, but he continually shut her out. It vexed her greatly that he blindly took the words of the priest without ever opening his mind to the possibility that he might be the one deceived. But she would continue to try.

Anne retired soon after to her own bedchamber and hoped fervently that Thomas' sour mood would keep him from one of his conjugal visits. In the months since she and Thomas had returned to Friskney, his visits had become fewer as his disenchantment with his bride grew. For her part, she found his change in mood entirely agreeable and secretly wished his visits would end altogether; but since Thomas had made it clear that he expected children, she had little reason to hope that their relationship would ever become platonic. The only thing that enabled her to endure her wifely duties was her belief that God had a higher purpose for her, a calling to which she must strive to be worthy.

In her mind, Friskney and all that it represented had become to her "the valley of the shadow of death." Everyday, she witnessed the vacant stares of the people around her, people without truth or hope. Convinced that God had sent her here as his messenger to "proclaim liberty to the captives," she studied her Bible diligently to prepare herself to go out among the people and impart the gospel to everyone she met. Thomas may not wish to hear what she had to say, but she was sure that there would be others who would.

A quiet rap on her door brought sudden panic to Anne's heart before she remembered that Thomas was not in the habit of knocking.

"Yes, come in," Anne called, closing the Bible she held on her lap.

Joane opened the door and bobbed a curtsey as she entered.

"Will milady be wanting anything more of me this evening?"

"No, you may retire if you wish."

The young maid turned to go, then looked back at her mistress. Anne saw a flicker of concern in the girl's eyes.

"What is it, Joane?"

"I… that is, 'tis plain that Master Kyme is harsh with you, but…" she hesitated, unsure of how much she should say. "But you must continue to speak the truth. I promise I will stand with you, no matter what comes." She bobbed again and hurriedly left the room.

Anne stared at the empty space where Joane had stood. Until this moment, she had not realized that those were the first kind words she had heard spoken to her in months; and her heart was starved for affection, any affection, even that from a young servant girl. She suddenly wished very much for Joane to return but could not bring herself to call to her. Setting the Bible on the night table, Anne rose and went to her bed. She slipped between the sheets and pulled the heavy quilts about her neck. Her longings for home intensified; and as the night stillness descended on Kyme manor, the quiet sobbing of its young mistress floated into the darkened halls.

November 1539

The late afternoon sun cast a long shadow behind Anne as she hurried along the well-worn path, gripping her Bible in one hand and her long velvet cloak in the other. A sharp November wind urged her forward as if warning her of Thomas' anger if she arrived late again for dinner. Although Anne did not concern herself with Thomas' tirades, for they had become routine; she nonetheless did not welcome them. If she could get home before he came in from the fields, she could at least hope for one quiet evening. She chided herself for staying so long at Sarah Lucas' tiny cottage, but her visits there were one of the few pleasures Anne had found in Friskney.

Anne had been in Friskney less than a fortnight when she began traveling the countryside oftentimes on foot, reading her Bible openly in the public square and declaring bolding that the priestly "miracle" of turning bread and wine into the actual body and blood of the Lord Jesus Christ was fraudulent and not founded on Holy Scripture. Denouncing Catholic doctrine, she taught the Reformed doctrine to any who would listen to what she had to say. But very few listened. Most turned away from her, either in fear or apathy. Some did so quietly; but many more did so loudly, vehemently voicing their hatred and condemning her as a heretic, believing as Vicar Jordan of the Friskney parish was quick to point out, only heretics read the Bible.

Yet Anne, convinced that she suffered the affliction for her Lord, refused to be intimidated. Indeed, the more opposition she met, the more determined she became. And, to her great joy, the Lord did not allow her zeal to go unrewarded; for though they were few in number, a small handful of women had listened and had come to believe the truth of which Anne so earnestly spoke. Sarah Lucas was one of those women.

As the wife of a poor tenant farmer, Sarah's life had been hard. She had borne seven children and buried five. The years of hard labor and overwhelming pain had crushed all hope from her heart, and although she dutifully went to mass, she found no comfort in the cold, mechanical words of the priest. Week after week, she stared at the paintings on the church walls—paintings depicting the saints of old gazing serenely at the nail-pierced body of Christ. But she could find no solace in those portraits, whose lifeless eyes reflected the emptiness of her own soul. In the weariness of her days, she often wondered whether God even knew she existed—or worse, whether He even cared. She never voiced aloud her thoughts for fear of the priest's condemnation, for apart from her own family and a few peasant friends, she was regarded as worthless by society. Then she met the strange young gentlewoman with an English Bible.

When Anne first tried to speak to her, Sarah retreated in fright. But Anne persevered, and eventually, her gentle ways and kind words broke down the wall of fear; and Anne found an open—though hurting—heart. As Anne read to Sarah from her Bible and shared the gospel of Jesus' love, Sarah dared not hope that such love could be directed toward her. But the day came when Sarah, sobbing and broken, understood God's love and accepted by faith alone the saving work of Jesus Christ.

Since that day, Sarah was a different woman. For the first time in her life, she knew peace. Though her days were still filled with back-breaking labor, each day became precious to her as she grew in her understanding of her new life in Christ. She listened in rapt attention each time Anne read from the Bible, and she begged her to repeat a verse over and over until she committed it to memory. Then, after Anne left, she continued to repeat the verse, lest she forget the wondrous words.

Anne's joy, too, overflowed; and she delighted in explaining scripture to Sarah and helping her memorize the portions that they studied together. News of Sarah's transformation brought curious neighbors to the Lucas cottage and opened new opportunities for Anne to speak; and within a fortnight of Sarah's conversion, Anne had the privilege of instructing four other women along with Sarah in the new theology.

Now heading home after a lengthy visit, Anne quickened her pace. She smiled with satisfaction as she recalled Sarah's pride at being able to recite from memory the first three chapters of Philippians—no small feat for a woman who had never learned to read. But with Anne's help, she had patiently listened and repeated the verses over and over until they were burned into her memory—and her heart. Tears brimmed Anne's eyes as Sarah, her own voice quavering slightly, finished reciting the last verses.

For our conversation is in heaven from whence also we look for the Saviour, the Lord Jesus Christ, who shall change our vile body, that it may be fashioned like unto His glorious body, according to the working whereby He is able even to subdue all things unto Himself.[9]

The glow on Sarah's face washed from Anne's heart the pain of a loveless marriage; and for the first time since coming to Friskney, Anne offered up a prayer of thanksgiving for her new circumstances. *When I meet with Sarah again, we will begin to memorize chapter 4*, she thought to herself as she hurried along.

As she approached the manor, Anne looked anxiously around. From this side of the house, she could not see the barns to tell whether the sheep had yet been driven into the paddock for the night. She hoped they had not because Thomas always oversaw that task, not trusting his underlings with the care of his livelihood. She strained to hear the sheep's telltale bleating as they were herded up the path to the gate, but the wind came from her back, whisking any sounds away from her.

Anne entered the cross-passage and glanced toward the large hall. Two place settings lay at either end, but there was no sign that one meal had been consumed. Anne sighed with relief and hurried toward the stairs. Over the months, she had learned to ascend and descend the steps to avoid any loud creaking, and now she crept softly upward toward the second floor and the safety of her bedchamber.

She reached the landing. Relieved, she leaned back against the wall to steady her rapid breathing. A creak! The door across from her swung open, and Thomas' stocky silhouette appeared in the doorframe. Anne almost fainted with fright! Yet determined not to show her fear, she quickly composed herself, nodded slightly to him, and stepped forward to pass him. In one side step, he blocked her path.

"Please move aside and let me pass," she said.

Thomas answered by stepping closer, his face inches from her. The strong smell of ale hung on his breath, and his wild eyes burned with anger.

"Where have you been?" he demanded.

Though the odor from his breath and his unwashed body assaulted her senses, Anne stood her ground and glared back at him.

"I have been calling on some of our neighbors as the good mistress of Kyme Manor ought to do."

"Do not lie to me, woman! You have been out spreading your heretical ideas again! I have told you repeatedly that I will not have it."

"And I have told you repeatedly that nothing you can say will deter me from doing God's bidding."

"You shame me before the entire countryside with your behavior!"

"Rather you than my Lord."

Thomas' anger exploded. He grabbed Anne by her shoulders and shook her with all his strength. Anne's head snapped back and searing pain shot through her body. Involuntarily, she cried out. At her cry, he abruptly released her, and she slumped to the floor. Thomas stared at her crumpled form, but made no move to assist her. Instead, he simply stepped back and hissed through clenched teeth, "Ye best be learning your place, woman!" Then turning on his heels, he retreated to his room, slamming the door behind him.

The pain that shot through Anne's body left her feeling fuzzy all over and unable to think. She was vaguely aware of strong, but soft arms encircling her waist and lifting her to her feet. She peered up into the frightened eyes of Joane, who had stooped beside her mistress for better balance in helping her to her feet. Leaning heavily on Joane, Anne stumbled toward her room and collapsed on the feather mattress of her bed. Her head pounded. She meekly submitted to Joane, who pulled off her shoes and stockings and gently urged her under the quilts.

Anne closed her eyes against the pain. When Joane applied a cool wet cloth to her forehead, Anne opened her eyes again, grateful for the cooling relief. Joane paused a moment, a shy smile on her face. Suddenly very thankful for her presence, Anne reached out and grasped Joane's hand in hers. She smiled warmly at her faithful companion. Joane smiled back, then gently disengage Anne's fingers.

"I will go and fetch you a supper tray, milady," she whispered. "You must rest now. You will need your strength. There are still many in the shire who must hear the truth."

January 1541

Francis sat at the desk in the second-floor study, reading again the letter he had received just that morning from Anne. A deep frown creased his forehead as he reread her words. Her letter disturbed him; but in truth, it was not what she wrote that concerned him—it was what she didn't write. She inquired after the health of their father, Elizabeth, and Francis' new young wife, Elizabeth Hansard, granddaughter to their stepmother. She wrote at length of her weekly meetings with Sarah and the other fledging converts, her continued efforts to proclaim the gospel, and the growing opposition among the local clergy. Finally, she commented on the bitter cold and the hope that spring would come early. But not once, even in passing, did she make any mention of Thomas.

It had not always been so. Anne's first letters to her brother after her marriage did speak of Thomas, though not always in the most glowing of terms. Primarily, she had written of her concern that Thomas adamantly remained closed to the truth. She had frequently requested that Francis might pray for Thomas and for her as she sought to be a goodly testimony to him. But as months passed, she mentioned him less and less; and now his name was omitted altogether.

Francis lay the letter on the desk and sat back against the straight-backed armchair. Anne was not happy. She had not said as much in her letters, but he knew her well enough to interpret her unwritten words. Her marriage to Thomas had been a mistake, one for which he personally took responsibility as he had been instrumental in convincing her that it was the right thing to do. Now he realized too late that the ill-matched pair would know nothing but misery in their life together.

He wondered to himself just how far the misery stretched. An earlier letter from Anne spoke of Thomas' outbursts of anger against her for her "irreverent wanderings" as he called them. And though Anne did not write it plainly, there was the hint that his display of anger had gone beyond words to violent harm, but Francis could not be certain it was so. Indeed, if he could confirm that Thomas has treated his sister harshly, Francis would not hesitate to confront him. And his standing as a nobleman would easily enable him to make the life of the young farmer quite uncomfortable. Yet, without evidence or provocation, he could do little more than write back and try to encourage Anne from a distance.

Francis sighed. The wind rattled the window panes, and he suddenly felt chilled. Rising from his chair, he went and stood before the fire in an effort to warm himself. Though he knew he must, he was not anxious to pen a response to Anne; for when he did so, he would wish to write a letter that would uplift her spirits, but the circumstances at South Kelsey Hall provided little fodder for an encouraging letter.

Two doors down from the study was his father's bedchamber. Within that bedchamber lay Sir William, his once strong body shriveled and useless. Throbbing pain was his constant companion though he valiantly tried to hide it. As time passed, however, it became increasingly difficult; and his anguished moans could be heard throughout the house. Adding to the old man's misery was a mind that remained strong and alert, ever aware of his lost dignity and robust strength. He was totally dependent on others to care for him, and he despised every moment.

Sir William's decline in health had taken a serious toll on his family as well as they waited for his inevitable death in hopeless anticipation. Though Elizabeth dutifully attended her ailing husband, there was no warmth or tenderness in her care. Indeed, she showed no kindness or affection toward any family member. For in her heart, she had ceased to live when on a summer's day eighteen months prior sixteen-year-old Thomas Askew, reckless and daring, had urged his horse to jump a ravine too wide. At the last moment, the panicked steed shied from the jump, throwing its young master over its head. The boy had died instantly from a broken neck—and, emotionally, Elizabeth had died with him.

In the months following that tragic day, it seemed to Francis that Elizabeth resigned from the real world, resembling more of a shadowy specter haunting the halls of the great manor, obstinately detached from those who still chose to seek some pleasure from life. The younger Elizabeth—Betsy to her adoring husband—distraught at seeing her grandmother so consumed with grief, tried in vain to offer some comfort. But all her attempts were thwarted by cold aloofness or scathing tirades. The older woman would not be consoled. She rarely spoke, and when she did, her voice was devoid of the spark it once held. South Kelsey Hall lay shrouded in gloom.

A quiet rap sounded on the door.

"Come in," Francis called.

Young Betsy Askew entered. He smiled when she came to him, a feeling of warmth spreading through him that the fire's heat had failed to produce. From under her headdress, smooth black hair neatly framed her delicate face; and her big brown eyes shimmered with love for the man she had married less than a year before. She looked tired; but when she smiled, the dark circles under her eyes vanished. She said nothing. She simply walked to him and laid her head against his chest. In response, Francis enclosed her in his arms and held her close to him.

Finally, she whispered, "I simply needed to have you near to my heart."

She turned her face up toward his. Francis responded to the invitation in her eyes. His arms tightened around her, and his lips pressed tenderly against hers.

The gloom at South Kelsey Hall began to dissipate.

Chapter X

March 1541

Thomas locked his arms over his chest in a futile effort to shield himself from the biting wind as he hurried through the village square. The countryside around Friskney was virtually devoid of trees, giving the harsh winter winds freedom to howl mercilessly across the white crystallized bogs, scouring the barren landscape and chilling to the bone every man and animal unfortunate enough to be caught in their path. The winter had been unusually bitter; and although it was March, it showed little sign of relinquishing its tenacious grip on the desolate land.

With his head lowered against the onslaught of the wind, Thomas pressed forward, driven on by the delicious thought that a warm tankard of ale awaited him at the local tavern.

"Thomas Kyme!"

Thomas stopped abruptly at the sound of his name, annoyed that someone would dare delay his intended pleasure.

"Thomas Kyme, I would have a word with you."

He turned toward the direction of the speaker. Vicar Jordan stood in the open doorway of the parish church, his priestly garments flapping in the wind like the wings of an ensnared crow. With his long bony fingers, he beckoned Thomas to join him. Thomas suddenly wished he had feigned a hearing loss when his name had been called, but it was too late now. Reluctantly, he strode toward the tiny limestone church.

Stamping his feet to shake off any half-frozen mud, he quickly entered the drafty parish, the priest right behind him. With some effort, Vicar Jordan secured the door against the wind, then turned and hurried toward the back of the church and into a small room that served as his study. Thomas assumed that he was to follow. When he entered, the vicar had already taken up his position before the blazing fire, rubbing his arms and shoulders in an attempt to rid his bony frame of the ubiquitous chill. Thomas waited politely, though his annoyance at this intrusion on his time grew with the passing moments.

"You must do something about your wife, sir," Vicar Jordan said at last, still facing the fire. "She poisons the minds of my parishioners with her heresies. As a loyal follower of the true faith, you cannot allow this to continue."

Thomas felt his face redden.

"I assure your grace, this cold weather has kept her at home...."

Vicar Jordan spun around and growled, "Has it? Or are you so ill informed of your wife's whereabouts? And even if she has remained at home these few days, do you think it will continue? Once the spring thaw comes, will she be kept at home then? Or will you allow her once again to venture forth to spread her lies and heresies?"

"She is not easily persuaded, sir. She is very headstrong and refuses to obey...."

"Then you must make her obey! The Church is firm that the wife must be in submission to the husband, not the husband to the wife!"

The accusation stung, and Thomas felt his anger swell within him. Showing his anger before the vicar was a foolhardy move, but his words tumbled out unbridled.

"Aye, sir, but the Church has never taken a wife! 'Tis an easy matter for you to sit in judgment when you have never had to face such a raging sea, but 'tis no easy matter to husband such a willful woman, I assure you. What would you have me do? Chain her to a chair and lock her in her bedchamber?"

"If need be, yes! She too easily sways the minds of these weak-willed peasants who grasp at every new wind of doctrine that comes along. Indeed, I have even heard they have dubbed her 'the fair gospeller.'"

"Begging your pardon, your grace, but she has convinced but a handful..."

"A handful whose wretched souls are now eternally damned! Will your conscience bear this out? Nay, sir, I rather doubt it will. But, perhaps, I should wonder at your own loyalty. Have you, too, been persuaded...?"

"I have not, sir! Nor shall I ever be! I am and always shall be a faithful follower of the true Catholic Church!"

"Then give evidence of it! Restrain your wife, sir, or the bishop shall hear of the matter."

Thomas paled at the threat. He glared at the man before him, realizing all too well that he would make good on his words. The vicar returned his glare, steadily staring at him as if he could see into the depths of Thomas' own soul. Thomas shifted uneasily; and reading the vicar's silence as his dismissal, he headed for the church door. But as he reached the sanctuary door, he paused. Momentary courage laid hold of his heart, and he turned abruptly and snarled, "If the parish priests did a better job at proclaiming the truth, weak-willed peasants could not be persuaded."

Before the startled priest could reply, Thomas stomped out. The biting cold slapped him full in the face; yet still, he paused momentarily on the parish steps, trying to decide his next move. Perhaps he should return home immediately and confront Anne—again; but the thought of another confrontation repulsed him. Glancing down Friskney's main road, he saw the tavern, its warming light beckoning him through its windows and the smoke from its roaring fire rising seductively over its rooftop.

A man needs shelter from this wind, he thought to himself and darted down the road to his waiting ale, which promised to shelter him from much more than the wind.

When Thomas emerged from the tavern several hours later, he was feeling greatly encouraged. The cheerful fire, the abundant flow of ale, and the hearty banter of friends had lifted his spirits as much as they had warmed his body. He could face anything now—even an obstinate wife.

The thought of Anne sobered him slightly, but not enough to take away his newly acquired fortitude. He stumbled as he stepped down from the tavern door, but quickly regained his balance. He wasn't drunk. He just felt confident—and a little light-headed.

Thankfully, the wind had died down; and although the night air was bitter, the ale warmed him down to his toes. He crossed the square to the livery stable, stumbling only once, paid the liveryman enough coinage to cover the care of his horse and to buy a pint, and mounted his bay gelding, with a little assistance from the grinning attendant. Nodding his thanks, Thomas then turned the horse toward the road that led to Kyme manor. The steed seemed in no hurry to return to the Kyme barn as its stomach was more than satisfied with the hay and oats it had eaten at the Friskney livery; and receiving no prodding from its master, it settled into a comfortable, easy gait.

Despite the cold, the ride home began pleasantly. The full moon, its luminous sphere frozen against the black sky, cast a distorted shadow of horse and rider across the hardened trail and illuminated the hoary frost that clung to the deadened grass that lined each side. And every time Thomas exhaled, his crystallized breath hung momentarily in front of him before dissolving into the night air. The rhythmic plodding of horse hooves lulled his already dull senses, and his head drooped against his chest.

A startled movement? An anguished cry? Thomas was never quite sure, but he was suddenly wide awake. His horse, sensing his master's tension, whinnied and pranced forward. Thomas reined him back and glanced around him. The icy moonlight bathed the fens in its ghostly light, but no apparition arose to greet him. For now, the world was silent.

Thomas exhaled in great relief and tried to still his pounding heart. His fuzzy thoughts could not discern what had alerted him, but as he drew closer to Kyme manor, his apprehension grew. The moment he had forestalled by hours spent in the tavern was now descending upon him, and his fortitude began to fade. Before him lay his timber-framed farmhouse, silhouetted against the frosty landscape. He tensed. The very place that should have welcomed him rose up as his adversary in the darkened night. It wasn't the structure but the woman within that Thomas dreaded.

As he stared at the familiar buildings, he wondered again how he had come to be in this situation. For certainly, this was not the marriage he had envisioned for himself. His mother had been a meek, hardworking woman, who kept the family home in perfect harmony. If she had ever disagreed with his father, she had shown her husband his due respect and kept quiet about it. His father had ruled his family firmly, but not harshly; and he had raised his children to believe in the true faith, hard work, and the value of a coin—in that order of priority.

Perhaps it had been this last tenet that had been Thomas' downfall. The handsome dowry offered by the wealthy and influential Sir William had entrapped him to the point that he willingly, even eagerly, married a woman of whom he knew little, convinced that she would be the very image of his mother in her demur demeanor and her earnest devotion to the running of his household. Had Martha lived, it may have been so, but Anne was neither demur, nor devoted—at least not to him.

In the two years since their marriage, Thomas could not remember one happy occasion between them. From the first day, she had held him at arm's length, defying his authority and withholding her affection. They were as different as two people could be. He understood farming; she understood Latin and Greek. He wanted to discuss market prices, she, social issues. He wished to remain untouched by his lowlier neighbors; she wanted to evangelize them. Their relationship had no hope of finding common ground.

And even in the physical union that should have made them one, there was estrangement. Unbeknownst to Anne, Thomas had come to loathe their intimate moments as much as she; but as he wanted children, he dutifully continued to make the conjugal visits, though it had become more difficult as months passed. Yet, even if this had been the extent of their differences, he may have found some peace in his own home had it not been for one exasperating and appalling truth—Anne was fanatical in her convictions to the Reform theology. Had she kept her beliefs to herself, he could have borne it. But she did not. It was bad enough that she humiliated him before the townspeople by openly espousing these heresies; but that she dared to instruct him, her husband, in religious matters was more than Thomas could bear. And as he possessed neither her sharp wit nor keen intelligence, he more often than not found himself on the losing side of every discussion in which Christian doctrine was the main topic. But for all his outrage, he was incapable of forcing his will upon her. Anne simply would not be ruled, and he despised her for it.

As Thomas rode up to the house, scrunching footsteps on frozen grass echoed as a servant scurried out from the darkness to meet him and take his horse to the barn. Thomas dismounted easily, his head fully recovered from the ale he had drunk. He handed the reins to the man and turned for the house. A soft orange glow filtered through the front parlor window. The hour was late. Surely, Anne would have retired by now—a comforting thought, though he knew the morning would bring him face to face again with his odious task. He entered the cross-passage, pushed opened the door, and stopped short.

A lone figure sat facing the dying fire. If Anne heard him enter, she made no indication of it, but, instead, continued to stare at the dancing flames as though transfixed by their flickering movements. For a moment, Thomas considered exiting quietly and retreating to his own room; but doing so seemed rather cowardly, and he realized that such an action would only delay the inevitable confrontation, not avoid it as he vehemently wished to do.

Summoning the dwindling confidence that had been his in such abundance when he left the tavern, he marched across the room. Anne did not look up. As he approached, he saw she held a letter on her lap, probably from Francis or Jane. He hoped it was from Jane, for letters from Francis always concerned him though he wasn't quite sure why.

"Wife, I would speak with you."

Still, Anne did not acknowledge him. Emboldened, Thomas went on.

"I will tolerate no more your gospelling throughout the village. This very afternoon, Vicar Jordan warned me, and now I warn you, that this matter will come before the bishop unless it ceases immediately! You claim to be a goodly Christian woman, yet you have no respect at all for the command, 'Wives, obey thy husbands.'"

Anne's gaze never left the flames, but lacking her usual tartness, she quietly replied, "I have as much respect for it as you have of the command, '*Husbands, love your wives, even as Christ also loved the church and gave Himself for it; that He might sanctify and cleanse...*[10]"

Thomas grabbed her arm, yanking her to her feet. He had no intention of allowing her to best him again.

"A man cannot love a disobedient wife! Nor can I abide a heretic! You shall stop if I have to beat you into submission," Thomas thundered.

Anne looked straight into his eyes, her face distorted by an emotion Thomas could not read. He braced for the verbal assault he was sure was coming. But to his astonishment, she burst into tears and fled from the room. He heard her sobbing as she raced up the stairs to her bedchamber. A moment later, the door to her room slammed shut.

Thomas was stunned. He had seen—and been the recipient of—Anne's fury, her biting wit, her sarcasm, and her maddening logic; but never had he seen her tears. This was totally unexpected, and he had no idea what he said that triggered such a response. Then he saw the letter.

It had slipped from her lap when he yanked her up and now lay inches from the fireplace. He retrieved it, recognizing Francis' bold script. For a moment, he thought to throw it into the flames; but, instead, he began to read...

My dearest Anne,

My heart is grieved within me that I must be the one to bear you the sad tidings that our beloved father died early this morning...

Thomas read no further. A measure of remorse swept through him as he thought of his harsh words. Had he known of the news she had just received, he would have forgone the confrontation—at least until the morrow. In frustration, he crumpled the letter and threw it on the dying embers. He watched as it blackened, ignited, and finally burned completely, leaving only silver-gray ashes aglow with orange edging.   Thomas turned and trudged up the stairs to his room.

Anne did not go down for breakfast the next morning.   She wished to stay as much away from Thomas as she could.   Sitting by her window, she stared out across the bleak landscape, her Bible in her lap.   Even when Joane brought her a breakfast tray, Anne did little more than glance at it.

Though she tried, she could think of little else than the heart-breaking news that had arrived the evening last.   She knew her father's health had been failing, so his death came as no surprise; but still, Anne ached at the thought of never seeing him or hearing his voice again.   And she wondered whether he had truly come to faith.   In his letter, Francis had stated that he believed he had; and Anne took comfort from that, but she would have liked to have known for certain.   And she desperately wanted to go to South Kelsey for the burial, but that was an impossibility, even if Thomas would allow it—which he probably wouldn't.   At this time of year, the roads between Friskney and South Kelsey would be far too hazardous to make such a journey, so she had to deal with her grief alone.

She opened her Bible.   She had no verse in mind to read, so she merely continued reading where she had left off the day before. I Peter, chapter 3, verse 1.

"Likewise, ye wives, be in subjection to your own husbands; that, if any obey not the word, they also may without a word be won by the conversation of the wives; while they behold your chaste conversation, coupled with fear."[11]

Anne stopped.   These were *not* words she wished to read.   She started to turn to another passage, but a piercing conviction stopped her.   Reluctantly, she read on.

"But let your adorning be the hidden man of the heart, in that which is not corruptible, even the ornament of a meek and quiet spirit, which is in the sight of God a great price."[12]

Anne winced and snapped the book shut. Desperately, she sought to shut out the crushing conviction that flooded her heart, but the Spirit of God would not relent. True, she had witnessed boldly to Thomas of the truth, but there had not been even the smallest measure of meekness or quietness about her. In the days following her marriage to Thomas, she had convinced herself that she was not bound to submit herself to a man who rejected God's word, but that was not what this passage said.

"He is a heretic," she argued to herself.

He is a man whose eyes have not yet been opened.... Francis' words echoed in her mind.

"Dearest Lord," she pleaded, "how can I submit to such a man?"

"Abide in me, and I in you. As the branch cannot bear fruit of itself, except it abide in the vine; no more can ye, except ye abide in me."[13]

"Then teach me, Gracious Father, how to abide in Thee."

Summer 1541

The same year Anne Askew married Thomas Kyme, the Reformation in England was dealt a formidable blow. Wishing to alienate England's troublesome king, the Pope formed an alliance with the king of France and the emperor of Spain. War threatened English shores. Henry, having neither the time nor the desire to deal with internal factions and realizing that England must be unified, urged the passing of the Six Articles of Faith, which upheld the most controversial of Roman Catholic doctrine and which, he hoped, would put an end to the divisions that threatened to tear his realm asunder. Any person found to be in opposition to these articles was in danger of forfeiting both land and life to the king.

To the great concern of evangelicals, it appeared for a time that the great forces opposing the Reformation were unstoppable. By 1541, Thomas Cromwell, a dedicated and powerful advocate of the Reform movement, had fallen from the king's favor and been executed; Anne of Cleves, fourth wife of Henry and a devoted Protestant, had been summarily divorced; and Henry, determined to find his own happiness, had become enamored with and married the beautiful, young Catherine Howard, who to the triumph of the Roman party was herself a staunch Catholic. To the established faction, the most favorable result of this new union was the whole-hearted return of Henry to Catholicism—albeit minus the Pope. And with the king's conversion came the power to effect laws that would make the Roman Catholic Church triumphant once and for all.

But if the political winds blew against the Reformation, the winds of spiritual unrest fanned the flames of spiritual revival, and thousands among the English gentry as well as the lower classes came to embrace the Reform theology. And though alarmed at the government's attempt to abolish all Protestant thinking from England, the evangelicals were nonetheless persuaded to hold fast their faith, even in the burning flames of the growing persecution.

Anne made good her conviction to be more submissive to her husband. In her desire to be obedient to God, she ceased arguing with Thomas and endeavored to spend more time at home, though not necessarily in his company. Thomas was surprised, and more than a little suspicious, at the change in his wife's demeanor, but he attributed it to the grief she bore at the loss of her father. But whatever the reason, he was glad of it and began to believe he had finally triumphed over her.

Although she was more temperate in her dealings with Thomas, Anne could not bring herself to submit to his orders that she forsake her evangelistic efforts—she simply purposed to be at home before Thomas came in from the fields. Though the Articles of Faith had been passed by Parliament in the summer of 1539, news of the event had been slow in reaching Friskney. When word first arrived early in 1540, several of Anne's young converts recanted their new faith, fearful of losing what little they had, or worse, being condemned as a heretic. But Sarah had held firm; and under Anne's patient tutelage, her faith continued to grow. Anne simply could not abandon her now; and so, each week, Anne faithfully made her way to the tiny Lucas cottage for prayer and Bible study.

If the Articles of Faith were meant to discourage Reformers, they had no such effect on Anne. Quite the contrary, she became more determined to continue her boldness in proclaiming her faith despite the possible consequences; and on almost every excursion into the village, she proceeded to the Friskney parish and read from the great English Bible chained to the altar, even if no one stopped to listen. Vicar Jordan, incensed by her audacity, took every opportunity to draw Anne's attention to the painting on the church wall depicting the "irreverent woman despising the host" and her just condemnation. Anne merely responded that such superstitious beliefs only grieved her heart and that she would not be silenced when it came to delivering God's truth.

And once again, Thomas discovered that he could not bridle his headstrong wife.

March 1542

Anne sat by her bedchamber window, eagerly reading the religious pamphlets that Francis had smuggled to her. The pamphlets were illegal; but knowing Anne was starved for intellectual stimulation, Francis had hidden them inside books of classical literature he had sent to her. Apart from her Bible, which had become quite worn from constant use, Anne had little access to any Christian material that could encourage her and build her own faith. And not since her marriage had she been able to read any of the writings of Reformation preachers, such as Hugh Latimer or Robert Barnes. Now, she drank in every word, thankful for Francis' thoughtfulness toward her. Anne was so engrossed in her reading that she failed to take notice of the heavy footsteps ascending the stairs.

The door of her bedchamber suddenly flew open, and Thomas stepped in, a look of triumph on his face. Startled, Anne shoved the pamphlets into the folds of her skirt, but it was too late.

Anger flickered in Thomas' eyes as he caught sight of the papers, and he strode toward her.

"What do you hide in your skirts, woman?" he demanded.

Anne bit her tongue, trying to hold back the tart words. When she did not answer, Thomas seized her by the shoulders and pulled her from the chair. The pamphlets scattered over the floor. Thomas bent to retrieve them.

"What is this? More of your heretical lies? Well, no more!"

To Anne's horror, he turned and threw the pamphlets into the fire, where they immediately took flame.

"And no more of this!" Thomas snarled and snatched up Anne's Bible.

"Destroy the pamphlets if you must," she begged. "But do not profane God's Holy Word." Anne reached her hand toward the sacred book.

Thomas held it aloft away from her reach and sneered.

"I have just come from the parish where I had a visit with Vicar Jordan. He received the good news this morning that Parliament has passed a new bill—one that forbids any lay person, *especially women*, to read this book." Taunting, he held it up just beyond her grasp. "By their decree, only a priest now has that right. By my faith, I now have the full weight of the king's law on my side. Therefore, as your husband, I forbid that you read either this Bible or the great Bible in Friskney; or I swear, I shall drag you before the ecclesiastical council myself and have you charged with heresy!"

Abruptly, Thomas turned and strode from the room, still clutching Anne's beloved Bible. With his threat reverberating in her ears, Anne sank into the chair, her anger welling up.

"You are *not* my husband!" Anne hissed, though Thomas was out of earshot. "You are an adversary of the truth, deceived by the papists who opposed the true servants of God. God shall surely judge you for your acts against His saints!"

Spring 1543

The months gave way to a new year, but much to Anne's dismay, fiery coals did not descend on Thomas even though it was clear that he had set himself totally against her. After suffering more than three years of humiliation, he had had enough of her fanaticism; and to ensure that she stayed well within the confines of his home, he ordered a manservant to watch over her to prevent her from taking anymore of her evangelistic excursions throughout the countryside. Though she chafed under the constant supervision to which she was subjected, the poor manservant who had been assigned the dreadful task suffered as much, for Anne's verbal abuse could be biting. But though he begged to be released from the task, Thomas was firm that Anne should not be free to spread her detestable lies any further than already done.

But more than the watchful eyes that guarded her every move, Anne grieved the loss of her Bible. At first, she feared that Thomas had burned the precious volume, but when she inadvertently overheard a servant tell another that the "master has well hidden that heretical book," she was greatly relieved. From that point on, she was resolved to find where Thomas had stowed it. But as she was under constant surveillance, she had little opportunity.

Yet if Thomas thought he had won by taking Anne's Bible away from her, he had greatly underestimated his wife. For even though she could no longer read the Bible for herself, he failed to realize that from the time she was a young girl, she had memorized huge portions of scripture. And with these secreted in her heart, she found strength.

"Blessed are they which are persecuted for righteousness sake; for theirs is the kingdom of heaven. Blessed are ye, when men shall revile you, and persecute you, and shall say all manner of evil against you falsely, for my sake. Rejoice and be exceeding glad; for great is your reward in heaven, for so persecuted they the prophets which were before you."[14]

For Anne, the issue had become quite clear; and she took comfort in her belief that she was, indeed, being persecuted for her unwavering faith in God's word. By his actions, Thomas had declared himself her enemy, her persecutor, a man bent on opposing the truth in which she so fervently believed. But he would not have the victory. She would hold fast to the truth, even if it meant suffering at the hands of this man whom the Catholic Church recognized as her husband—though she no longer acknowledged him as such.

And suffer she did. Apart from the humiliation of being under constant guard, she grieved that she had no freedom to visit Sarah or any of the village women whom she had been discipling. Whenever she was able to justify a trip to Friskney, her "shadow" went along to ensure she went nowhere near the parish church. To make matters worse, Thomas took away all her books—declaring they were the cause of her haughty spirit—leaving her with nothing to read at all. Nor did she have anyone with whom she could converse intelligently. Anne was more miserable and lonely than she had ever imagined being. The timber-framed structure of Kyme Manor became her prison, stifling and unbearable.

Thomas, however, smugly congratulated himself at having finally subdued his willful wife, though he soon discovered that his victory came at a high price. A bitter poison had enveloped the two, a poison that neither one felt responsible for nor took any measure to remove. Thomas, gloating over the triumph of the Roman Church, took every opportunity to mock Anne's religious beliefs. Though Anne could easily have defended herself, and crushed him with her keen wit, she chose not to respond; but, instead, she refused to sit at the table with him at mealtimes or even occupy the same room in which he was present. In retaliation, he ordered that unless she sit down to dine with him, she would not be allowed to eat at all. But after Anne went a week without eating and was forced to her bed, he begrudgingly relented, not wishing to have her death on his hands.

Thus, within this atmosphere the final break came.

September 1543

Joane crept cautiously along the upstairs hallway. She listened carefully for any sounds that would indicate the presence of another servant. All was quiet. Having waited all morning for an opportunity, she knew she had to move quickly if she were to have any hope of success and not be discovered. Glancing one more time down the hall, she drew a deep breath, quietly opened the door to Thomas' bedchamber, and slipped in. Quickly surveying the room, she made her choice and approached the large oak armoire that stood opposite the master's bed. Her heart pounded so hard, she feared she would faint; but she was determined to see her task through. The door to the armoire creaked as she began to open it. Joane froze. No sound of footsteps. Gently, she eased the door open further. Reaching inside, she ran her fingers over the bottom boards, praying she would be able to discern a distinction.

Yes, she felt it!—one board slightly misaligned with the others. She pressed eagerly, but nothing budged. Sliding her fingers along the edge of the board, she continued to press down. A small movement! She pressed harder, and the board jutted upwards. Under the board in a hollowed-out space was Anne's beloved Bible! Her hands trembling, Joane grabbed it up, pressed the board back into place, and hurried across the room. She paused only a moment to tuck the Bible under her apron and to make sure that the hallway was empty, then she exited as quietly as she had entered. Once outside, she drew a deep breath and tried to steady her racing pulse. Then she hurried to find her mistress.

The tingling breath of the autumn breeze tugged playfully at Anne's headpiece as she sat under the only tree that grew near to the house. Though Anne had never preferred needlework, she now found that it was one of the few diversions Thomas allowed since confiscating her books, and so she impatiently plied her needle to the linen. Her stitches were uneven, but she really didn't care. It was a way to pass the time.

When Joane came running up to her, her face flushed and her breathing rapid, Anne could not hide her alarm. But before she could say anything, Joane pulled a familiar black book from under her apron and held it out.

Anne was ecstatic! To Joane's great surprise, Anne leapt to her feet, threw an arm around the young girl's neck, and hugged her tight.

"How ever did you find it? Oh, my dearest friend, how can I thank you!" Anne cried as she held the startled servant close. Just as suddenly, Anne released her, sank back into her seat, and gazed lovingly at the book in her hands, gently caressing its cover.

Seeing Anne so happy was reward enough for the young servant girl, who had for so long feared for her mistress' well being. For four years, Joane had been a silent, and often trembling, witness to the harsh treatment Thomas had time and time again let loose toward Anne; and she had been a helpless bystander. Now, she had become an instrument of joy to her mistress, and Joane thought it well worth any punishment that may befall her should Thomas discover her ruse.

Anne looked up again, awaiting Joane's explanation.

Taking a quick glance around, Joane dropped at Anne's feet, leaned forward, and spoke in a low voice. "Ever since the master took your Bible from you, I have kept an open ear to any words that may be spoken in unguarded moments. Four days ago, I over-heard Humphrey bragging to James that though milady may try, you would never discover the secret compartment in which the master hid your Bible. I listened carefully, hoping he would divulge the whereabouts of this compartment, but he did not. Still, I made up my mind to find it. While the others were about their work, I have secretly searched every room and piece of furniture in the house. The master's bedchamber was the last place I looked because I greatly feared discovery; but this morning, I searched his armoire and found this!"

"You should not have taken such a chance," Anne scolded mildly, but smiled and grasped Joane's hand. "Yet, I am so very grateful that you did! But, we must be careful that Master Kyme does not find us out. I shall find another hiding place. One that only we shall know about."

The two young women laughed nervously at their secret and headed toward the house, Anne clutching her precious bundle close to her heart. Neither one saw the figure hunched behind a nearby hedge, nor did they see him slip away toward the paddock as they entered the cross-passage.

Chapter XI

Anne frowned as she stared about her room. With such sparse furnishings, finding a hiding place for her Bible would be difficult. She knew that it was only a matter of time before Thomas discovered the missing book and came looking for it—and she wanted to be absolutely sure he would not find it. Joane offered suggestions, but Anne was convinced that hiding the book in her own armoire or among her belongings would be too obvious. No, it must be a place where Thomas would not think to look.

Downstairs, a door slammed. Anne and Joane froze. Heavy footsteps pounded across the floor and began to ascend the stairs. Fear washed over the two women and sent them into frenzied activity. Anne desperately sought a place for her Bible. As the footsteps reached the landing and started down the hall, Anne thrust the book into Joane's hands, spun around, and quickly gathered up her skirt.

"Quick, tuck the book between my bodice and chemise!" she ordered.

The footsteps entered Thomas' room and momentarily stopped.

Her hands trembling, Joane hastily shoved the book up until it lodged securely against Anne's back.

The footsteps retreated to the hall.

Joane hurriedly smoothed the gown, hoping the pleats in the back would conceal the book's form. Anne hastened to the window chair, sat down, and snatched up her needlepoint.

Thomas burst in the door. Joane paled with fright. Anne merely looked up.

"Where is it?" he demanded.

Anne gave him a quizzical look. "Where is what?"

"Think me not a fool, woman! I know you have stolen your Bible from my room!"

"Pray tell me, how is it possible that I could steal something that by your own confession already belongs to me?" Anne asked quietly.

Thomas went purple with rage. He charged Anne, yanked her from the chair, and, in a mighty heave, threw her against the wall. An involuntary cry escaped Anne's lips as she hit the wall and slumped toward the floor. Joane hastened to help her stunned mistress, but Thomas blocked her path and drew back his arm. With one swift strike, he sent the young servant girl sprawling backwards.

"I shall have you beaten for this! You, who dared to enter my private bedchamber!" He stepped forward, but Anne darted past him to shield the sobbing girl from her master's wrath. Though inwardly terrified, Anne refused to allow her fear to be evident to Thomas. She faced him squarely, being careful not to show her back.

"If you beat anyone, then take your rod to me. Joane conducted herself as my true servant whose loyalty is toward me!"

"Loyalty! What do you know of loyalty? What of a wife's loyalty to her husband? Or of a subject's to her king?"

"My loyalty lies with my God. He alone owns my allegiance!"

"Then He alone shall have it!" Thomas thundered as he turned and tore open Anne's armoire. "I rid myself of you!"

Enraged, he grabbed her gowns and threw them to the floor in a crumpled heap. "I want no more to see your face or hear your voice! Pack your trunk and take your leave of this house! You are no wife of mine!"

As he turned from the armoire, Thomas flung his hand at the small side table. A gold candlestick clattered to the floor; and a delicate glass vase flew across the room, shattering on the opposite wall. Joane squealed and buried her head in her arms. Anne crouched protectively beside her, staring in horror at the violent outburst.

Then, just as suddenly, Thomas stopped. He glared at the two women huddled against the wall.

"I curse the day I ever agreed to make ye my wife!" he hissed and stomped out.

"Humphrey!" Thomas roared as he strode down the hallway. "Hitch the horses to the carriage. Mistress Kyme is leaving!"

The heavy footsteps retreated down the steps, across the hall, and ceased. The downstairs door slammed shut.

After four years of strife and bitterness, Anne was finally going home. As she settled into the carriage, she gave not one thought to the house—or the man—she was leaving behind. She never even glanced out the carriage window as the horses jostled forward. Her thoughts stretched toward the road ahead, the road that promised renewal, the road that led to South Kelsey Hall. In her lap, she clasped the well-worn Bible that had been her life-line and the final instrument in forcing the separation. Joane sat beside her, equally relieved to be leaving the place that had caused her so much fear and brought her mistress so much sorrow.

In their haste to leave, Anne had ordered that only one trunk be packed, as she had no desire to linger longer than necessary, lest Thomas have a change of heart. But Thomas, stomping around the paddock, had no intention of changing his mind. For him, the sooner Anne left, the better. His only thoughts were the longings for a home in which he would once again know quiet and comfort in the evenings after a hard day's toiling. For husband and wife, there were no regrets or second thoughts.

The carriage bumped along, making good time. The roads were dry, and the horses fresh. In a little town several miles north of Friskney, the driver stopped at a wayside inn where Anne and Joane could transfer to another coach that would take them on to South Kelsey. The two travelers took advantage of the stop, ordering some refreshment and taking a brief walk. Anne also penned a hasty note to Francis announcing her imminent arrival and hired a courier to ride on ahead of them to deliver the letter. Within a half hour, the coach was on its way.

With every mile that distanced her from Thomas, Anne felt herself grow freer and stronger. The heaviness and sorrow that she had worn around her like a shackled chain dropped link by link with the rhythmic clip-clop of the horses' hooves on the hard ground. For the first time since her wedding day, Anne knew the simple joy of being alive. She inhaled deeply the sweet scents of the autumn air, sank back against the side of the carriage, and allowed the gentle rocking motion to drain away the remaining tension.

As she watched the fens give way to rolling hills, a firm conviction took hold in her heart. She would never again return to Friskney—or to Thomas.

At long last, the carriage mounted the last rise, and Anne eagerly looked out the window. At the first glimpse of South Kelsey Hall nestled among the autumn trees, Anne's heart leapt with joy. The sun, just beginning its descent below the horizon, cast a fiery glow across the land. South Kelsey Hall was awash in crimson as the fading sun's rays painted the sky, the manor, and the landscape in brilliant reds and orange. Anne could not recall having seen anything so beautiful.

She impatiently awaited the footman to assist her and bounded out the moment he opened the carriage door. Just as she stepped down, the heavy oak doors of South Kelsey Hall swung open and Francis and Betsy emerged. Smiling broadly, Francis strode toward her. Anne rushed to him and flung her arms around his neck, embracing him heartily.

After a long moment, Francis gently disengaged her arms, stepped away, and held her at arm's length.

"Let me have a good look at you, dearest!" he said. But one glance told him more than he wanted to know. Though the day's light was fading, the evening twilight was enough to reveal the stark change in his sister's appearance. The vibrant young woman to whom he had said goodbye four years earlier was gaunt and pale. Dark circles under her eyes betrayed the pain she had suffered. His heart broke within him.

Then Anne smiled. And in her smile, Francis saw the saucy spirit and indomitable will that he knew so well. He smiled, too. *Anne may have been mistreated, but she is not broken*, he thought with satisfaction.

Anne turned to greet Betsy, who had waited patiently while brother and sister were reunited. Stepping toward Anne, Betsy welcomed her warmly.

"Francis and I were so delighted when we received your note telling us of your forthcoming arrival. We hope you plan to stay long with us."

"I shall be delighted to stay as long as you will have me," Anne responded, smiling broadly. She decided it would be wiser to tell Francis later that she had no intention of ever returning to Friskney.

"Let us not tarry here in evening air, my dears," Francis said, leading the ladies toward the door. "You must be tired and hungry from your journey, Anne. Your room has been prepared; so if you wish, you may retire now. Betsy will see to it that a tray is sent up."

"Oh, no, Francis, I am too happy to be tired. Even if you and Betsy have dined, I would enjoy taking my meal downstairs with you instead of alone in my room. The good Lord knows I have eaten enough meals alone! And, I confess, I am as hungry for intelligent conversation as I am for meat!"

"Then you are fortunate, for we have not yet dined. As soon as you have freshened yourself, we shall gather for dinner in the hall."

Anne grinned and turned toward the stairway. Then, stopping abruptly, she turned again toward Francis.

"What of Elizabeth?"

Betsy glanced sideways at Francis, who hesitated only a moment before replying.

"Elizabeth has taken to her room and refuses to see anyone but her personal attendant. 'Tis best that you not try to see her while you are here. 'Twould only upset her."

"Aye, but I shall continue to remember her in my prayers," Anne replied softly, then ascended the stairs with Joane following close behind her.

Anne headed toward her former bedchamber, eager to be settled into that dear, familiar room; but just as she was passing Elizabeth's room, the door opened. A startled servant, with tray in hand, gaped at her for a moment before quickly closing the door behind her and hurrying past, but not before Anne caught a glimpse of the withered figure hunched in the bed and the bitter eyes that bore into Anne's own with a hatred that chilled Anne's very soul. Stunned, Anne moved quickly down the hall, hoping that she would not again be passing when that door was opened.

As she approached her bedchamber, she slowed, then gently turned the doorknob, and entered. The fire crackled and burned brightly, washing the room in its warm, golden glow. As Anne stepped in, a long-forgotten happiness surged through her as she remembered the years she had spent here. Up to this moment, she wondered if this were all a fantastic dream from which she might suddenly awaken. Now, she felt secure that she was truly at home again. She crossed to the window seat and gazed out over her beloved hills, now silhouetted black against the purple sky. She promised herself that tomorrow morning she would be sitting there when the sun rose to greet her in her new life.

With Joane's help, Anne changed quickly out of her traveling clothes and into a dinner gown and hurried back downstairs. Francis and Betsy, waiting in the front parlor, rose in unison when Anne entered. Betsy came forward in greeting, entwined her arm through Anne's, and walked beside her as they went into the dining hall.

"You must tell us all your news," Betsy said, then suddenly broke off, embarrassed at her indiscretion.

"I shall tell you everything," Anne quickly assured her. "You and Francis are the dearest people in the world to me. I have no secrets to hide, nor anything of which I am ashamed."

As soon as the blessing was said, Anne could wait no longer and decided the moment had come to be forthright in her plans. She drew a deep breath.

"You expressed earlier your desire that I stay long with you. I hope you were sincere in your invitation because I have decided not to return to Thomas—ever." She paused, waiting for their reaction. Betsy almost dropped her fork, but Francis only gazed evenly at Anne, awaiting her further explanation. Anne obliged.

"To pass the time on my journey, I read my Bible. While doing so, I believe the Lord led me to the verses in I Corinthians, chapter 7. In these verses, Paul speaks of marriage between believers and those who do not believe. He makes it quite clear that if any unbelieving husband is content to live with a believing wife, then she should not depart. However, if the *'unbelieving one departs, let him depart. The brother or sister is not under bondage in such cases.'*[15] Though I am the one who departed, I did so only because Thomas drove me most violently from the house. Joane will attest to this confession as well. His treatment of me these past four years has been most harsh; and though I endeavored to speak truth to him, he would not hear it. Therefore, I believe the scriptures affirm my decision to seek an annulment of my marriage to Thomas."

Francis' goblet froze midway between table and mouth. "An annulment! Anne, do you know of what you speak? The church will never allow such a thing. I realize that you have been unhappy—"

"Unhappy? You think I choose this path merely because I have been unhappy? Dare I tell you how much I have endured at the hands of Thomas? On more than one occasion he threatened me with physical harm. And though I was loath to write you of such matters, on another occasion during one of his drunken stupors, Thomas shook me 'til I feared my neck would snap. Other times I was thrown against a wall or to the floor because I dared to read my Bible or because I boldly proclaimed the truth to those who were dead in their trespasses! His conduct does not defend an unbelieving husband content to live with a believing wife. Even so, had these things been the extent of my suffering, I would gladly have borne it for sake of my Lord. I freely confess that I may not have been the wife that Thomas wished me to be, but I sought to be an obedient wife until obedience to Thomas meant disobedience to my Lord. Surely, Francis, you understand that I can no longer live with a man who stands opposed to God's Holy Word and His saints! Nor do I believe it is what the Lord requires of me. If our gracious Lord grants me success in my cause, then I shall be free to give my life to His service. I assure you, I shall not marry again!"

Francis sighed. He saw the fierce determination in her eyes and knew that once she was persuaded, it would be a dauntless task to convince her otherwise. And, in truth, in his own heart, he was unwilling to do so. He had regretted her marriage to Thomas almost as much as she, and he realized that there was little hope of their reconciling.

And, as always, her argument was compelling. Yet, even when Francis pointed out that he had heard of others who had made similar argument before the ecclesiastical counsel and been met with little success, Anne was not persuaded.

Francis cringed inwardly as he imagined the court battle that lay before Anne. The priests of Lincoln were steadfast in their doctrine that a wife was to be subjugated to her husband in matters of religion as in all else. Anne would find little, if any, sympathy among them. But he would not make her task more difficult. He sighed, then smiled.

"If you are convinced, dearest, then you have my word that I shall stand with you."

Anne had not been back at South Kelsey long before she realized that, as in Friskney, she was the center of gossip—and great debate—throughout the county. However, much to her encouragement, several prominent Protestant families, like Francis, supported her in her decision to seek an annulment of her marriage to Thomas. Indeed, these families were whole-hearted in their conviction that she was right in placing her loyalty to the Lord Jesus Christ above everything else, even an unbelieving husband.

The Catholics, on the other hand, took quite a different view. They argued vehemently that it was a wife's duty to be obedient to her husband in all matters – religious or otherwise. Anne, they said, must return to her husband at once.

But Anne had no intention of returning to Thomas, nor did she have any intention of distancing herself from this controversy that embroiled the county—though Francis tried vainly to persuade her that discretion dictate that she do so. Strengthened by the support of friends, Anne boldly made known her cause to anyone who would listen. With a renewed heart and a firm conviction that her cause was good, she eagerly rekindled her evangelical efforts, making regular visits to town to share her faith openly in the square.

The gossipmongers buzzed. Anne paid no heed. Her new-found freedom had given her the opportunity to live as she had always longed to live. Her heart belonged to no man; she was wholly the Lord's.

When Thomas saw Vicar Jordan striding down the path toward Kyme Manor, his first inclination was to duck into the barn and hide. But his conscience stopped him. Such a cowardly action would surely be a sin; but even more distressing, it would be only a postponement of the inevitable. He had long since regretted his impulsive decision to drive Anne from his house. Not that he wanted her back. He didn't. But he had been unprepared for the repercussions that resulted from his hasty action. News of Anne's forced departure spread rapidly; and much to his shame, he realized that he was now the primary topic of every gossip in town. Wherever he went, sideward glances and whispered conversations followed him; and many a one-time friend now shunned him or treated him with polite indifference.

And if that weren't enough, the local priests and their loyal supporters brought serious charges against him, accusing him of having sheltered a heretical wife and failing as a husband to subdue her wild fanaticism. Thomas was miserable, even more so than when Anne still inhabited Kyme Manor. His hopes of quiet solitude vanished in the controversy that engulfed him like a snake swallowing its terrified prey. But he could not hide from the vicar, no matter how much he wished to.

When Vicar Jordan was in earshot, Thomas called out to him, in the most pleasant tone he could muster.

"Good day to you, Vicar. Fine weather we're having. If this continues, we can all look forward to a plentiful harvest."

Vicar Jordan scowled. "I did not come hither to discuss the weather or the harvest, Thomas Kyme. I came to discuss what you intend to do about your most unfavorable circumstances."

There was no use trying to feign ignorance, however much Thomas was tempted to do so. And with great effort, he also resisted the temptation to speak the words that rushed unbridled into his mind. He was in enough trouble as it was. Instead, he studied a rope he held in his hands as if it were the first time he had ever seen such an object. Finally, he answered, though somewhat weakly. "I have thought of writing to Anne...."

"Write to that heretic! What nonsense! Do you honestly believe she would return simply because you write to her? I daresay, she is only too glad to be free to spread her detestable doctrine throughout the entire county! Sending her away was a grievous error, Kyme, a grievous error."

Thomas winced at the verbal lashing, but held his tongue. "Your grace, my duty–"

"Your duty, sir, is to insist that your wayward wife return to you immediately and submit herself properly to your authority—even if it means taking a rod to her and beating her senseless!"

Stunned, Thomas stared at the robed figure before him, aghast at the priest's harshness. Even though Thomas had threatened to do just that on more than one occasion, he did not expect such counsel from the clergy.

"You think that too hard a matter, Kyme? Or does it surprise you that I, as a man of God, would affirm such action. Nay, do not be surprised. Your wife's eternal soul hangs in the balance. Which is worse? To suffer a beating in this world that may bring her to her senses, or to suffer eternal damnation because you are too soft a man?"

At this last insult, prickling anger against this man—priest or not—ignited within Thomas' heart. Vicar Jordan had attacked his manhood before, and he chafed under this latest admonition. What could a priest know of the trials of being a husband, especially to a woman as willful and headstrong as Anne? Yet before he could respond, the priest continued.

"I, along with the other priests, have decided that you have but two choices: bring her back and force her to submit or denounce her to the local authorities. Let them decide her fate."

Thomas' anger vanished, replaced with stunned amazement. Though he had to admit he had often entertained such thoughts, in truth, to denounce his own wife to the authorities was unthinkable! Anne was a gentlewoman of noble standing, a lady of one of Lincolnshire's most prominent families. While he may vehemently disagree with her opinions, he could not imagine actually bringing charges of heresy against her! Francis Askew would never tolerate such an act; and for all the power the priests held, Thomas feared the lord of South Kelsey Hall much more than the local priests. Francis could ruin him financially; the priests could merely make life uncomfortable. Thomas turned away from the vicar in disgust, aware that he had few options.

"I shall write to Francis Askew immediately, demanding that he send his sister back to Friskney," he snapped as he strode toward the house.

A sinister smile settled on the thin lips of the priest as he watched Thomas walk away. *So easily intimidated*, he thought with smug satisfaction. *So easily manipulated....*

November 1543

There was no point in showing Anne the letter, Francis rationalized as he finished reading the parchment that lay before him on his desk. He knew instinctively her response. She would not be persuaded to return to Thomas, no matter how grand the promises. The letter, its script evidence of the inferior education of its writer, was full of apologies and statements of contrition—and fervent promises of greater understanding and more sympathetic treatment. Then, as graciously as his poor writing skills would allow, Thomas entreated Francis to send Anne back to Friskney within the fortnight.

Francis heaved a sigh and sat back in his chair. Such a disagreeable business. He wondered whether he should write Thomas himself and inform him of Anne's decision to seek an annulment. As far as he knew, she had not communicated with him at all since arriving at South Kelsey Hall; and Francis felt that, at the very least, Thomas deserved an explanation and a letter apprising him of the proceedings that Anne was determine to undertake. But, no, that was truly Anne's responsibility.

He pulled the servant cord. Immediately, a manservant entered.

"Please tell the Lady Anne that I wish to see her in my study."

The servant bowed and left.

As Francis waited for Anne to arrive, he framed in his mind the words he would say. A gentle knock sounded.

"Come in," Francis called.

Anne entered, crossed the room to where he sat, gave him her prettiest smile, and waited politely for him to speak first. Francis couldn't help but notice the marked improvement in her appearance since her arrival at South Kelsey Hall. Her face had filled out, the dark circles had vanished, and the blush on her cheeks had returned. Seeing her so vibrant made his task all the more odious. He hated telling her of the letter's contents, but what choice did he have? He rose from his chair, taking the letter in hand.

"I have received a letter from Thomas. He asks that I send you back to Friskney."

"And how have you replied?"

"I have not—as yet. But I must and soon. But I would rather you write to him first."

"I have nothing to say to him."

"On the contrary, you have much to say to him. The man deserves to know the course you have chosen to follow. 'Tis not as though he were a disinterested third party."

"He will only protest."

"Aye, but he deserves to know nonetheless." He extended the letter toward her; Anne made no move. "He says he is willing to mend his ways."

"And you believe him? He fears you, Francis, for he knows you are powerful. Therefore, he will promise you anything, but I daresay, that once I reside under his roof again, the circumstances will be as before; perhaps even worse, for he has suffered humiliation before his friends and neighbors, and Thomas is not a forgiving man."

Instead of answering, Francis reached into the top drawer of his desk and pulled from it another parchment. He then turned toward Anne, frowned slightly, and said, "I have just last evening received these orders from the king's counselor that my services are required by the king to assist him in his war with France. I must leave shortly after the New Year." He paused, then said, "I will not be here to stand with you in your cause, Anne. And I fear that you do not know what you are up against."

"I may not know the mind of the council, but I believe I know the mind of God; and He will stand with me," Anne responded firmly. Then seeing the troubled look on Francis' face, she softened. "Dearest, I know you worry so for me, but I am strong and I believe my cause is good. I must see this matter through on my own, no matter what the outcome. God will not forsake me."

Francis studied the earnest face before him, then smiled gently. Taking Anne's hands in his, he spoke quietly, "Aye, that He will not; and, one way or the other, I have no doubt that you shall prevail."

Chapter XII

August 1544

Anne did not prevail. Though she presented her case strongly and had the support of many of the leading Protestant families in the county, the priests of the Bishop's court in Lincoln summarily ruled against her and ordered her to return to Thomas. But Anne, convinced even more so that in the eyes of God her marriage to Thomas was invalid, refused to accept the counsel's decision. Indeed, not only did she refuse to accept it, she had the boldness, or—as the counsel declared it—the audacity to challenge the priests to prove their case from scripture.

Upon hearing the outcome of the case, a friend wrote to Anne advising her to keep a safe distance from Lincoln as it was rumored that the priests were very much "bent against her" and may even bring charges of heresy against her. But undaunted, Anne went straight way to Lincoln to hear from the priests themselves. She later wrote to a friend:

> I was warned that if I did come to Lincoln, the priests would assault me and seek to do me great harm. But when I heard of the matter, I went forth indeed and was not afraid because I knew my matter to be good. I remained there nine days and continually read from my Bible in the Minster. Eventually, the priests did come, sometimes by twos, by fives, and once by six, yet none spoke a word to me. Finally, one priest did speak to me, but his words were of small effect.

Shortly after Anne returned from Lincoln, she received yet another letter from Thomas. In the months following Francis Askew's departure from South Kelsey Hall, Thomas' letters had not only become more frequent but also much stronger in their demands that she put away her foolish thinking and return at once to Friskney. His letters had no effect on her, except to cause her irritation, because she knew what lay behind them. *No doubt,* Anne thought, *he wants me back because he suffers greatly at the hands of the local clergy.* But after scanning his latest epistle, Anne tossed it into the fireplace just as she had done with every other letter she had received from him. His threats did not concern her.

What did concern her, however, was the course of action she should now pursue. Having lost her battle before the Lincoln counsel, she realized that staying at South Kelsey would avail her nothing. And as to returning to Thomas, that option was unthinkable. After being separated for the better part of a year, she had no illusions that Thomas would receive her kindly or treat her well once she was under his roof again. Indeed, she had absolutely no doubt that were she to return, she would bear most cruelly the brunt of his anger and frustration brought about by the humiliation he had suffered since her departure. Furthermore, in her mind, such an act would be an admission that she had wrongly interpreted scripture, something she was quite unwilling to acquiesce. No, after considering all alternatives, she saw that only one road lay before her now, and that road led to London.

December 1544

The first snow of winter had just begun to fall as the carriage in which Anne and Joane rode rumbled into the bustling streets of London. Thick white flakes swirled through the air in the same way the swarms of people, bundled against the chilly air, jostled each other as they went about their business—street peddlers hawking their wares, merchants trying to entice prospective buyers into their store fronts, and children darting between carts and stands in a lively game of tag. Roars of deep, booming laughter resounded in the taverns. Dogs barking, pigs squealing, and chickens squawking compounded the cacophony of the streets.

Neither young woman inside the carriage had ever witnessed such a fray of people or heard such commotion, and each craned her neck to see as much as possible. Joane, who preferred the quiet countryside, felt somewhat panicked by her surroundings, but Anne was exhilarated. Her father and brothers had often told her exciting tales of this great city; and now, at long last, she was seeing it all for herself. She could hardly wait to begin her quest that would release her from her old life so she could soon enjoy to the fullest her new.

Though Christopher Askew had died a year earlier, Anne's brother, Edward, still resided in London and was now firmly entrenched in Thomas Cranmer's inner circle. Upon hearing of her plans to come, he had taken pains to secure lodgings for Anne that were comfortably close to Westminster. From here, Anne could easily visit the homes of friends and relatives living in the inns of the court and be under the protective care of Edward and other male kinsmen in residence nearby. When her carriage pulled up to the front gate, Edward was there to greet her.

"Dearest Anne," he exclaimed as he helped her alight. "You are certainly a delight to the eyes!"

Anne could hardly believe her eyes as she gazed lovingly at the tall young man before her. When she had last seen him, he was still very much a country gentleman. Now, he bore all the elegance and sophistication of a man of the court. She beamed her prettiest smile.

"Oh, Edward! 'Tis such great joy to see you again! And, I can see that you have become quite the fashionable gentleman. So dashing and debonair! I imagine all the young ladies of the king's court are heartbroken that you are an old married man instead of an eligible bachelor!"

Edward only grinned and extended his arm to escort up the steps. "And you are still the charmer I have always known!"

Inside, he led her on a tour of her new apartments, which she found quite satisfactory, then he turned to her and said, "I shall give you time to rest from your journey, then I shall send a carriage for you at eight this evening. Margaret is most anxious to see you again; and tonight, we dine at the home of Lord and Lady Neville, who made me promise that I would introduce you first thing upon your arrival. So, I shall take my leave of you now, but I shall look forward to hearing all the news of South Kelsey." He bent and kissed her cheek. "Until this evening, dear sister."

Anne ardently wished that Edward could visit longer with her, but she understood that his duties as one of Crammer's assistants were considerable and vastly important; and she wouldn't dare think of asking him to put her wishes above the biddings of his master. So, she would have to content herself with waiting until evening and sharing him with others.

In the meantime, she had letters to write to friends and acquaintances, informing them of her arrival and her earnest desire to renew old friendships. One such dear friend was John Lascelles, a Lincolnshire neighbor who had come to London several years earlier. She had heard that he held great influence at court and, more importantly to Anne, was well known for his devotion to the evangelical movement. If she entertained any hopes of success, she must seek out those who would easily sympathize with her cause and be in a position to offer assistance. John Lascelles was such a man.

Though it had happened quite by accident, John Lascelles had unwittingly played a key role in the downfall of Catherine Howard, Henry's fifth wife. In September 1541, the king and his young queen had taken an extended trip to the north of England. John Lascelles was among the king's entourage, who were all merriment and laughter. When the king and his party passed through the county of Sussex, John took advantage of the opportunity and stopped to pay a visit to his sister, Mary, who had formerly been in the service of the Duchess of Norfolk, the young queen's grandmother. As they visited, John suggested that, considering her former relationship to the Duchess, Mary should seek a position among the queen's ladies; but, to his surprise, Mary was adamantly opposed.

"I shall certainly not do such a thing; for when I think of the queen, I cannot do so without great sadness," she told her brother.

"But why?"

"Because she is so frivolous in character and in life! Why, when she was no more than sixteen, she was known to be intimate with Francis Derham, an officer in the Lord Duke's house! And if that weren't enough, she was quite familiar with another, a man by the name of Manox, I believe. No, I would not serve such a queen. 'Twould grieve me too deeply."

John, greatly astonished at this news, realized immediately the import of it. He also realized the uncomfortable position in which it put him. If he kept it quiet, he could be accused of conspiring against the king were the information ever to be discovered through other means. Reporting the information also carried risks; but in his mind, those risks seemed far less likely to do him great harm. Therefore, he immediately wrote Thomas Cranmer, revealing the entire matter to him. Thus marked the beginning of the end for the beautiful and vivacious, but foolish Catherine. Within a few months, the scandalous truth came out; and Catherine was convicted of high treason and beheaded on the Tower green, just as her cousin Anne Boleyn had been six years earlier.

The ramifications of his decision were far reaching, more so than he could have imagined at the time. Though highly esteemed in Protestant circles for his part in the demise of the Catholic queen, Lascelles paid a high price. Those of the established leaning were not forgiving, and he gained as many enemies in the king's court as he did friends. But he was not a man who was easily cowered. He boldly continued his efforts to advance reformation doctrine throughout the city; and when he received Anne's letter, he was more than delighted to help her.

The small meeting room was already packed, and a little stifling, when Anne, escorted by John, entered through the double doors. As John greeted those closest to him, Anne could not help but take notice of the odd assortment of people—artisans, merchants, courtiers, students, even common men and women—gathered together in the cramped lodging. Yet, even more striking was the fact that although the gathered individuals were from very different social classes, they intermingled freely, greeting one another with genuine affection and sharing conversation as though they were old friends.

"There is no distinction of class here, Anne," John explained in response to her astonished look. "We are all the same in the sight of our dear Lord. We gather together because we each love Him and want to serve Him with our whole hearts. It matters not to us one's background or social standing."

Anne's heart was warmed by his words. Immediately, she felt at home among the people at this gathering. And as John introduced her to the "members of my flock" as he was wont to say, she experienced a thrill and a sense of kinship that she had heretofore never known. Here were people who truly believed as she believed, loved as she loved, understood as she understood. She could scarcely contain her excitement. Yet, this proved to be only the beginning. From the moment John stepped forward to preach the Word to the assemblage, Anne sat spell-bound, hanging on every word the man of God had to say. Until now, she had not realized how starved she had been for sound teaching, and she eagerly soaked in every new revelation.

When the meeting was over and the group began to disperse, Anne lingered, hoping John would be willing to discuss more fully the passage of scripture he had taught that evening. He was talking to a small group of men, but when he saw her waiting patiently on the other side of the room, he left the group and walked toward her.

"I trust you were blessed by coming," he said as he approached.

"Indeed, more than I have ever been! In South Kelsey, we had a small group of believers who met together, but never did we have such inspired teaching. If it be not an inconvenience, may I ask you some questions on the text? There is so much I desire, nay, rather, need to learn."

John smiled as he studied the young woman before him. He had heard that she was highly intelligent and possessed a quick wit, but he wondered whether she truly had the heart of the Lord. He decided to find out.

"I shall be more than happy to discuss whatever you wish if you do not mind a bit of a walk. I have others in my flock who are unable to come to the meetings but who must be ministered to as well. You may join me if you wish, but you must help me carry one of these bundles." He stooped to pick up one of several large sacks neatly piled by the door.

Anne accepted the invitation—and a sack—without hesitation. As they stepped into the evening air, the stinging chill caught her breath. She shivered under her heavy cloak, but as she welcomed the chance to have John's undivided attention, she would not be put off by the cold night air. As they walked along, she peppered him with questions. John was impressed by her questions and even more astounded at her understanding of the answers. She truly was a unique young woman. But he would see whether she could put feet to her faith. As they made their way through the narrow streets, Anne became so engrossed in her conversation with John that she never noticed when the fine houses of the elite gave way to the merchants' homes, which in turn, gave way to the artisans' homes.

At last, John came to a stop; and, for the first time, Anne took genuine notice of her surroundings. An involuntary gasp escaped her lips. The tatterdemalion shacks and lean-tos could hardly be called homes, and the squalid living conditions were the worse she have ever witnessed, even more so than some of the peasant cottages around Friskney. Women and children with unkempt hair and soiled and thrice-patched rags for clothing stared in silence at the finely dressed pair. Anne was suddenly very conscience of her polished wool gown and heavy velvet cape.

But John, oblivious to any discomfort Anne may have been experiencing, warmly greeted the small gathering. He fondly patted dirty cheeks, and the children eagerly pressed close about him. Pulling sugar treats from his pockets, he made sure that every grubby, outstretched hand received one. As she quietly followed John into the nearest hovel, the stench of unwashed bodies, human excrement, and burning dung assailed her senses. With great difficulty, she stifled the gagging sensation in her throat and resisted the temptation to cover her nose with her handkerchief.

In an effort to conceal her initial reaction, Anne flashed a smile at the curious onlookers. None returned her smile. Vacant eyes only stared back, unwilling to trust one so lavishly outfitted. For several agonizing moments, Anne felt totally alone and lost in their midst.

Then she saw her: a young woman, not much older than Anne but clothed in a frayed and thread-worn dress, opened at the waist. She huddled close to a dying fire, holding a squalling baby boy. Strands of unwashed and uncombed hair fell across her face, hiding her features; but a low, somewhat desperate, cooing sound issued from her lips. Rocking back and forth on her heels, she kept trying unsuccessfully to coax the infant to feed. The baby only hollered louder. As soon as Anne saw her, she went and knelt beside the distressed mother.

"May I hold your baby?" she asked softly.

Surprised, the wary mother looked suspiciously at the well-dressed woman before her, then glanced toward John for affirmation. He nodded slightly. Reluctantly, she offered Anne the very unhappy child. Ever so gently, Anne took the boy, wrapped a portion of her cloak around his squirming body, and pulled him close against her. Softly, she crooned a lullaby as she rocked the infant in her arms. The comforting warmth from the cloak and Anne's body soon quieted the exhausted child; and within minutes, it was sleeping peacefully in Anne's arm. After several more minutes, Anne handed the baby back to his grateful mother. The baby whimpered, but before the cold could jar him fully awake, Anne removed her cape and draped it around the astonished young woman's thin shoulders and pulled it close over her body, shielding mother and child from the frigid air. Contented, the child immediately began to suckle.

"This will help keep the chill off," Anne replied to the silent question in the woman's startled eyes.

John looked on with satisfaction. Anne, indeed, was a woman whose faith ran deeper than intellectual debate. He nodded toward her then turned to open one of the sacks. From its depths, he pulled several smaller bundles tied about with string. Eager bodies surged forward, hands outstretched. With Anne's help, he distributed blankets, shawls, caps, and woolen stockings until the supply ran out. When all was gone, he sat down, opened his Bible, and began to read. The grateful recipients, holding their precious new clothes tightly against them, huddled close round the fire and listened raptly. For many, it was the first time they had heard God's word in their native tongue, and they were awed by what they heard. Anne studied their faces in the dwindling firelight. Faces whose eyes were sunken from hunger gazed steadfastly at John, and Anne thought she saw in some the dawn of understanding and the peace that follows.

The walk home was quiet. John instinctively knew that the evening had to have had an impact on Anne, and he was mindful not to intrude on her thoughts. In her thoughts, Anne reflected on the evening's events and considered the impoverished families living in the drafty and stench-ridden shacks, so far removed from anything that Anne had known in her short years. In the span of a few brief hours, her perspective had completely changed. She had come to London to seek an annulment. The Lord had led her here to be His servant among those who were lost—regardless of their social standing.

As long as Thou would have me here, use me to Thy glory, she prayed silently. She knew she could trust Him to answer this prayer.

Spring 1545

From the highest members of the king's court to the lowest illiterate commoner, Anne Askew—as she preferred—was soon well known and talked about. She had been in London scarcely four months, but had already made a profound impact. Her wit, unyielding convictions, and outspoken manner endeared her to the progressive side of society and secured the disdain of the established circle. Through her brother and John Lascelles, she was introduced to many influential members of the court, and, most exciting to Anne, the queen's own ladies. But these encounters paled in comparison to the day Anne first met Queen Catherine Parr.

Anne waited anxiously in the chamber outside the queen's apartments. She tried to still her racing pulse, but to no avail. Impulsively, she smoothed her skirt for the tenth time. Then the great doors opposite her swung open and the queen emerged, followed by several of her ladies. Anne immediately sank to the floor in a low curtsey, hardly daring to look up. Her heart pounded. As a young girl, she had imagined such an event, but now, here she was in the actual presence of Her Royal Highness. A soft voice spoke.

"Rise, Anne Askew, and let me look at you." Anne arose. Standing before her was a comely woman, whose deep blue eyes shone bright with both intelligence and grace. Though slight in stature, she was quite regal in posture. The queen reached a soft hand toward her, cupped her chin, and quietly studied her a moment, then smiled and said, "As of late, you have been much the topic of discussion. Now, here you are at last for my inspection."

"Your Majesty, I am honored by your favor."

"I have heard it said that you are well-versed in your knowledge of Scripture. I particularly enjoy lively debate and would be pleased to have you join with me and my ladies at the Bible studies we hold in my apartments. Often, I invite Drs. Latimer or Crome to give a sermon."

Anne was more than delighted to accept the gracious queen's invitation, and soon afterwards she became a regular and enthusiastic participant in the oftentimes lively discussions of Scripture with the queen and her ladies, many of whom could match Anne's wit and spirited jibes. One such lady, Catherine Brandon, Duchess of Suffolk, even named her favorite pet spaniel "Gardiner" in a deliberate jab at Stephen Gardiner, Bishop of Winchester and sworn enemy of the Reform movement.

Anne thoroughly enjoyed the company of her new friends, but she soon came to understand that in aligning herself so openly with the progressive movement, she was exposing herself to great risk. She had not met the king, but learned that Henry, though fond of his newest wife, did not tolerate any religious thought opposed to his own. Therefore, the meetings, though lively, were held discreetly, but with great regularity. Anne, however, gave little thought to any perceived danger; her joy overthrew her fear. And Anne's influence and reputation grew.

Among the Protestants, she was adored; and as the story of her hapless marriage came to light, she was held in the highest regard as one who had "truly suffered for righteousness sake." She won the respect of all who came in contact with her as they quickly realized that although she was very much the well-bred lady, she did not allow her station to separate herself from any who were in need of the gospel even if they were below her in society. She confidently moved in the most elite circles with grace and charm, but was just as comfortable entering the humblest riverside dwellings to minister to the poor and needy.

But just as the number of those who loved her grew, so did the number of those who hated her. Among the established faction who adamantly opposed the Protestant thinking, she was regarded with scorn and contempt. As she had done in Friskney and Lincoln, she now did in London. For to Anne, the most important work she had was to ensure that truth prevail. Therefore, she quite willingly, even eagerly, engaged any priest, bishop, or doctor of theology in debate to promote the views of the Reformists and expose the fallacies of the Roman Church. And with her vast knowledge of Scripture, her logical arguments, and spirited jibes, she was indeed a formidable debater. As quickly as she made friends among the Protestants, she made enemies among the Catholics. And through it all, she had no realization that she had begun a walk on very dangerous ground.

February 1546

Sitting at his desk, the craggy-faced man hastily finished the document before him. Then, dipping the quill once again into the ink, he scrawled his jagged signature across the bottom of the parchment. He glanced once more over his words. Satisfied, he quickly folded the letter, sealed it by pressing his ring against a drop of softened wax, and handed it to the young man standing nearby.

"For the Lord Chancellor," he clipped. The obedient attendant immediately took the document, bowed, and strode out of the chamber.

As he watched his servant go, the man scowled. For Stephen Gardiner, Bishop of Winchester, a great matter weighed on his mind and, indeed, had become quite serious. Over the winter months, he had received numerous reports that the Protestant movement had, in alarming numbers, grown in strength; and, much to his consternation, it was even reported that the queen, herself, gave evidence of moving steadily in that heretical direction. Something must be done, for it was in the queen's power to hold much influence over the king and his young prince; but Gardiner had not yet encountered the right opportunity that would enable him to act. Such things must be handled delicately, and timing was of absolute importance. Certainly, there was much talk and rumors abounded, but one could not destroy a queen based on mere hearsay. No, he must watch and wait. The time most assuredly would come. And he would be ready for it.

Chapter XIII

March 1, 1546

Though only forty-one, Thomas Wriothesley had risen high in the ranks of King Henry's court, due as much to his determination as to his abilities. Trained under Lord Cromwell, he managed not only to survive his former master's downfall, but also to manipulate the circumstances to his advantage with consummate skill. During his years of service to Cromwell, he was counted among the zealots of the Reform faith; but when the tides of power shifted in favor of the established party, Thomas Wriothesley—to advance himself—shifted with them. From that moment on, taking every available opportunity to commend himself to the king, he eventually found himself in the enviable position of being one of the king's closest confidantes. Now, as Lord Chancellor of England, having denounced any connection with the New Learning, he viewed the Reform movement as a great threat and was determined to do all within his power to see that it was crushed. To this end, he had gathered dossiers on many of the most outspoken Reformists, hoping that through them, he could make an example to all of the terrifying wrath that would descend if others followed their suit.

As he sat in his private Westminster chambers, he studied with particular interest the parchment pages of the dossier on the young woman who had, since her arrival sixteen months prior, gone out of her way to insult, scorn, and ridicule the most prominent and respected Catholic defenders. Indeed, she had openly dared to challenge and to treat with contempt every tenet of the true faith. But that would soon change.

A smile of satisfaction spread across the Chancellor's normally brooding face. His young employee of the Chancery court had done his job well. For months, the young man had shadowed the troublesome and outspoken woman, taking careful note of where she went, with whom, and what she said and did. The evidence was quite damning, more than he had hoped. But, he sighed inwardly, in all probability he would not have need of it. Wriothesley knew the woman's reasons for coming to London and had also made it his business to know the full extent of her legal proceedings in his court. Her case was finally scheduled to come before the Chancery Court the next morning; and if it went against her, as he thought it surely would, she would be sent back to her husband where she belonged and would pose no further threat. But, however remote, there existed the possibility that the court might rule in her favor. And if it did, he would be ready for her. He wondered, with smug confidence, whether she would be as ready for him.

March 2, 1546

Anne stood ramrod straight, her head high, her eyes directly forward as the judges of the Chancery Court filed solemnly back into the courtroom. Her face, devoid of emotion, was resolute; yet inwardly, her heartbeat quickened. To her alarm, she felt her palms becoming moist, but she resisted the urge to pull her handkerchief from her sleeve. She was determined to give no evidence that these men in any way intimidated her. Her cause was good. God would vindicate her.

The judges, all clad in identical heavy black robes and judicial caps, took their time in settling themselves in their respective seats. They relished the power they exercised over nobleman and commoner alike, and they were never in hurry to dismiss the one who faced them from the court floor, even when they ruled in the person's favor. No, it was far more enjoyable to make the hopeful, and quite often, anxious defendant squirm a bit.

But Anne did not squirm. She stood confidently—or, as the judges perceived it, arrogantly—as she awaited their pronouncement.

"The court of His Most Gracious Majesty, King Henry VIII, is now in session. All manner of persons having business with this court, come forth and be ye heard," a loud voice announced. An expectant hush fell on the room. In the upper chamber loft overlooking the court proceedings below, a well-dressed man sat attentively, his face shrouded in shadows.

On the floor, the court came to order. Lord John Kettleby, speaking for the judges, cleared his throat, shifted once more in his seat, and glanced down at the parchment before him. After a moment of study, he raised his head and peered sternly at Anne. Anne did not cower.

"Mistress Kyme," his gravelly voice began.

Anne involuntarily winced at the address, but the judges seemed not to notice.

"You have brought before this court a petition asserting that your marriage to one Thomas Kyme of Friskney is invalid and should be considered null and void. You have based this petition on your own understanding of the Holy Scriptures and the testimony of yourself and those who have spoken on your behalf. In accordance with our understanding of the laws of this the great Sovereign Realm of England, we, the lawfully appointed judges of the court of his Grace, King Henry VIII, and of his most loyal subjects, have thoroughly examined your case and your witnesses and have reached our verdict. We are not without sympathy; however, we have concluded that, notwithstanding the treatment you testify to having received at the hands of your husband, your marriage to Thomas Kyme is in all ways lawful, both in the eyes of the Church and of this court. Therefore, we are dismissing your petition and ordering you to return forthwith to your husband."

A gavel slammed down.

"The case of Anne Kyme against Thomas Kyme is dismissed," the same disconnected loud voice intoned.

For a moment, Anne could not move. Surely, she had not heard right. Perhaps, they had not truly understood. She started to speak, but already the judges had turned their attention from her; and the immediate buzz of voices from spectators and court officials drown her words in sea of commotion.

"Anne," a gentle, familiar voice beside her broke through to her thoughts. "Come away, Anne. 'Tis over. There is nothing more for you to do here." Edward's hand tugged softly on her arm. Still in a daze, she submitted to Edward's leading and allowed him to escort her from the courtroom floor. As she left, the tall man hidden by the shadows, watched her leave, a victory smile fixed firmly on his chiseled face. *One less heretic to bother about*, he thought with satisfaction.

March 8, 1546

Edward Askew paced the parlor floor of his Tudor home, trying to compose his thoughts. For the hundredth time, he fervently wished that Francis were there. Francis knew how to handle Anne; Edward only knew that she could be difficult to handle. But however much he wished it were otherwise, Francis was in South Kelsey; and Edward was in London, where Anne still was and where she had made it abundantly clear she intended to stay. Court order or no, Anne was *not* going to return to Thomas. Not that he really blamed her. She had been forced against her wishes to marry the man; and over the months, Edward had learned much of the harsh treatment Anne had received from Thomas. He was also aware that since her arrival in London, Thomas' letters had become increasingly threatening toward her. But Edward had served at the king's court long enough to know all too well that defying a court edict was a dangerous thing to do. People ended up in the Tower for far lesser offenses.

As he rehearsed his words again in his mind, Anne swept into the room, defiance dancing in her eyes. Before Edward could open his mouth, Anne spoke.

"'Tis of no use for you, brother, to lecture me concerning my duty either to the man whom some would call my husband or to the king. My duty is to God, and to Him alone shall I pledge my allegiance. And though this temporal court has given me leave to return to Thomas, I shall not. For I acknowledge only a higher court, one that does not abide a servant of Christ to be joined with a heretic!"

Edward sighed, and promptly forgot his prepared speech. Stepping toward her, he gently clasped Anne's hand in his own. The defiance in her eyes appeared to lessen.

"Dearest, I would not ask you to return to Thomas. I heartily despise him for the harm he has done you and would not betray your love by asking you to subject yourself again to such cruelty; but 'tis folly, nay, 'tis dangerous, for you to remain here in London. Your tongue has made you enemies, and I fear that they may set themselves against you if you tarry here much longer."

"Why should I fear the enemies of God? They are of no concern to me. But I am greatly concerned for the poor and needy and ignorant, who daily die and enter eternal torment because no one has told them the truth that can set them free. If these, whom you say are my enemies, assail me; then in truth, they assail the One in whom I have been given new life. It is His truth they oppose, not mine."

"I argue not against that, but of what good are you to those in need if you are shut away in prison? Who will minister to the heathen then? Who will bring them the message of God's salvation? Anne, I do not ask you to forsake your ministry, but to carry it on in more secure environs. If you return to South Kelsey, I am sure there are as many in Lincolnshire who are as much in need of your message as would be here."

Anne's brow knitted into a frown. She turned from her brother, crossed the room, and gazed out the parlor window. For several moments, she did not speak. Then slowly shaking her head, she turned and faced him again.

"I cannot, Edward," she replied softly. "Please, do not make such a request of me. To leave would be to admit defeat. And I firmly believe that this is where I am to serve my Lord now. Whatever happens to me, I am in God's good hands. He shall not forsake me."

"I pray He will not, for if your enemies prevail, I shall not be able to help you," he replied gravely.

Anne understood and smiled gently at him. The discussion was over. Sadly, Edward knew that any further words would only drive her from him, a price he did not wish to pay. He opened his arms to her and she went to him. As he held her, he offered up a silent prayer on her behalf as a growing fear gripped his heart. He hoped that the dread he felt inside for her safety would prove ungrounded, but he was almost certain that it would not.

March 9, 1546

"My Lord Chancellor," the young man bowed in humble submission at the entrance to his master's quarters. He hoped his trembling hands went undetected, but he knew this powerful man rarely missed anything, especially the fearful reactions of a subordinate.

"Yes, yes, Wadloe. Come in," Thomas Wriothesley barked, without bothering to look up. Ralph Wadloe hurried forward. "What news have you?" Wriothesley asked.

"'Tis Mistress Kyme, milord. She remains in London."

Wriothesley's head shot up. "Still? Even though the Chancery Court ordered her to return to her husband?"

"Yes, milord. 'Twould seem she believes that the court has no jurisdiction over her. At least, that is the word rumored among her friends. She has declared that she has God's work to do here in London and will not leave."

"Arrogant woman! She dares to defy the king's court!"

Wadloe wisely made no comment.

"Tell me, Wadloe," the older man continued, raising an eyebrow. "Has she the support of the queen and her ladies?"

Wadloe hesitated before answering. "I do not know, milord. She has not been seen in their company these past few days. Rather, she spends her time gospelling among the poor who live near the river."

Wriothesley snorted at this last statement. "Well, 'tis of little matter. We have proof enough that she regularly attended many of the queen's private gatherings. No doubt, she is party to that subversive element that seeks to undermine the authority of the Church and her priests. Her heretical opinions are widely known as she makes little pretense at hiding them, so it shall be a small matter to bring her to justice."

The Lord Chancellor snatched a blank parchment and inked his quill. With his bold script, he scrawled across the paper, then handed it to Wadloe.

"Take this. Draft a formal writ, and bring it back for my signature. I want to see this matter dealt with on the morrow, so make haste."

Wadloe took the parchment, bowed low, and scurried out to fulfill his master's wishes.

March 10, 1546

The first rays of sunlight had not yet scaled the high walls that surrounded the barren courtyard below. Yet in the morning twilight, seven men arrayed in the bright red royal livery took up their arms and assembled themselves in rigid pairs, with one man at the head. As they did so, a door on the far side of the yard opened, and the captain of the guard stepped out. He strode across the yard, walking directly to the man at the head and handed him a rolled parchment tied with a red cord. The man took the extended edict and bowed his head slightly in respect. The captain nodded in return, and the man stepped back. On his word, the entire guard moved forward as one. With swords to shoulder, they marched out through the prison gate, intent on making good time to their ordered destination.

Anne fidgeted as Joane worked at plaiting her thick, dark hair. Normally, she did not mind the task; but this morning, she was impatient. Within the hour, she was to meet John Lascelles and several others of their congregation to take a barge down the Thames to villages and farms where the gospel had not yet been proclaimed.

"Hurry, Joane," Anne urged. "They will leave me if I am not there on time."

Joane sighed. "'Twould be easier, milady, if you sat still—and if your hair were not so thick!" But, in response to her mistress' request, Joane plied her fingers more quickly, then assisted in arranging Anne's cap and veil. "There," she said when all was finished. "'Tis not a perfect job, but 'twill do for your outing today."

Anne agreed. She did not need to wear the finery that would be expected at court on this day, and she was glad. The simple gray woolen gown with its soft white underskirt was more comfortable and less confining then her more courtly wear; and today, she wanted to be comfortable. She stood and gave an approving glance at the polished glass, then tugged at her bodice.

"Loosen my laces a bit," she said, turning her back to her maid. Today, I want to be able to breathe easily."

The guards stepped in perfect time, eyes straight ahead, the cadence of their measured footfall announcing their presence. As they marched through the streets, people started at their appearing and scurried to get out of their way. Yet, the moment after the seven men had passed, heads huddled together and terse, whispered conversations speculated as to whom the intended victim might be. Curious children, careful to keep their distance, followed behind, hoping to see at whose door the armed guard would stop. The orderly men paid no mind; they just kept marching.

Anne checked once more to make sure that she had everything. A sizeable basket held assorted dried fruits, breads, cheeses, and a large flask of wine. More than enough for her and those with whom she would be traveling. The morning air held a chill so she reached for her woolen shawl and wrapped it loosely around her shoulders. Now, she was ready. But no, where was her Bible? Oh, yes, there it was on the table beside the entry way where she had laid it the night before so she would be sure to see it. Taking it in her hand, she made one final check. Then, confident that she had all she needed, she opened the front door and stepped out into the welcoming sunlight.

The guards turned the last corner toward their destination, a considerable gathering of curiosity-seekers following on their heels. As they approached the modest, but stylish lodgings of the young noblewoman, the front door swung open as if in expectation of their coming. In perfect order, the guard drew up and stopped. The head guardsman stepped forward toward the startled young woman dressed in simple gray.

For a moment, it did not register with Anne what was happening.

"Mistress Anne Kyme, by order of his grace, the Lord Chancellor of England, we have come to place you under arrest," the guard said without emotion. He handed the parchment to her.

As Joane watched in shocked horror, Anne fumbled with the cord that secured the rolled paper. She finally slipped the knot loose and, steadying her hands, unrolled the order. In bold letters, the edict announced that she, Anne Kyme, was to be taken under guard to Sadler's Hall where she was to give answer before the king's council on the charges of heresy and fomenting discontent.

Anne felt her knees weaken and whispered, "Dear Lord God, help me."

The prayer was no sooner out of her mouth when a surge of strength coursed through her. She stood erect, lifted her chin, and eyed the guard directly.

"I shall gladly go with you," she said calmly, then turned to Joane. "Tell my brother what has happened – and John. Ask them to pray that I remain strong."

Anne took her position in the midst of the guard. As they began the march back to the prison courtyard, Anne, with great joy flooding her heart, realized that she still clutched her worn, beloved Bible in her hands.

Chapter XIV

Sadler's Hall, London
March 10, 1546

"**A**re you aware of the severity of the charges brought against you, Mistress Kyme?" the thin-faced, long-nosed man asked, his eyes lowered as he studiously poured over the papers before him. He reminded Anne of a badger, a badger in search of prey.

Well, she would not be prey for this hunter. So, she did not immediately respond but waited patiently until her examiner, puzzled, looked up.

"Did you not hear my question, mistress?"

"I heard you well enough, milord, but I wish to see a man's eyes when I am talking to him." A sniggering of laughter rippled through the crowd of onlookers.

"You best be wishing that your circumstances be improved for yours now place you in gravest peril," he replied tartly.

"My circumstances are ordered by my Lord God. I am here only by His great design."

Christopher Dare grumbled under his breath. He had heard much about this outspoken young woman and fervently wished that another had been assigned the task of her examination before the Royal Quest. But the lot fell to him, and he could not avoid it. He returned to studying his papers.

While she waited, Anne glanced around at her surroundings. Sadler's Hall, the room in which she currently found herself, was quite large; yet despite its size, the hall was empty of all furniture save the chair she sat upon, the table and chair provided for her examiner, and the six chairs on which the jurors hearing the case sat. In like manner, the walls were bare of any tapestries or ornament; and the hall's only light filtered in through the clerestory above. Three stone pillars on each side of the room and two in the back separated the inner chamber from the gallery. Wooden railings connecting the pillars served to keep the curious spectators at a respectable distance and force those who had come to watch the proceedings to stand shoulder to shoulder and jostle each other for the best position.

As she looked around, Anne was gratified to see several familiar and friendly faces smiling and nodding encouragement to her from the gathered crowd.

Dare looked up again, mentally assessed the prisoner, and then shoved his chair backwards. The sound of the scraping wood on the stone floor reverberated through the huge chamber. He rose, came around the table, and positioned himself on its edge. Folding his arms across his chest, he summoned his sternest face. As he eyed her squarely, he hoped inwardly that his stance would work to unnerve the accused woman. Anne merely lifted her chin and returned his stare, thinking to herself, *not even a badger has such beady eyes.*

"This inquiry," he began, "has been ordered to determine whether you have knowingly and willfully committed acts of heresy against the Church of England. I have here a report of the things you have been heard to say. What say you to these charges?"

"I cannot answer charges unless I am informed as to their content, milord. But I assure you that whatever you ask, I shall speak truthfully."

The defiance in her manner warned Dare that this was not going to be easy. To collect his thoughts, he again picked up the dossier and leafed through it. Christopher Dare was by no means a theologian, and he felt more than inadequate for the task before him. Still, as an examiner for the quest, he was responsible for asking the questions that could lead either to her acquittal or—as he had been greatly urged—her conviction. He cleared his throat and leaned forward in his most imposing manner.

"Then speak plainly now. Do you confess that the sacrament that hangs over the holy altar is indeed the very body of our Blessed Lord Jesus Christ?"

Anne paused a moment, then responded "Can you tell me why St. Stephen was stoned to death?"

Confused, Dare stuttered, "No, but that has nothing to do with…"

"Then," she replied, a note of triumph in her voice, "neither will I answer your vain question."

Roars of laughter exploded in the room. To the delight of the crowd, Anne had successfully demonstrated that the man called to examine her had neither the knowledge nor the understanding of Scripture to question her—or anyone—regarding her beliefs. Dare felt his face grow red, first from humiliation, then rage.

"Silence! Silence, all of you!" he demanded. The onlookers gradually settled themselves. "I will not tolerate such outbursts during these proceedings. One more such scene and you shall all be put out!"

Whispered murmurs punctuated with snickering betrayed the crowd's knowledge that the royal examiner had no such authority, but Dare ignored them and returned to his chair behind the table. He picked up another list. Unwilling to place himself in a position of ridicule again, he decided a better course of action would be to call witnesses to testify against the accused.

"I call Mistress Alice Brewster to testify," he announced loudly.

Scuffling sounds in the back echoed through the room as the crowd parted to let a middle-aged woman step forward. She hesitated a moment, but a nod from Dare encouraged her; and she strode toward the front of the room to stand to the left of Anne. The name meant nothing to Anne, so she turned her head to face her opponent and was surprised that she did not recognize the woman's face either. But from the woman's attire, Anne assumed she was the wife of a merchant; and because many merchants and their wives attended the assemblies of which she had been a part, it was entirely possible the woman had been present at one time or another.

"What is your testimony, good woman?"

Mistress Brewster kept her gaze straight forward. She swallowed hard, then said, "I heard this woman scorn the holy sacrament, saying it was false and that 'God dwells not in temples made with hands.'"

"Are you willing to swear to this statement?"

"I am, milord."

Dare turned to Anne. "How do you answer? Did you say such?"

"For my answer to that, I would tell you to read chapters 7 and 17 of the Book of Acts[16] and see for yourself what St. Stephen and St. Paul said in regards to this statement."

Dare hesitated. He did not wish to take the time to read these chapters. Indeed, he had never read any of the Bible at all, and if requested to do so, would not have been able to even find the Book of Acts. And though fearful of the answer, he asked, "And pray, tell us, what is your interpretation of these scriptures?"

Anne now held the audience firmly in her favor, and they all leaned forward to listen intently for her reply.

"Oh," she smiled prettily at Dare. "I have learned not to cast my pearls before swine. Acorns are good enough."

Guffaws and hoots rocked the chamber. And although he tried, Dare could not raise his voice loud enough to be heard over the din. In frustration, he stood, banged his gavel repeatedly, and once again demanded silence. Finally, the crowd acquiesced.

As the hall quieted, Dare snatched another sheet from the table. Brandishing it before her face, he snarled, "I have here the testimony of another that accuses you of saying that you would rather read five lines from the Bible than hear five masses in the Temple Church. Is this true?"

"'Tis as you say," she replied simply. "For the one edifies me and the other does not. The Bible speaks plainly, but as for the Church, 'tis as St. Paul says in I Corinthians 14 'If the trumpet give an uncertain sound, who shall prepare himself for battle.'"[17]

Dare tried another angle. "You have also been heard to say that if a priest who is ill ministers the sacrament, it becomes the body of the devil and not that of God!"

"I never did speak such a thing. But this is what I did say: that whatsoever a priest believed when he ministered to me, his spiritually ill condition could not hurt my faith. I nevertheless in my spirit receive the body and blood of our Lord Jesus Christ."

"And what say you regarding the confession of your sins?"

"'Tis as St. James has spoken in his epistle. 'Confess your faults one to another, and pray one for another, that ye might be healed.[18]'"

Does this woman have an answer from scripture for everything? Dare wondered with despair. Then hoping to catch her in a treasonous remark regarding the king, he asked, "What do you think of the king's book?"

"I can say nothing about it for I have never read it."

By this point, Dare realized that he was losing more ground than he wished to admit. He glanced down at his notes and caught sight of a statement of another Protestant group, the Anabaptists, who believed that they were above human law because they answered only to the leading of the indwelling Holy Spirit. Dare smiled.

"Answer me this, Mistress. Do you have the Spirit of God within you?"

"If I did not, then I would be no more than a reprobate or castaway," Anne answered, looking directly into his eyes.

The intent of the jab hit home. Dare was at his wits' end. Angered, he turned away and motioned with his hand. A priest stepped forward and bent his ear to Dare's lips as the examiner whispered to him. Then he straightened and faced Anne. Anne was ready.

"What do you say concerning the sacrament on the altar?"

"I have already answered Master Dare concerning that matter."

"You answered him not at all! But I would have you tell me your meaning of the sacrament!"

Knowing that anything she said would be completely misunderstood—or worse, misconstrued—Anne decided inwardly that it would be best not to allow herself to be forced into a theological debate. Therefore, she simply said, "I beg you to excuse me concerning that matter. I am not a priest; therefore, it is not for me to say."

The priest tried again, but to no avail. Anne simply would not answer his questions. Dare glanced over at the men who sat as jurors. *Have they heard enough to reach a verdict?* he wondered. Their faces gave no evidence of their thoughts, so Dare chose to ask one more question: one he knew was a strong point of contention between the Protestants and the Catholics.

Returning his gaze to Anne, he asked, "Do you believe in the efficacy of private masses for the departed souls?"

Anne bristled. "'Tis great idolatry to believe that private masses are of more benefit than the death of Christ on the cross for us!"

Christopher Dare was hopelessly outside his league. He could no more argue with such a learned woman than he could argue with the Pope himself. Had she been a serving girl or weaver's daughter, he would have had no trouble. But not only was Anne far more educated than anyone he had examined before; she was a gentlewoman of a renowned family. And he was loathed to take responsibility of sending her to prison. Therefore, he did the only thing he could do. He decided to pass the decision to another.

He slammed down his gavel.

"This inquiry is over. Mistress Kyme, you shall be escorted to the House of the Lord Mayor for further questioning."

A rumble of discontented voices rolled through the room, but Dare paid no mine. Summoning a guard, he ordered that Anne be taken under guard to the Lord Mayor. As she was escorted away, he fervently hoped he would not encounter this troublesome woman again.

When a messenger from the Royal Quest arrived, Sir Martin Bowes, Lord Mayor, was enjoying a tankard of ale. The messenger handed him the folded parchment. Sir Martin set his cup down, broke open the seal, and scanned the note's contents. A grin spread over his face. So Christopher Dare was sending Anne Askew to him. For his part, he was more than happy to question this woman for he, too, had heard of Anne and was anxious to see for himself this eminent heretic who had come to London. Then he paused. Her reputation warned him that she was a woman of great wit and a tart tongue. Perhaps it would be wise to have a learned scholar with him during the questioning because, like Dare, the Lord Mayor did not consider himself well versed in matters of theology. Taking his quill, he scribbled a note, folded it, and handed it back to the messenger.

"Deliver this immediately to Dr. John Standish, the Bishop's Chancellor."

The courier bowed and promptly left. When he was gone, Sir Martin realized that it would be quite an accomplishment if he were able to secure from Anne a statement that she held firmly to Roman Catholic teaching. Yes, Bishop Bonner would be quite pleased with him indeed.

Anne arrived well before Dr. Standish, so she was made to wait in a small room at the back of the house. While she waited, she read her Bible and prayed for wisdom.

At length, she was summoned before the mayor. Entering the lavish room, she immediately saw Dr. Standish, sitting comfortably across from the Lord Mayor, his brooding eyes fastened critically on Anne. Though she did not know he was to be there, she was not surprised. *They gather their forces,* she thought.

Before he had dismissed the guard, Christopher Dare had given the head guardsman a list of questions he had asked of Anne during the earlier session. He knew the Lord Mayor would want to know what had already transpired. And he was right. Once Dr. Standish arrived, the two men went over the questions to be sure the Lord Mayor understood each one. So when Anne entered, Sir Martin was confident that this matter would be disposed of quickly. Anxious to prove his authority, he wasted no time in beginning the examination. He began with the same questions that Dare had posed to her, and Anne answered each just had she had earlier. For more than an hour, the two men tried to unnerve her; but in the end, it was Anne who managed to vex her examiners by her both pointed and evasive replies.

In exasperation, Sir Martin finally brought up an old argument that had at one time been used by a Protestant faction, known as the Lollards, to expose the fallacy of the bread and wine becoming the actual body of Christ when the priest blessed it. At the present time, anyone using the argument was automatically branded a heretic.

"Tell me, madam, what say you to the question: If a mouse were to eat the sacred Host, would it receive God? Many testify that you have used this question on more than one occasion to deceive your opponents."

"I never ask anyone such a question."

"But what do you believe? Does it or no?"

Anne only smiled. She knew what the Holy Scriptures taught of the Lord's body and blood, but refused to be led into such an obvious trap. At her persistent silence, Dr. Standish exploded.

"This is an outrage," he stormed. "What arrogance you possess, mistress! You forget your place and show no respect for those in authority over you. You, a mere woman, bandy scripture around in front of men, who are obviously your superiors both in education and society, thinking to prove them false. In all your studying, have you failed to read of St. Paul's admonition that women are expressly forbidden to speak or to talk of the work of God?"

"I know well St. Paul's meaning, sir. In I Corinthians 14, he says that a woman ought not to speak in the congregation by way of teaching.[19] So I ask you, sir: How many women have you seen go into the pulpit and preach?"

Dr. Standish fumed silently a moment, then finally admitted, "I have never seen any."

"Then, you ought to find no fault in a poor woman unless she had indeed transgressed the law."

"Indeed you have transgressed the law! You speak of things of which you have no authority to do so and you propagate heresy," Sir Martin bellowed and reached for paper and quill.

"Well, perhaps some time in prison will make you think better of your position."

"What surety do you require for my release to my own home?" Anne asked, fully aware of the law.

"None. There will be none and I will accept none," he snapped. "Guards!"

Anne's escort immediately appeared.

"Take this woman to the Counter on Bread Street," Sir Martin ordered. To Anne, he growled, "If you are truly wise, you will reconsider your answers and your actions."

Anne did not respond, but simply turned and followed the guard out.

The Lord Mayor's prison on Bread Street was only a short distance, and as the armed escort approached, Anne felt a knot growing in her stomach. Walking through the arched doorway, she could hear the clanking of iron gates somewhere down a poorly lit passageway. The jailer, a scruffy man who reeked of ale, quickly read the Lord Mayor's message.

"This way," he said gruffly, turning toward a narrow stairway.

Anne was led up the stairway to the second floor. The jailer, unaccustomed to seeing a gentlewoman, sneered at her as he thrust the key into the lock. The door groaned on its hinges as it opened. A rough hand from behind shoved her forward. The door swung back and clanked shut. The footsteps of the jailer and guards faded away.

The day had demanded the best of her, and she had held her own. But now, in the dark and musty cell, Anne finally released her pent up emotions. Dropping to her knees beside the well-worn mattress, she burst into tears. Never had she felt so alone, so abandoned. Sobbing, she choked out a desperate prayer.

"Gracious Lord, comfort me in my hour of need! And grant me Thy strength to stand firm against my adversaries."

Fear threatened to overwhelm her; and between choked sobs, she recited over and over the precious promise of God to which she had clung so many times in the past.

I will never leave thee, nor forsake thee.[20]

The hours slipped by, but gradually the truth of God's word lay hold of her; her sobs quieted and her tears ceased. Her heart grew still.

I am not alone, she thought as a final tear ran its course down her cheek. *I am not abandoned.*

Chapter XV

hroughout her first night of captivity, Anne was on her knees in prayer. Although she was exhausted by the day's events, sleep eluded her; but she attributed it mostly to the wretched condition of the straw mattress. Yet, she could not dismiss the stark reality that as the darkening gloom and unsettling night noises invaded her cell, fear invaded her heart. So on her knees she cried out to the Lord as she battled the forces of terror that threatened to overwhelm her. When at last the gray dawn shed its dim light into her small space, Anne finally collapsed on the mattress and slept, totally oblivious to the lumps and smells that had kept her awake hours before.

She awoke with a start. A key in her cell door jangled loudly, and the door swung open. A new jailer appeared, just as scruffy and odorous as the first one she had encountered, but this one at least did not sneer at her. He carried a small bowl of food, utensils, and a goblet, which he set on an unsteady table. He said nothing to Anne, but motioned toward the door.

"Well, git ye in here, woman, if yer comin'!" he called toward the passageway.

Timidly, Joane stepped in, her eyes wide with fear. Anne was on her feet in a moment. She rushed toward the servant girl, taking her somewhat by surprise, and embraced her, then stepped back.

"Dear Joane," Anne exclaimed. "What are you doing here?"

Habit forced Joane to bob a curtsy, then she said, "When your cousin, Britain, heard that you were confined, he went straightaway to the Lord Mayor and insisted on seeing you. But he was refused. However, the Lord Mayor did concede that a lady such as yourself should not be without her maid, so I was sent forth-with," Joane explained, still casting wary eyes around the room.

At her explanation, the jailer snorted. "Little good a maid is in a place like this," he muttered and exited. Anne ignored him. She was very grateful for Joane's company.

As the door clanked shut, Joane jumped. She looked on the verge of tears, so Anne quickly made her sit down and assured her that she was perfectly all right. Joane smiled weakly, then suddenly, her smile brightened.

"Oh, I almost forgot. I brought you some of your things, milady," she said, opening up a large satchel. From the bag, Joane pulled out Anne's hairbrushes and pins, one fresh dress, a woolen shawl, two changes of underclothing, a quill and parchment paper, and a book of Luther's sermons. "This was all I had time to gather," Joane apologized.

Anne grinned. "'Tis so much more than for what I could have hoped! You are a good and faithful servant."

Joane beamed under the praise. Then, as if she suddenly remembered her place, she asked, "Shall I brush your hair, milady?"

Anne nodded and turned her back to her. *God meets our needs in mysterious ways*, she thought as Joane's nimble fingers loosed Anne's long dark hair.

For six days, Anne had no company but Joane. And though she longed to see her brother or cousins, she realized that if they stayed away, it was because they were not allowed access to her. To pass the time, Anne occupied herself in prayer and Bible reading and recording on the parchment what had transpired thus far. Joane busied herself with washing their few clothes and keeping their tiny cell as neat as possible.

Secretly, Joane marveled at her mistress, who seemed unperturbed at her dismal surroundings. But though Anne showed no fear outwardly, she battled it inwardly and spent hours in silent, but earnest, prayer to overcome the dark emotions that threatened to undo her.

On March 17, the jailer unexpectedly admitted a visitor—though not one for which Anne had hoped.

At the sound of the lock turning, Anne glanced up from the table where she had been writing. It was not mealtime; therefore, someone must finally have been given permission to visit. She held her breath. The door swung open, and a priest stepped in. Anne groaned inwardly.

"Mistress Kyme," he began, his voice gentle. "I am Father Bennett. The Lord Bishop has sent me here to ask you some questions and give you my good advice."

Anne doubted whether that was possible, but said nothing. Her silence prompted him to speak again.

"Tell me, good lady, for what reason were you imprisoned here?" he asked as he cast his eyes around the white-washed chamber.

"I cannot tell you, sir, for I do not know."

"'Tis a great pity that one should be imprisoned without knowing the cause," he said, giving her his most compassionate smile. He crossed the cell and settled himself on the straw mattress. "Indeed, I am heartily sorry for you."

Anne doubted that as well, but again refrained from commenting.

"But perhaps I can be of good service to you and help secure your quick release."

"'Tis too late for a quick release," Anne replied tartly.

The priest did not respond to her remark, but merely smiled again. "Well, the Lord Bishop has hopes, as do I, that your time here has given you opportunity to reconsider your position and your opinions. 'Twould certainly be to your advantage to do so. Neither his lordship nor I wish to see you so cruelly treated, but even more so, we are in earnest to see your soul delivered from the horrors of hell."

"My soul has been delivered. You should be as concerned for your own."

For the first time, the priest frowned, but he did not allow his irritation to thwart his purposes. Instead, he composed his face, leaned forward, and said, "Answer me well a few questions, and I shall recommend to his lordship that you be released immediately."

He paused. Anne said nothing, so he continued. "I have been told that you deny that the sacrament on the altar is the Body of the Lord Jesus Christ. What say you to this?"

"I have answered that question before. Speak to Christopher Dare or the Lord Mayor for my response."

"I would like to hear it for myself," he urged gently. But Anne remained adamant in her refusal to enter into his game. Realizing the futility of pressing her further, he switched tactics.

"Would you make your confession then?"

"Most assuredly, as long as I can make it to Dr. Crome, Sir William Whitehead, or John Huntington for I know them to be men of wisdom."

The priest bristled inwardly at the names of the well-known Reform clergy and replied, "If I or any other priest were asked to hear your confession, 'twould be as good, for we are as honest as they be. If it were not so, the king would not allow us to preach."

"Nay, 'tis rather as Solomon declares in Proverbs that in the company of wise men, I may learn wisdom, but in speaking to a fool, I receive only harm."

Father Bennett no longer concealed his growing agitation. "And what say you concerning a beast who eats of the Host that has fallen to the floor?"

"Seeing as you have taken such pains in asking the question, I desire that you answer it yourself. For I will not because 'tis plain that you come only to tempt me, and I will not be led so."

"Do you intend on receiving the sacrament at Easter?"

"If I did not then I would not be a Christian woman. Indeed, I rejoice that the day grows so near and that I can celebrate again my Lord's glorious resurrection."

The priest studied her a moment, then sighed heavily. He stood and gazed down at her; and for the first time, Anne saw true compassion in his eyes. "You do yourself great harm, mistress. I shall pray that you see the error of your ways lest it be too late."

Summoning the jailer, he departed. When he had gone, Anne rose and went to the solitary window, her only source of sunlight. "And I shall pray for you," she whispered.

March 23, 1546

Twelve days had passed since Anne's arrest and still no friend or relative had been admitted to see her. She often wondered how long her imprisonment would last, realizing that others of the Reform faith had been locked away for years. Yet once again, the sound of the turnkey brought hope. The jailer unlocked the door, and Britain Askew, Anne's cousin, strode in, a look of anguish on his face. But Anne's face lit up, and she immediately went to him and embraced him warmly. When he drew away from her, he studied her closely.

"Are you fairing well? Have they treated you with kindness?" he asked.

"As kind as any prisoner, I suppose," Anne replied, trying to make light of the matter. But Britain was not amused.

"Edward sends his love, but 'tis impossible for him to come to you."

Anne understood. In his position under Cranmer, he could not risk assisting her. And had he not warned her of these very consequences if she would not leave London? No, she knew all too well that association with her meant that anyone coming to her aid would also be suspect. She held no bitterness.

"I am working to obtain your release on bail," Britain continued, "but 'tis no easy matter. I went to the Lord Mayor, and he sent me to the Lord Chancellor. As you well know, neither one sympathizes with your plight. The Lord Chancellor advised me that you could not be released without the consent of a spiritual officer. So I went in search of Dr. Standish. But he also cares little for your circumstance. He told me that he was not at liberty to recommend your release for he considered it a very heinous matter!"

Anne sighed and sank onto the stool by the table. "I am not surprised. He was quite angry at the examination."

Britain was astonished. "He was present at Sadler's Hall?"

"No, he was with the Lord Mayor at his house, where they questioned me a second time. I fear my answers did not suit him well."

Britain was downcast. The situation was far more serious than he had imagined, but not wanting to alarm Anne more, he simply said, "Take heart, my dear. I will continue to do all I can to see that you are released quickly. But you must promise us all that when you are, you will leave London at once!"

Anne started to protest, but thought the better of it. She understood Britain's fears for her, having encountered them herself; but still, she was unwilling to give her enemies the satisfaction of a victory. Keeping her thoughts to herself, she smiled up at her cousin.

"I am in your debt, dear cousin. Remember me in your prayers."

March 24, 1546

Edmond Bonner, Bishop of London, stared out of the large window that overlooked the bustling courtyard below, his portly frame casting a bulbous shadow behind him. Yet for all the activity occurring before his eyes, he saw none of it, his mind consumed with the troubles that plagued his diocese. Despite all his efforts to crush it, the Protestant movement flourished; and daily, he heard fresh reports of the growing number who embraced this popular—albeit heretical—teaching. Yet, even so, he was not without hope. Many of their leaders had already perished at the stake for their heresy, and it was only a matter of time before their followers abandoned their ideology in effort to spare their own lives. And even if they did not, there were other ways to fight this enemy. As he considered the situation, he realized that he had before him in the form of a young, headstrong woman, a powerful weapon that, if handled in the proper manner, could effectively discourage these new believers.

Anne Askew had come to his attention months before when he, too, heard of her outspoken and often lively debates with many of the leading conservative scholars. Since her arrest, he had made it his business to closely follow her trial; and though dismayed at her audacity, he nonetheless believed that she could be of significant value to his cause. If she could be persuaded to recant, her recantation would do more to demoralize those of the Reform thinking than a thousand heretic executions. *And*, he thought with pious satisfaction, *it would save her soul as well.*

But the matter had to be handled delicately—and without Anne being condemned as a heretic. As much as he despised her beliefs, Bishop Bonner did not want Anne to be burned for her faith, knowing all too well that would make her a martyr in the eyes of the people and only increase their religious fervor. No, he must move carefully and precisely. This was a matter he must take care of himself to ensure a good outcome.

He turned from the window and crossed to his desk. Settling his huge frame into the cushioned chair, he took a quill in hand. When he had finished writing, he called to his assistant, who instantly appeared.

"See that the Lord Mayor receives this message and arranges to have the prisoner, Anne Askew, brought to me at three o'clock tomorrow afternoon for examination. And see also that her friends are notified and that Doctors Crome, Huntington, and Whitehead be present as well to testify that she is not handled unjustly."

The assistant took the extended parchment and hurried away to do his master's bidding. Bishop Bonner leaned back, folded his hands across his bulging middle, and smiled. Yes, having three of the most renowned Reform clergy at the examination would add a nice touch. Their presence would demonstrate his sincere interest in a fair and honest hearing, and it would encourage the prisoner to speak forthrightly. Yes, before them, she would let down her guard; and when she did, he would have her.

March 25, 1546

As in her previous exams, Anne sat with her back straight and her eyes sparking confidence. Upon entering the Bishop's chamber, she was greatly encouraged to see her cousin who had come with a large gathering of friends to show their support. Anne breathed a prayer of thanksgiving. Although she was determined not to show it, fear clutched at her heart for she knew that a hearing before the Bishop of London was a serious matter— much more so than to what she had been subjected thus far.

For several minutes the assembly waited, tension thickening. Finally, the door leading to the Bishop's private offices opened, and the Bishop lumbered in, followed by Dr. Standish and several archdeacons.

He, too, brings a show of power, Anne thought, and then reminded herself, *If God be for us, who can be against us?*[21]

Bishop Bonner settled himself at an oaken table opposite Anne, folding his hands in front of him. He gazed at her gently for several moments, then spoke quietly.

"Mistress Kyme, I wish first to say that you are among friends. Oh, not just those who gathered here." He nodded his head toward Anne's cousin and supporters. "But I, likewise, am here to assist you in every way possible. But I am unable to help you unless you speak freely of the things that burden your conscience. I gave my word to them and now to you that that I shall in no way use any words you say against you."

"I have nothing to say, my lord, for my conscience, I thank the Lord, is burdened with nothing.

Bonner tried again.

"Now, pray tell me, if a man has a wound and goes to a surgeon, he cannot receive treatment until the wound is uncovered. In just the same way, I cannot give you wise counsel until I know with what your conscience is burdened."

"I say again, my lord, my conscience is clear concerning all things. Would it not appear to be folly if a surgeon were to lay a plaster on healthy skin?"

Bonner shifted in his seat, and his face became sterner. "Very well, then, you leave me no choice but to lay to your charge your very own words, which are these: you said that he who receives the sacrament from the hands of an evil priest receives the devil and not God."

"I never spoke such words. But as I said before to both the quest and to my Lord Mayor, so say I now again to you. The wickedness of a priest cannot hurt me; for in spirit and in faith, I receive no less than the body and blood of Christ."

Bonner eagerly leaned forward, realizing that she was very close to denying the church's teaching on the very presence of Christ in the host. "What type of saying is this? 'In spirit?'"

"My lord, without faith and spirit, I cannot receive Him worthily."

"But did you not say that after the holy bread has been consecrated, it nonetheless remains only bread?"

"No, my lord. I did not. When I was asked that question by the quest, I told them that I would not answer unless they first told me why St. Stephen had been stoned to death. They could not answer me, so neither did I answer them."

"Yet you quoted certain passages of scripture in order to refute the doctrine of the mass."

"I only quoted St. Paul's words to the Athenians that 'God lives not in temples made with hands.'"

"And how do you interpret these words?"

"I believe as the Scriptures tell me, my lord."

"Then if the Scriptures say that the holy bread is the body of Christ?"

"I believe as the Scriptures teaches…"

"And if the Scriptures say that it is not the body of Christ?"

"I still believe as the Scripture…"

"Well, what then, in your opinion, does the Scripture teach?" Bonner snapped.

"Whatever Christ and His apostles taught, I believe."

Scowling, Bonner leaned forward and demanded. "And what did they teach concerning the sacrament on the altar?"

Anne said nothing, but only stared straight ahead.

"Now, you seem to have very few words. Why is that?" Bonner asked, sensing victory in his grasp.

"God has given me the gift of knowledge, not of utterance. And, as Solomon attests in Proverbs, a woman of few words is a gift from the Lord."

Throughout the room, smiles flickered on the faces of the onlookers. But Bonner did not smile. He rose from his seat and paced the floor. Then he moved to where Anne sat and glared down at her.

"Did you or did you not say that the mass is idolatry?"

"No, I did not. When the Quest put that question to me, they asked if private masses relieved the souls of those departed. I answered, 'What idolatry is this that we should trust more in private masses than in the healing death of the dear Son of God?'"

"What sort of answer is that?"

"A poor one, my lord, but good enough for the circumstances."

Bonner turned away in exasperation. No matter how hard he tried, Anne would not give him the statements he needed to bring charges of heresy against her. Of course, he had no doubt that she was a heretic; but without clear statements as to her beliefs, he had no way of proving it. Were she an ordinary woman, he would throw her in prison and leave her there until she confessed. But Anne was no ordinary woman. She had powerful and influential friends who would not allow her to be held without a formal charge.

Bonner made one final attempt. "There are many who read and know the Scriptures, yet they do not follow them, nor do they live on after death."

"My lord, I desire that all men know from my conversations and from my life that I do believe Scripture. I am so sure of myself in this that I know of none who are able to prove any dishonesty in me. If you know of such a man, pray, bring him forth that I might answer him."

At her answer, Bonner exploded in rage. He charged from the room and returned to his own office, Dr. Standish quick on his heels. Out of the hearing of the assembly, he stormed, "What kind of woman is this? She neither confesses nor asserts her beliefs! Well, I will know once and for all her mind on these matters!"

As Dr. Standish looked on, Bonner took parchment and quill and began to write out a document of orthodox doctrine. One way or the other, he would wring a confession from her. If she refused to sign it, he would then be able to legally bring charges of heresy against her. And if she signed, her recantation would be enough to destroy her in the eyes of her fellow believers. When he finished, he ordered Anne to be brought to him.

Anne's heart pounded as she entered the room where the Bishop sat, glaring at her from behind his desk. She immediately knew what the early Christians must have felt as they were led into the arena of ravenous beasts, for she realized that this man had every intention of devouring her. She whispered a prayer and stepped forward to face him. Dr. Standish offered her a chair; and though she would have preferred to stand, she felt her knees weaken. Garnering her courage, she sat and gazed evenly at the large man before her.

"Since you refuse to make your position known," Bonner began, "I have written an article of faith that if you truly be a good Christian woman shall have no hesitation in signing. If not, then you will prove yourself the heretic you are."

Anne paled and her hands grew clammy. Yet, she waited in silence. Bonner took up the parchment and read thus:

Be it known to all faithful people that as concerns the blessed sacrament of the altar, I do firmly and undoubtedly believe that after the word of consecration be spoken by the priest, according to the common usage of the Church of England, there is actually present the body and blood of our Savior, Jesus Christ, whether the minister who does consecrate it be a good man or a bad man. Also, whenever the said sacrament is received, whether the receiver be a good man or a bad man, he does receive it really and corporally. And moreover, I do believe that whether the said sacrament be then received of the minister or else reserved to be put into the pyx yet there remains the very body and blood of our Savior. So that whether the minister or receiver be good or bad, and yea, whether the sacrament be received or reserved, there always is the blessed body of Christ in actuality.

And this belief with all other beliefs concerning the sacrament and other sacraments of the Church, and all things concerning the Christian belief that are taught and declared in the king's book, lately set forth for the erudition of the Christian people, I, Anne Askew, otherwise called Anne Kyme, do truly and perfectly believe and do here and now confess and acknowledge. And here I do promise that henceforth I shall never do or say anything against these tenets. In witness thereof, I, the said Anne, have subscribed my name before these present.

When he had finished, he shoved the document across his desk toward Anne and waited for her response. Anne swallowed hard. Her choice was clear: either she sign the parchment and be released or refuse and face the consequences. She summoned the last of her waning courage.

"I believe as much of what you have written as is supported by Scripture. Therefore, I desire that you add that to what is written."

"Do not tell me what to write, mistress," he replied, his voice cold.

Taking up the document again, he rose, and returned to the outer chamber. Anne had no choice but to follow. Before the assembled group, he once again read the document aloud. The priests nodded their approval. Anne's friends looked worried.

"If you truly be this woman's friends, you will counsel her to sign for her own sake," Bonner advised them.

Britain rose from his seat and went to Anne. Taking her arm, he pulled her aside out of earshot of the bishop and his colleagues. Her other friends surrounded her as well. Speaking softly, Britain urged, "Anne, I know your faith and how ardent you. No one will think the worst of you if you sign this document, especially those who know you."

Anne was shocked. "How can you say such? Would you truly ask me to deny all that I believe?"

"All who know you know your heart and know that you would deny nothing. But you must be reasonable. What good would come from your imprisonment or worse, your death?" Britain pressed.

Another spoke up. "And if you sign, then you can return to Lincoln and continue your work there among those who have not yet heard the gospel truth."

"Truly," Britain added, "you are of far more value to the cause of Christ by your life than by your death. And make no mistake, Anne, this man *will* convict you of heresy if you do not sign! Do you really wish to burn?"

Anne paled at the thought and shook her head. Yet, everything inside her said this was wrong. She had not come this far to abandon her beliefs now. But as those around her continued to press, she felt herself weakening. The days in prison and the long interrogations she had been through had wearied her, and she had no wish to prolong them. With great misgivings, she finally agreed to sign.

Britain heaved a great sigh or relief. A murmur of approval passed through the crowd of priests. Bishop Bonner could not conceal his satisfaction at such a victory. He ushered Anne to a seat, handed her an inked quill, and peered over her shoulder as she put her hand to the document. She wrote:

> *I, Anne Askew, do believe all manner of things contained in the faith of the true Church of Christ.*

Reading her words, Bonner boiled over in rage! Snatching the parchment from her, he flung out of the room. *Is this woman incapable of straight dealing?* he thought in exasperation.

In horror, Britain watched him go, then quickly decided to follow him in hopes of assuaging his anger. Behind closed doors, Britain and Dr. Weston, another Reform thinker, reasoned with the agitated bishop until at long last, they persuaded him to accept both Anne's signature and postscript.

But Bonner had no intention of letting Anne off easily. He would hear no talk concerning bail and ordered her to be returned to the Lord Mayor's prison. To accentuate his victory, the next day, he once again ordered her to appear, this time in Guildhall, where he publicly read her confession, being sure to leave off her final words. Throughout the reading, Anne hung her head, fighting to hold back tears of humiliation. At the end, she was escorted back to her cell, where she fell on her mattress and wept bitterly.

Finally, on March 27, after much discussion with the Bishop's officers, Britain secured the Bishop's warrant that allowed for Anne's release. He hastened to the prison, but the news did not bring a smile to Anne's face. Silently, she accompanied him back to her apartments, where Edward greeted her. He extended his arms toward her. Anne collapsed in his arms, torrents of tears streaming down her cheek.

"Hush, dearest. 'Tis over now. You are safe, and I will see you safely home."

Three days later, a weary Anne boarded a carriage accompanied by Joane and several other attendants. She was not the same woman who had come to London two and half years earlier. Emotionally and physically, she was exhausted. Her heart was broken, broken by her ordeal in prison, but more so, by the knowledge that her signature was inscribed at the bottom of a document whose espoused doctrine she knew beyond doubt was false. She had failed her friends—but worse, her God. Now, she longed for nothing more than time alone to read her Bible and to find peace again with her Savior.

The Chancery Court had ordered her to return to Thomas, but as the carriage bumped along, it traveled the road that led not to Friskney, but to Lincoln – and South Kelsey Hall.

Chapter XVI

April – May 1546

Stephen Gardiner, Bishop of Winchester, was not a patient man, but he was a politically wise one. In the hope that the right opportunity may present itself to rid London, indeed all of England, of the wretched heretics who continued to grow in number, he had bided his time; but time was running out. Henry VIII, though still a formidable king, was growing weaker; and though it was treasonous to utter it aloud, everyone knew that the king could not survive much longer. And once Henry was gone, the throne would pass to Edward, the young prince with a decided Protestant leaning. No, if these enemies of the Church were going to be stamped out, Gardiner must act quickly before it was too late. True, there were risks involved, but to hesitate would surely give the Protestant movement the momentum it needed to flourish unchallenged.

And, of course, there remained the most exasperating problem with the queen. Reports of the Bible studies Catherine Parr held in her private apartments were numerous, and her growing allegiance to the Protestant movement had to have a great influence on the young prince. The only way to thwart that influence would be to discredit her before the king and the country. So he waited and watched for his chance to pounce. He could only hope that if he were successful she would eventually go the way of her predecessors, Anne Boleyn and Catherine Howard.

So in the waning months of Henry's reign, the Catholic bishops, with Gardiner and Thomas Wriothesley leading the charge, declared war on the troublesome Reformers. Men and women, both of high class and low, were summoned before the Council to defend or recant their beliefs. John Lascelles was among them, much to the delight of the Howards, who had never forgiven him for his part in the downfall of Catherine, Henry's fifth wife.

Though he defended himself well and refused to fall victim to his examiners' attempts at trickery, he was, nonetheless, thrown into prison to await further judgment.

But Gardiner, not content to limit his inquest to London, sent couriers to outlying areas with letters that demanded that questionable persons appear before the Council. Thomas Kyme received one of those letters.

May 26, 1546

Thomas was not alarmed when he received the summons; in fact, he had been expecting it. For over two years, Anne had refused to come back to Friskney though he had made numerous attempts to persuade her to do so. He long regretted his hasty action in driving Anne from his home, not because of any feelings of remorse at having been an unfit husband but rather because of the scathing attacks he had received from the local priests in dealing inappropriately with a confessed heretic. But another situation weighed heavily on him, for Thomas found himself in the most disagreeable circumstances. In the eyes of the church, he was legally married, yet he had neither the comfort nor the help of a wife. The years of separation had only served to increase his bitterness toward the woman to whom he was pledged; and the invidious position he now found himself in led him to the decision that one way or another, he would be rid of the troublesome wench; for as long as Anne lived, he could not marry another.

So when Anne once again refused to heed the Council's admonition that she return to her husband, Thomas took a step that two years prior he would have been loathed to do. With the support and urging from the local parish, he denounced Anne as a heretic and sent his denouncement to the London Council. That was all Stephen Gardiner needed. On the pretense of trying to reconcile a failing marriage, Gardiner sent a summons to Thomas demanding that both he and Anne appear before the Council within ten days of receipt of the summons.

Thomas grinned when he received the expected summons and wasted no time. He immediately sat down and wrote to Sir Francis Askew, urging him once more to send Anne back to Friskney. Though he endeavored to keep the tenor of the letter respectful, his bitterness and anger seeped through. He wrote:

> *I implore you, Sir, that you see to it that your sister, my wife, be ready to depart with me without delay upon my arrival. Should you be tempted to conceal her from me, I remind you that this summons comes with the king's authority and ask that you consider gravely the results of incurring His Majesty's displeasure. Be assured, good Sir, that if Anne persists in evading me, I am not without friends who will aid me in seeking her out.*

May 27, 1546

Francis held Thomas' letter in his hands, his throat tightening as he reread the words. The matter had indeed become quite serious; and he knew the risk was great, but he was determined to do all he could to save Anne from both Thomas and the Council. He was completely aware of what lay behind the summons, and he could not willingly surrender the sister he loved so dearly to a fate he shuddered to even imagine. So, after waiting three days, he replied:

> *I fear I am unable to assist you in the matter of which you wrote, for I do not know my sister's whereabouts at this time. Though she returned here at first, she decided it was to her advantage to stay with friends, and she did not inform me as to which friends had offered her their hospitality.*

June 1, 1546

Thomas was enraged! Was Sir Francis so arrogant that he believed himself above the law of the Church and the king's pleasure? Well, he would not win this time. With the summons clutched in his hand, he called for his horse and quickly mounted. Yanking hard on the reins, he turned his horse toward the road heading north and urged his steed to a gallop.

When Francis was informed that Thomas was, indeed, on his way to Lincoln, he was astounded. He had not expected so bold an action on the part of the boorish, if well to do, farmer; and, for the first time, Francis realized how grave a danger this posed for Anne. He hastened to look for her.

Francis found Anne just where he expected her to be – sitting under the ancient willow by the moss-covered stonewall. He sighed as he approached her, noting again how her appearance had changed. She looked so tired, and the sparkle in her eyes had vanished. Quietly, he slipped up beside her. When she detected movement out of the corner of her eye, she looked up from her reading and smiled, but even her smile had lost its vivaciousness.

"What are you reading, now?" Francis inquired, settling himself on the stony ledge.

"A collection of sermons. Some by Luther and diverse other well-known reformers."

When Francis made no further conversation, she returned to her reading but glanced up again when she sensed him studying her.

"Have you come out merely to keep me company, or is there another issue weighing on your mind?" she asked.

Francis' brows knitted together as his face grew solemn. Drawing a deep breath, he said, "I have received word that Thomas is on his way to Lincoln, presumably to meet with the Bishop of Lincoln and his officers."

Anne said nothing.

"I should have known he would come, and I should have sent you away when I first received his letter," Francis apologized.

"But I foolishly assumed that my position in Lincoln would keep Thomas from making so daring a move. And now, 'tis too late to make arrangements for you to go elsewhere, but there is Tanner cottage. You could go and hide there, at least until the danger has passed."

"Do you really think that is necessary?"

"Yes, dearest, I do. For it has also been reported to me that Thomas has denounced you as a heretic…"

Anne stiffened. "So he means to be rid of me for good."

"If you go to Tanner cottage immediately, you will not be found. I promise you that." Francis said and leaned over to take her hand in his.

"I shall have Joane pack what I need at once."

June 2, 1546

Dean Heneage, one of the bishop's officers, studied the determined red-haired farmer who stood angrily before him. He then glanced down to read for the second time the contents of the summons Kyme had presented to the Lincolnshire officers. Although Heneage abhorred heresy in all its forms, he was loathed to make a move against one of the most influential and powerful families in Lincolnshire. Without saying a word, he passed the parchment to a fellow officer on his right, who also quietly read its contents. This continued until each officer present was fully informed of the situation. The last officer in turn handed the document back to Heneage. Throughout this proceeding, Thomas stood stock still, his face hardened and angry. Finally, Heneage spoke.

"This is no easy matter, Kyme. While we sympathize with your plight, you must understand that Sir Francis Askew is well known and quite powerful in these parts."

"Are you a friend of Sir Francis or an officer of the bishop, milord?"

"I would hope to call myself both."

"Perhaps in other circumstances you may, but in this matter you must choose. And I might add, choose as well whether you are a friend of Sir Francis or a loyal subject of His Majesty."

Heneage shifted uneasily in his chair. The summons did bear Gardiner's seal, which could only mean that the king's approval had been secured before it was issued; therefore, to act in defiance of the summons would mean acting in defiance against the Catholic Church and His Grace, King Henry. Leaning forward on his desk, his balled fist pressed against his lips, Heneage eyed the young man squarely. Then abruptly, he stood.

"We will ride to South Kelsey first thing in the morning," he announced, and the other officers immediately rose in unison. "You, no doubt, will wish to ride with us, sir?"

Thomas nodded. He wouldn't miss this for anything.

June 3, 1546

As the bishop's officers along with Tomas Kyme dismounted in the courtyard of South Kelsey Hall, Francis could not help but remember the terrifying October night almost ten years earlier when angry, zealous men had come and dragged him and his younger brother away from these sheltering walls. Now, it was happening all over again; only this time, their prey was Anne, and he was all that was standing between her and these men who were bent on destroying her.

Thomas dismounted first and strode toward the massive oak doors, but Heneage hastened to step up before him.

"Kyme, as the bishop's officer, 'tis my duty to handle this matter," Heneage asserted.

Thomas reluctantly stepped back, glaring at the man who chastened him before the others.

Heneage approached and pounded on the door. A few moments later, a male servant opened the door a crack.

"We will speak to Sir Francis," Heneage ordered.

"If you will be so good as to wait…" the servant began to close the door.

"We will wait in the inner hall," the officer retorted and pushed the door back. The startled servant stumbled backwards and the officers and Thomas entered.

Hearing the clatter of men in the entryway, Francis, who had been listening from the back sitting room, took a deep breath and opened the double doors to the hallway. He glanced at Thomas, whose face was almost as red as his hair, but chose to ignore him. He instead approached Dean Heneage.

"Heneage, this is rather early for a social call."

"This is no social call, sir, as you are well aware. I have a summons here from Gardiner, Bishop of Winchester, that demands that Anne Kyme return with her husband," he motioned toward Thomas, "immediately to London as they have been called to appear before the king's council."

Francis looked surprised. "But, I have already informed Master Kyme that Anne is not here, nor do I know her whereabouts. She left here sometime ago, and I have not heard from her these past few weeks."

"He lies!" Thomas snarled.

"Hold your tongue, Kyme! We will search out the place to know if he speaks true or not."

"Search if you must, but you shall find nothing."

Heneage turned to the other men; and with a nod of his head, they fanned out to search each room of the house. Servants scurried to keep out of their way as the officers, followed closely by Thomas, moved from room to room and out into the gardens, but neither Anne nor anything that could be identified as hers was found. As the men continued their search, Heneage questioned Francis further.

"How long was Mistress Kyme here?"

"I suppose 'twas little more than a week, perhaps ten days at the most."

"It does seem strange that she should leave and not inform you of her whereabouts."

"Anne is accustomed to choosing her own way. If you knew my sister, you would know that she has quite an independent spirit."

Heneage studied Francis. If he was lying, he was good at it, but he had to make sure.

"You know, of course, the consequences of interfering with an official royal edict."

"I know only too well, sir. I have witnessed the consequences of those who are accused of opposing the king," Francis replied, remembering with anguish the fate of Thomas Moigne.

"Well, 'twould serve…"

The sound of feet scuttling down the stairs made Heneage stop in mid-sentence. William Gibson, a fellow officer, rushed into the room, a small folded note in his hand. He extended his hand to Heneage. Francis' face grew suddenly pale.

"We found this, sir!"

Heneage took the proffered note and unfolded it. He read:

> *Dearest Brother,*
>
> *I am safely settled in the cottage and wish you not to worry for my sake. God will not forsake me to mine enemies. I shall wait until I hear from you that it is safe to return.*
>
> *Anne*

Heneage looked up and stared evenly at Francis. When he spoke, his words were ice. "So, you do not know your sister's whereabouts. What say you now, Sir Francis?"

Francis could think of nothing to reply. Feeling suddenly weak, he sank into a nearby chair. Heneage turned away from him in disgust. To Thomas, he asked, "Do you know of this cottage?"

"I believe there are several cottages on South Kelsey land, but it shall not take long to search each one. We shall find her even without her brother's help," Thomas replied, triumph resounding in his words.

With only Joane to serve her, Anne found herself doing more domestic chores than to what she was accustomed, but she really didn't mind. Most chores were rather mindless, so Anne could sing and pray as she worked. This morning she had decided to bake bread, a task she undertook with great enjoyment. She dumped the soft dough onto a kneading board. Then flouring her hands, she sank her hands into the plump ball, and began kneading the soft mound. In front of her on the table lay her open Bible so that she could read as her fingers plied the elastic dough.

Suddenly, the kitchen door burst open. Anne jumped, startled by the sudden appearance of Samuel, one of the stable hands at South Kelsey. He leaned heavily against the doorframe.

"Milady," Samuel gasped, clearly out of breath. "You...must leave...at once!"

"Leave? Why? What has happened?" Anne demanded to know.

"They are comin', milady. Master Kyme...and the bishop's officers!"

Anne froze, then the terrifying impact of the news pushed her into action. She glanced at the table, grabbed her Bible, and started for the door. But then she stopped abruptly. If they found the Bible on her, she would be accused of possessing heretical material. But where could she hide it? Thinking quickly, she turned back to the kneading trough, thrust the Bible into the dough, and folded the soft dough over top of it. Placing it quickly on the baking paddle, she turned to the oven beside the brick hearth, yanked open the door, and slid the paddle into the hot interior.

Samuel, eyes popping, stared at her as if she had suddenly gone mad. Anne ignored him as she brushed past him and raced to find Joane. She found her faithful servant hanging out clothes on a grassy knoll beside the cottage.

Anne didn't even take time to explain, but grabbed the young woman's hand and dragged her behind her as she headed for the nearby woods. Branches whipped at Anne's face as she plunged through a thicket of small trees and bushes, but Anne's steps neither faltered nor slowed. Stumbling behind her, Joane struggled to keep up, not knowing why she was being dragged into the woods but very certain the reason was valid. Finally, the two women, breathless, came to rest in a deep ravine overgrown with dense underbrush. Anne borrowed out a hole in the thick grass and brush and shoved Joane in, then scooted in behind. Hearts pounding, the two women listened for any sound of approaching horses.

Thomas was determined to take the lead in the search for Anne, so when the riders dismounted in front of Tanner cottage, Thomas was the first to reach the door. Shoving it open, he stormed inside. He quickly surveyed the small front parlor and then headed toward the back. The other men followed on his heels, once again spreading out to search each room. Heneage sauntered in last of all. He'd let the others do the work and take the credit when the fugitive woman was apprehended. But after only a few minutes, all the men gathered again in the front room, one man dragging Samuel with him.

"'Twould seem she has been forewarned," the man growled, holding Samuel by the scruff of his collar.

"Which way did she go?" Thomas demanded.

"By your leave, sir, I do not know. She left so quickly, I did not take notice," the frightened man stuttered.

Outraged, Thomas sent the back of his hand flying and struck the trembling man across the jaw, causing him to fall to his knees and cry out as much from fear as from pain.

Heneage stepped forward. "Enough of this! 'Twould be impossible for her to go far on foot. If we spread out, we should find her within the hour."

Grumbling murmurs rippled through the group as they realized their work was not yet done; but they filed out obediently, leaving the terrified Samuel behind them. Once outside, they mounted their horses and split into four groups, each group heading in a different direction. Thomas was with the group heading toward the woods.

Anne held her breath as she strained to listen. Were those voices she heard? She waited, her heart pounding so hard she knew it would come right through her chest. The voices were clearer now, but she could not recognize to whom they belonged.

Then a voice all to familiar called out, "Over here! The grass has been trampled down!"

Anne felt herself stiffen. He was so close, but if she bolted he would surely catch her. The blood pulsed rapidly through her veins. Beads of sweat tickled down her face.

The thrashing of footsteps through the thick grass came closer. Anne pressed herself back against the wall of undergrowth behind her, willing herself to be invisible. The footsteps paused. Then a thud shook the ground as two booted feet landed on the ravine floor just a few feet away.

Anne looked up into the sneering face of Thomas Kyme.

Chapter XVII

𝕱rancis sat alone in his study, his shoulders sagging forward, his head cradled in his hands. Though he tried desperately to block the invasive image from his mind's eye, he knew that as long as he lived, he would never forget his last glimpse of Anne and the horror he felt as he watched her ride off toward London. Thomas, insolent in his triumph, rode on one side of her; and Dean Heneage, sneering in disdain at Francis, rode on her other side. But Francis cared not at all what those men thought of him; it was Anne's terrified eyes that pierced him through to his soul. She had trusted him to protect her, and he had failed her. In his heart, he knew he would never see her again; and he also knew his failure would haunt him throughout his days on earth.

He moaned and wearily sat back, his eyes still closed. Then slowly he opened his eyes and gazed mindlessly at a huge mirror that hung over the great fireplace in the room. His eyes focused on nothing, but then his gaze fell on a golden illumination that grew and took shape. Suddenly, he bolted upright. In astonishment and fear, he stared at the polished glass. He shook his head as if to waken himself fully, then stared again. A translucent yellow-orange flame flickered and glowed in the mirror. He spun to see what burned behind him. Nothing. He turned back. The flaming apparition burned brighter.

"Oh, Anne," he sobbed in anguish and fell to his knees. "Dearest Anne… what have I done?"

June 1546

Although Thomas urged the riding party to hasten without delay to London, by the time the couple arrived, they had missed their ordered ten-day schedule. Therefore, they were forced to take lodgings in London and wait almost two weeks before the Council called them to appear. While they waited, the tension between them bristled. Though the couple shared living quarters, they spoke little and only when absolutely necessary. Thomas refused Anne any visitors, so she spent the days closeted in her room rather than suffer his company. Realizing full well that the summons was not about her marriage, she spent much of her time in prayer as she prepared herself for what she knew was coming. She sorely missed having her New Testament with her, but her years of discipline paid off. As she sat quietly in her room, she reviewed in her mind the countless passages of Scripture she had memorized and was thereby strengthened. *This time*, she told herself, *I shall not falter. Even if I should perish, I will not deny Thy truth.*

Anne was serene; Thomas, restive. He felt completely uncomfortable in London's bustling surroundings. Born and bred a simple country farmer, he preferred the endless stretch of fields and boundless horizon to the chaotic streets and confining structures. The constant activity and mass of humanity of London set him on edge, and the few words he spoke were biting and harsh. He loathed spending time with Anne, but he feared that if she were out of his sight, she would somehow slip back to South Kelsey and his plan to be rid of her would fail.

Finally, on June 19, 1546, Thomas and Anne Kyme were summoned before the Council in Greenwich. Thomas Wriothesley sat on the Council among others, but it was Stephen Gardiner who took charge.

"Mistress Kyme," he began. "I have documents here that testify that on March 2 in this, the year of our Lord 1546, you brought a case before the Chancery Court against your husband, one Thomas Kyme, claiming your marriage invalid. Yet, your case was heard, and the judgment was that your marriage was and is in the eyes of the Church and His Majesty's court lawful in every regard. You were thus ordered to return to your husband forthwith. Yet, you disobeyed that order and remained in London where you involved yourself in illegal affairs for which you were arrested and ordered to appear before the Royal Quest again on March 10."

Gardiner paused and peered at Anne, who sat stoically, her face calm. She returned his stare without flinching. Gardiner muttered something under his breath, then continued. "Because your answers were found to be insufficient, you were retained further. On March 25, you were called before Bishop Bonner, where your answers again proved most unworthy. But, the Bishop, being a merciful man, allowed you your freedom to return to your husband; yet, once again, you revealed your flagrant disregard for the law and returned instead to your brother in Lincolnshire!"

At this point, Gardiner sat forward and glared at her. "What say you to all of this?"

"'Tis as you say, milord. Your facts on the matter are correct," she replied evenly.

"I am not asking for a confirmation of the facts, madam, but an explanation as to your actions!"

"It matters not to me what the Chancery Court or the Council has to say. I place my trust wholly on the Word of God that gives me freedom from this man. Thus, he is *not* my husband!"

"And on what Scripture do you base that opinion?"

"The Book of I Corinthians, chapter 7."

"And what does that chapter say?"

"'Tis not for me, a mere woman, to teach a man of the church what Scripture says," Anne replied, working to suppress a smile.

Gardiner glared; but before he could reply, Wriothesley demanded, "Speak plainly, mistress! What is your mind concerning your husband?"

"My Lord Chancellor, I have already spoken my mind concerning this matter."

"Your answer is not satisfactory. And if you were a loyal subject of His Majesty, you would speak plainly for it is the king's pleasure that you do so."

"If it be the king's pleasure to know my mind and hear what I have to say, then I shall gladly speak the truth directly to him."

"'Tis beneath the king to be troubled by one such as yourself."

"Milord, Solomon was considered the wisest king ever to have lived, yet he did not deem it unworthy to hear the complaint of two poor women. If he be so, then surely His Grace could hear the testimony of a simple woman of faith and his loyal subject as well."

Wriothesley's anger simmered, but he determined that he would not to be outdone by this woman. "Tell us, Mistress Kyme, what belief do you espouse regarding the Holy Sacrament?"

Anne hesitated, but only for a moment. She had rehearsed in her mind what she would say when, undoubtedly, this subject was put to her once again. She lifted her chin and gazed directly at the Lord Chancellor. "I believe that as often as I, in a Christian congregation, do receive the bread in remembrance of Christ's death and with thanksgiving, in accordance to His holy instruction, I receive the fruits of His most glorious passion."

"What sort of answer is that?" Gardiner rebuked her. "Will you not speak directly? Declare plainly your thoughts about the Sacrament. Is it truly the body of our Lord or is it not?"

"Milord, I will not sing a new song to the Lord in a strange land."

The Bishop snorted, "Now you speak in parables because you fear the truth."

"No, milord. I speak thus because 'tis best for you. If I were to speak the truth openly, you would not accept it."

"You are nothing more than a parrot, mimicking only the words you have been taught by others, of which you have no true understanding."

"I speak my own mind and none other," Anne declared firmly. "And I am ready to suffer all things at your hands, not only your rebukes but all that may follow hereafter, and that with great rejoicing!"

"If you suffer, 'twill not be by my hands, but by your own; for you are stubborn and possess a haughty spirit!" Gardiner snapped back. He then turned abruptly to Thomas Kyme, who had been watching the proceedings silently, but with great hopes that Anne would hang herself with her own words.

"Master Kyme."

Thomas started when his name was called but immediately rose to his feet.

"It appears, sir, that you are without guilt in this matter and that you have endeavored to be a goodly husband to this woman who accuses you without any honest allegation; therefore, you are free to go. This Council shall summon you should your presence be required again."

Unaccustomed to being in the presence of such august gentlemen, Thomas stammered his thanks and quickly departed. Outside the Council chamber, he leaned against the wall and heaved a sigh of relief. A priest noticed him and approached.

"You are Thomas Kyme, husband of Anne Kyme?"

"Aye, though I would rather not own her as my wife," Thomas grumbled.

The priest cast a furtive glance around then lowered his voice.

"'Twould appear, sir, that you may have your wish. I have heard that the Council is set against her. She has made powerful enemies. I would not wish to stand in her place." The priest nodded knowingly to him then quietly moved on.

As he watched him go, Thomas felt the hairs on the back of his neck prickle as the import of the priest's words sunk in.

After Thomas was dismissed, Anne was subjected to further questioning for four more hours. In an effort to trick her into admitting her heresy, the Council members came at her from all angles, asking repeatedly the same questions. But Anne held firm. She stuck with her first statement and refused to elucidate further. As the hours wore on, tempers flared. In truth, the members of the Council had no desire to sentence Anne to death.

A recantation would suit their purposes far more, but try as they may, she would not give in. They were astounded that she so willingly placed her life–and in their eyes–her immortal soul in such great peril, but though they cajoled, then finally threatened, they made no progress.

Finally, the confounded Councilors ended their questioning; and Anne, exhausted by the day's events, was lodged in the home of Lady Garnish, a devout Catholic, but also a kindly woman. The Council hoped by keeping her there she would be further persuaded to give up her opinions. But this only proved how little they understood the mind of the determined young woman for Anne was equally convinced that the Lord had brought her into these circumstances to test her faith, and she was resolved not to succumb to their wiles.

June 20, 1546

In a small antechamber in Greenwich Palace, Anne waited. She was tired, having slept little the night before, but she was determined as ever not to give in to her enemies. She could hear muffled voices in the outer chamber, and she could only guess that her examiners were preparing for another bout. Anne was preparing, too, praying as she waited and reviewing Scripture in her mind. The sound of an opening door made her sit upright, expectant. Stephen Gardiner entered, followed by William Parr, Earl of Essex, and John Dudley, known also as Lord Lisle. The latter two looked uncomfortable and avoided Anne's eyes, but Gardiner began just where he had left off the day before.

"I will ask you again, Mistress Kyme. Do you confess that the Holy Sacrament is indeed the flesh, bone, and blood of our Savior, the Lord Jesus Christ?"

"I have made my statement concerning that matter. I have no more to say."

"Mistress," Lord Parr implored. "Why do you make this so difficult? If you will but agree with the teaching of the holy church, you shall be released. Why do you remain so obstinate?"

Anne eyed him and Lord Lisle squarely. "And why do you counsel contrary to your knowledge? That is a very great shame!"

Gardiner, sighing heavily, changed tactics. "My dear woman, if you would only realize that I am your friend and desire nothing but your good."

"That, milord, was the exact attitude of Judas when he unkindly betrayed Christ!"

William Parr cleared his throat in a poor attempt to disguise the laughter that threatened to burst forth from him. The Bishop scowled. How dare she treat him, a renowned bishop of the church, with so much disrespect and in front of these two gentlemen with whom he had little friendship.

"If you would, mistress, I would speak to you privately," he urged, anxious to remove himself from further public ridicule.

"I cannot allow that, milord," Anne replied.

"But why? I only mean to ascertain more clearly your mind on these matters."

"According to the words of Christ and of Paul, 'tis in the mouths of two or three witnesses that every matter will stand. But I shall ask a question of you. How long shall you tread on both sides? You wholeheartedly rejected the authority of the Pope over the English Church, yet you so tenaciously cling to the Pope's doctrine of the mass."

Gardiner could contain his anger no longer. "Where do you learn such disrespectful ideas?" he snapped.

"I kings, chapter 18. king Ahab also sought to align himself with both Baal and God."

The Bishop reddened in rage. "Beware, woman," he rasped, "you are the one who treads on dangerous ground."

"And from what Scripture do you accuse me? For in truth, I have searched the Scriptures and find no place where Christ or any of His apostles condemn any person to death."

Gardiner had had enough of this Bible-quoting woman. In a fury, he rose and abruptly turned to leave. As he strode across the room, he yelled over his shoulder, "Take heed if you be so wise, for surely you will burn for your obstinacy!"

"God will laugh your threatenings to scorn!" Anne retorted to his departing back.

June 27, 1546

The morning sun wiggled through the lace curtains and splashed on Anne's face, but Anne could not bring herself to open her eyes. Instead she feebly turned away from the intrusive light as she lay on the bed in her room at the home of Lady Garnish. Anne's head throbbed. In fact, her entire body ached, and every move was anguish. Never had she felt so ill, and she truly thought-and perhaps wished-that she might die. Where this illness originated, she did not know, but Anne was convinced that the past week's ordeal contributed to her present agony. Throughout the week, one Council member after another had interrogated her, often for hours at a time, in an attempt to persuade her from her opinions. Indeed, two highly respected Catholic theologians, Dr. Richard Cox and Dr. Thomas Robinson, visited her twice, the second time bringing a document that set forth the orthodox doctrine of the mass for her to sign. But Anne stood her ground, vowing within her heart never again to put her name to anything that could be taken as a recantation. In the end, she even refused to answer any more of their questions, though they were relentless in posing them to her. Yet, still the Council pressed her.

Exhausted and aching, she now lay with her eyes closed, wishing only for quiet and rest. A pounding at the front entrance to the house made her groan. *Dearest Lord,* she prayed, *grant me Thy grace for I have no strength left of my own.*

Indistinct voices seemed to be arguing in the downstairs hall. She recognized the voice of Lady Garnish, but her words, though animated, were muffled. Then the voices accompanied by footsteps ascended the stairs; and two men, along with Lady Garnish, burst into Anne's room, not bothering to knock.

"Mistress Kyme, rouse yourself for you are herewith ordered to Newgate Prison. We are sent to escort you," one man ordered brusquely, ignoring the obvious pain etched in Anne's face.

"This is outrageous," Lady Garnish objected. "The poor girl is far too ill to be moved. Let her stay with me a few days longer until she has recovered herself."

"She does not appear ill to me," the same man replied wryly and grabbed Anne's arm and hoisted her to a sitting position.

Anne winced, but she was too weak and in too much pain to resist. Unable to protest, Anne was dragged from the house, heavily supported on both sides by the prison guards, Lady Garnish close on their heels protesting vigorously, but ignored.

Thirty minutes later, Anne was carried into a Newgate prison cell, having collapsed on the way. The guard unceremoniously dumped her onto the thin mattress set on a ledge against the cell's gray wall on the far side. But Anne did not care. She was lying on a bed again and that was all she wanted. She groaned softly and turned toward the wall, hoping her tormentors would leave her in peace. She heard them leave and sighed with relief. She closed her eyes and soon dozed.

A rough hand shook her violently as a gruff voice demanded, "Get ye up, woman!"

Before Anne was able to comply, the same hand grabbed her upper arm and dragged her from the bed. Anne, her head swimming, sought to gain her footing but stumbled and fell to her knees. The guard muttered a curse and yanked her once again to her feet. Anne stood unsteadily on her feet, fighting the dizziness and the aches that racked her petite frame. Her head drooped forward and her dark hair tumbled freely across her face, obscuring her vision. She never noticed the man standing directly in front of her.

Stephen Gardiner eyed the disheveled form in front him, pleased to see that for once her defiant insolence had left her. Perhaps she would be more pliable in her present condition and open to reason. He said nothing, but nodded to the guard who shoved Anne forward, his hand firmly holding her upright to keep her from collapsing again. He guided Anne out of the cell, through the narrow passageway, and down the steep steps, never once easing his brutal grip on her arm. And it was just as well, for it was only his strength that propelled her forward and kept her on her feet.

When Anne was thrust through the doorway into the prison courtyard, the glaring sunlight hit her full in the face, making her wince; she instinctively held up a hand to shield her eyes from the offending light. A dozen or so others, who Anne could only guess were also prisoners, were already gathered in the court-yard. As she glanced from face to face, she recognized many of them from the Bible studies and meetings she had attended in previous months. One young man, whom she remembered as having attended regularly, smiled shyly at her. His clothing was common, indicating he was probably a tradesman of some kind, which was why he didn't dare speak. She managed a slight smile and nod in acknowledgement, but felt too ill to pursue a conversation.

When the guards were satisfied that all appointed prisoners were gathered in the courtyard, they began herding the group out of the prison gates. Twice Anne stumbled and nearly fainted, but both times strong, though rough, hands upheld her and forced her forward. The group was led through a narrow street, which opened to a large green. Anne looked up. St. Paul's Cathedral loomed before them, its massive gray columns and delicate sculptures beckoning worshipers to enter. At St. Paul's Cross stood the open-air pulpit erected years before for sermons and important public announcements. On this day, the area was alive with activity at the anticipated event. People of every class and trade milled around, vying for a good position from where they could hear and see all that was going on. Anne's hapless group was escorted to the forefront.

From the graying portico on the north side of the cathedral, bishops, clergy, and high-ranking nobles emerged, among them Bishop Bonner, Lord Chancellor Wriothesley, and Thomas Howard, Duke of Norfolk. They strode forward, confident and triumphant in their steps. Then much to Anne's dismay, she spied Dr. Edward Crome, the noted Reform theologian, walking in their midst. While the former virtually swaggered forward, relishing the moment; the latter lagged behind, his head down, his shoulders sagging.

With sinking heart, Anne suddenly realized why she and the other marked prisoners had been brought to St. Paul Cross. As

Dr. Crome mounted the podium, he faltered a moment, took a deep breath, then proceeded. When at last he stood in the pulpit, his tired eyes and worn features revealed the heaviness of his heart, but when he spoke, his voice was firm.

"My friends," he began, "I have come this day to declare before you that I have in recent days come to a true and right understanding, according to my own conscience, of the Six Articles of Faith put forth by our gracious and magnificent king. I should have come to this understanding earlier but was kept from it by perverse-minded persons, who persuaded me otherwise, and by fallacious and ungodly books and writings."

The hot sun beat down on Anne's back, and her knees wobbled. Dr. Crome's voice droned on.

"For this, I am most heartedly sorry and desire that you, my good friends, be made aware of such books, for though they are fair in appearance, they hide within them a dangerous encumbrance to men of Christian consciences…"

The last thing Anne remembered before she passed out was the startled look on the face of the young tradesman beside her as he reached to catch her crumpling form.

A cool cloth on her head, a familiar voice speaking softly roused Anne from her blackness. She struggled to open her eyes, but a stabbing pain in her head forced them closed again. She tried to speak.

"Hush, milady," the voice chided gently. "Do not tire yourself further. You must rest."

Anne obeyed and lay still. The sweetly familiar voice comforted her, and the damp cloth eased the throbbing pain. Finally Anne opened her eyes. Joane's grave face peered down at her, a most welcome sight. Anne smiled weakly.

"Dearest Joane…"

"I am here, milady. Your brother, Sir Francis, has sent me to be with you. He is overcome with grief and did not wish you to be alone."

"'Tis not his fault. I am here because the Lord has brought me here."

"I shall pray that you are soon released from this horrid place, and we can once again go home."

"You shall go home, Joane, but I shall not accompany you. The Council is set against me. I fear…"

"Do not speak it, milady, for then it shall surely come to be!"

To ease her maid's heart, Anne did not speak it, but she thought it. And in her heart, she knew it was true.

June 28, 1546

The four prisoners stood at the rail facing the Council members. Every available space at Guildhall was jammed with curious spectators, eager to hear the outcome of the trial. Two of the prisoners were men of little renown, but the third man, Nicholas Shaxton, was the former Bishop of Salisbury. Yet as well known as he was, most of those gathered were there to catch a glimpse of the fourth prisoner, the well-known and well-discussed Lady Anne Askew. Hushed conversations rippled through the hall when the four had been brought in, but now the room was shrouded in deathly quiet.

Anne glanced sideways at the young man who stood at the farthest end of the railing. It was the same young man from Newgate Prison, whom she had since learned was a tailor by the name of John Hadlam. He stared straight ahead, his chin lifted, his eyes determined. Anne breathed a prayer on his behalf, then focused her attention back on the Council.

One by one, the three men were questioned as to their beliefs; and one by one, condemned for their opinions. Finally, the Council looked to Anne.

Thomas Wriothesley leaned forward in his chair and eyed Anne derisively. She merely returned his gaze.

"Mistress Kyme, you stand here before this Council as a heretic, condemned by the law if you insist on standing on your opinion."

"I am no heretic, milord. Neither do I deserve any death by the laws of God. But as concerning the faith which I have uttered and even wrote before this Council while imprisoned unjustly, I will not deny it for I know it to be true."

"Then you profess before this assembly that you deny the Sacrament to be the true body and blood of our Lord Jesus Christ?"

The moment had come; a prayer for courage ascended. As new strength surged through her, Anne lifted her voice so that all could clearly hear.

"Yes, for the same Son of God, who was born of the Virgin Mary, is now glorified in heaven, and He will come again from there in the latter day in the same manner as He went up. As for that which you call your God, 'tis merely a piece of bread. For proof thereof, let it but lie three months in the box, and it will become moldy and so become nothing good. Therefore, I am persuaded that it cannot be God!"

Astounded gasps and frenzied murmuring shattered the shrouded silence of the hall. Wriothesley banged his gavel to restore order. A judge on Wriothesley's right side bent toward him and whispered in his ear. He scowled, but said, "Do you wish a priest be sent for that you might make your confession, mistress?

Anne gave no reply. In the quiet gloom, she studied the assembled clerics and nobles who sat before her. Then slowly, an enigmatic smile spread across her face. Infuriated by her silence—and her smile, Wriothesley asked, "Do you find the offer of a priest objectionable?"

"I have no need of a priest for I confess my faults to God; and I am sure that He hears me with favor."

Almost as one, the members of the Council snorted in outrage, and the entire hall erupted in chaotic chatter. But when Wriothesley rose from his seat, the chatter came to an abrupt halt.

"Mistress Kyme," his voice solemnly intoned, "by your own words you stand condemned. 'Tis the judgment of this Council that you, by your own testimony, are a professed heretic; thereby, you are sentenced this day to death by burning. May God have mercy on your immortal soul!"

Chapter XVIII

Striding through the halls at Greenwich Palace, Bishop Gardiner could barely contain the triumphant feeling surging through him. The tide had finally turned in his direction; the queen had made a fatal mistake. His time to act had come, but he must do so quickly. He hastened to find Thomas Wriothesley.

Secluded in Wriothesley's private office, Gardiner told him of the morning's events.

"When I met with His Grace, I found him in a particularly foul mood. Thinking that the pain in his legs had worsened, I naturally inquired after His majesty's health. Indeed, his pain was increased, but his grumbling was not against the pain, but against the queen herself! 'Twould appear that as the queen nursed him last evening, she endeavored to remove his mind from his pain by engaging him in earnest conversation. As is her custom, she embarked on a religious topic, one to which she professed many opinions and to which she was not opposed to voicing those same opinions to His Grace. 'Twould seem she was more enthusiastic than usual in her expression of opinions, for this morning as the king related the event to me, his anger simmered and in his complaint, he said to me, 'A good hearing it is when women become religious clerks, and a thing much to my comfort to come in my old days to be taught by my wife!'"

Wriothesley grinned. The king displeased with his Protestant queen, indeed this was astonishing news. Gardiner, encouraged at the pleasure reflected in Wriothesley face, continued.

"Well, I could not suffer such an opportunity to pass, so I heartily agreed with him. Then declaring that I wished only to be His Majesty's humble and obedient servant, I told him that I had reason to believe the queen was deliberately undermining the stability of the state by fomenting heresy of the most odious kind and encouraging his loyal subjects to question the wisdom of His Majesty's government. Indeed, I said, the matter was grave enough that there would be no doubt in the minds of the Council to affirm that were the greatest subject in this land to speak the words that she did speak and defend likewise those arguments that she did defend, he would be with impartial justice by law deserving of death. To my pleasure, the king was rightly alarmed and has authorized an immediate inquiry into the orthodoxy of the queen's household. Furthermore, he has agreed that if any evidence of subversion be forthcoming, charges must be brought against Catherine herself!"

Gardiner sat back, reliving the encounter in his mind and relishing his moment of triumph. But he rested only a moment. Leaning forward again, he reasoned with Wriothesley as to their best approach in handling the matter. After a few minutes discussion, both agreed that it would be through the queen's own ladies that they best could orchestrate her downfall. Therefore, each lady should be questioned immediately and persuaded to give evidence of the queen's subterfuge.

"Undoubtedly, if we are able to secure confessions from those closest to the queen of her treasonous persuasions, we shall have no trouble in destroying her – and her vile influence."

"And Providence has smiled upon us for we have in our possession a most valuable weapon," Wriothesley suggested. Gardiner was quite attentive. The Lord Chancellor leaned forward and spoke aggressively. "Mistress Anne Kyme. If any of the queen's ladies have given her aid, it would be by the queen's consent. That alone 'twould be evidence that she is in sympathy with a condemned heretic."

A satisfied smile spread across Gardiner's face. "A most splendid observation," he agreed. "I leave it to you to secure the necessary warrants." He paused, then added. "And I leave Mistress Kyme in your expert hands as well."

"A pleasure, your grace. And, I give you my word, you shan't be disappointed."

July 5, 1546

The view from the Tower window was more pleasing to Anne than that which she had had at Newgate, but her transference only hours earlier to this London's most notorious prison brought with it a strong feeling of foreboding. She gazed out over the River Thames, remembering with bittersweet fondness the trips she had taken with John Lascelles down that river to share the gospel with those less fortunate. Now the river, its murky waters coursing peacefully along its bed, served as a reminder to Anne that life—her life—moved forward according to God's purpose and that He alone knew the final outcome.

A jangling of keys in the cell door brought Anne out of her reverie. A guard entered. "Come with me," he ordered. Anne obeyed, although she was wearied by the prospect that once again her captors meant to harass her. For just that morning, Richard Rich, the solicitor-general, along with Bishop Bonner and the quickly recanted Nicholas Shaxton tried feverishly to persuade her to abandon her opinions. But Anne had held firm. She had been particularly harsh toward Shaxton, telling him that "it would have been better for you had you never been born." She sighed. Would they never believe her true in her convictions and leave her in peace?

Anne followed the guard through the dismal hall, down the narrow stairs, and across the Tower green to a small, dark office located in the White Tower. When she entered, Anne groaned inwardly when she realized that once again she was confronted by Rich, this time accompanied by Sir John Baker, a member of the Council, who nodded to her to sit. As soon as she was seated, Rich began curtly.

"Mistress Kyme, we have need of information from you, which as a loyal subject to His Majesty, you are charged to give us. Do you know of any lady or gentleman of the court who has been, as you were, an attendant of your religious gatherings?"

This was not the line of questioning Anne expected, but she realized at once their intent. "No, milord. I know of none."

"Really, mistress, do not take me for a fool. Do you mean me to believe that in all the months you attended, you never once saw or recognized a lady of the court? Perhaps if I were to mention a few names, you might recall their attendance. What of the

Duchess of Suffolk, the Countess of Sussex, the Countess of Hertford? Or perhaps Lady Denny or Lady Fitzwilliam?"

"If I were to make any pronouncements against them, I would not be able to prove it."

"What an odd thing! For the king, himself, had been informed that if you were willing, you could name a great number of your religious sect."

"Then the king has been well deceived in this and quite misled by those who attend him."

At that moment, the door swung opened and a large shadow fell across the floor. Wriothesley, relishing his authority over this young condemned heretic, swaggered in. Rich quickly informed him of what had thus far transpired. Wriothesley scowled and settled himself on a chair opposite Anne. Leaning toward her, his face hard, his eyes cold, he asked her, "How were you maintained while you were imprisoned in the Counter? Who gave you money? Who visited you and willed you to hold fast to your heretical opinions?"

Anne, unintimidated by Wriothesley's stern countenance, replied, "No one visited me, milord, either to strengthen me or to give me counsel. As to the help I received, I owe that to my maid, who went throughout London and begged help from the street apprentices. Many were kind and did send me money, but who they were, I never knew."

"But not all were apprentices; many were ladies of the court, were they not?"

"There may have been, but I never learned their names."

"You lie, mistress! We know that many ladies sent you aid. Who were they?"

"I only know what my maid told me, sir. Once a man in a blue coat gave her ten shillings. He said it came from Lady Hertford. Another time, a servant in purple livery gave her eight shillings, saying that Lady Denny had sent it. Whether this is true or not, I cannot attest to for I do not know. This is only what my maid told me. I cannot, nor will I, swear to the truth of the matter."

"But you did receive help from members of the king's Council, did you not?"

"No, milord. I did not."

Wriothesley shoved back his chair in frustration, rose, and crossed to the guard standing by the narrow entrance. His voice lowered, the Lord Chancellor whispered to the man. The guard's eyes grew wide and his face paled.

"But milord…" he stammered.

"Do as I tell you, or you shall find yourself facing the same!" Wriothesley barked. The man bowed quickly and hastened from the room.

Turning back toward Anne, Wriothesley said, "'Tis most regrettable that you have proven yourself to be a most difficult witness, madam, but perhaps we can persuade you in other ways."

Anne suddenly felt cold, and an overwhelming fear swept through her. Immediately, she turned her thoughts to the Scriptures.

From my distress, I called upon the LORD; the LORD answered me and set me in a large place. The LORD is on my side; I will not fear; what can man do unto me?[22]

Wriothesley grabbed her upper arm and hauled her to her feet. He shoved her forward toward a door at the back of the office. Following behind Rich, Anne walked through a narrow hallway that led to another heavy oak door. Rich ordered a sentry to open it. The door opened with a shudder, creaking loudly on its hinges.

The LORD taketh my part with them that help me; therefore I shall look with satisfaction upon them who hate me. It is better to trust in the LORD than to put confidence in man. It is better to trust in the Lord than to put confidence in princes.[23]

The passageway narrowed, and their footsteps echoed eerily as they descended steep steps into the bowels of the Tower. The flickering flame from the torch sent ghostly shadows dancing on the damp, cold stone walls. Anne's pulse quickened, and she felt her hands grow clammy. She felt as though she were descending into the very pit of hell.

Whither shall I go from Thy spirit? Or whither shall I flee from Thy presence? If I ascend up into heaven, Thou art there; if I make my bed in hell, behold, Thou art there.[24]

At the bottom step, the passageway widened into a corridor, on which sides were small, dark cells. The rancid smell of unwashed bodies and decaying human waste assaulted Anne's nostrils; she struggled against nausea. As they passed one door, Anne could hear muffled sobs; from behind another, anguished groaning. Striding ahead of her, Rich inadvertently stepped on a rat's tail, causing the rodent to squeal in pain and anger. Anne jumped, and her eyes darted back and forth to see which way the foul creature had run, hoping it would not cross her path.

Deliver me, O LORD, from the evil man; preserve me from the violent man....[25]

The corridor abruptly turned, and once again the group descended a precipitous stairway. The bottom of this stairway opened into an undercroft only slightly larger that the cell Anne had most recently occupied. Anne's knees almost gave way as she, in horror, realized where she was. Standing approximately six feet out from the wall was a stout wooden frame, its center interwoven in a criss-cross pattern with thick leather strips. A third of the way down from the head of frame lay an open, heavy iron neck shackle. On either end of the frame lay thickly twined cords that wound around heavy rollers. On either side of the upper roller were spiked wheels used for turning the rollers in opposite directions. Though she had never seen one, Anne knew instantly that the horrifying contraption was a rack. In the half-lit chamber, the device appeared even more terrifying as the dancing torchlight made the shadow of the hideous frame writhe and twist as if to mock—or warn—its next victim of the fate about to fall. Beside the contraption stood a masked jailer and next to him, Sir Anthony Knyvett, the Lieutenant of the Tower, who looked quite unhappy and visibly nervous.

Fear thou not; for I am with thee. Be not dismayed, for I am thy God. I will strengthen thee; yea, I will help thee; yea I will uphold thee with the right hand of my righteousness.[26]

Wriothesley observed with satisfaction the astonished look of horror on Anne's face, but his satisfaction was short-lived. Drawing a deep breath and breathing a silent prayer, Anne straightened her shoulders and composed her face, willing all traces of fear to vanish.

If the world hates you, ye know that it hated Me before it hated you.... If they have persecuted Me, they will also persecute you.[27]

Wriothesley cursed and moved toward Anne. He reached for her headdress and veil and unceremoniously yanked them from her hair. Anne stifled a startled cry.

"Have you ever seen a demonstration of this device, madam?" he asked, his voice as cold as the massive gray stones walls. She made no reply. "No? Then allow me to demonstrate what this clever machine is capable of doing."

He handed her headdress to the sullen Sir Anthony. Obediently, he took it and laid it on the rack. His fingers trembling slightly, he attached one of the cords to each end and then signaled the jailer. The man stepped up to the wheel. Grasping one of its spokes, he turned it clockwise. The heavy rollers heaved and groaned; the cords grew taut. The headdress lifted slightly from the frame as it stretched. The jailer turned the lever again; and suddenly, the headdress tore asunder, the veil snapping backwards.

Wriothesley smiled sardonically. "Though it takes more pressure on the wheel to produce the same effect on the human body, 'tis certainly not difficult. And Sir Anthony has had considerable experience overseeing this means of truth extraction."

He nodded to the lieutenant, but Sir Anthony refused to return the acknowledgement. He could not believe that Wriothesley actually meant to proceed with this heinous act. Sir Anthony was by no means squeamish, having administered this form of torture on unfortunate men on numerous occasions, but he understood that the rack was meant only for male felons and traitors, not women—and certainly not a gentlewoman. And as Lord Chancellor, surely Wriothesley knew that such an act was illegal. No, the man meant only to frighten the poor woman into speaking. He would not, he could not follow through on such a shameful atrocity.

Across the room, Anne had watched the demonstration in stoic silence. But instead of the fear her enemies had hoped to instill, a new resolve coursed through her veins. Garnering her strength, she determined that she would prove to her tormentors that no amount of pain or suffering would weaken her faith or cause her to betray her friends. Just as her Lord was silent as a lamb before his tormentors, so would she be silent before hers. Her body may suffer, but her will would remain tensely inflexible.

Wriothesley saw the determination on her face and made his own determination. Just as Anne was firm in her resolve to remain strong, he was equally determined to break her will to pieces. He signaled toward the burley jailer, who immediately went to Anne and pulled her toward the rack. Expecting a struggle, he firmly planted his feet and bent to lift her. But to his surprise, Anne submitted to him and laid herself quietly on the frame. Grabbing the rope cords, he securely fastened one around each of her ankles. He moved to the other end and pulled both of her arms over her head and secured her wrists. Finally, he clasped shut the iron shackle around her small neck. Anne lay as if sleeping, but her lips moved wordlessly.

Dearest Lord Jesus, Thou who suffered most greatly at the hands of evil men, yet neither fainted nor surrendered Thy Father's will, grant me Thine abundant grace to endure. I place myself in Thy lovingkindness. Do not forsake me, now, O Lord.

Sir Anthony whispered to the jailer, "Give her only a pinch. She will relent soon enough."

The heavy rollers creaked; the ropes grew taut. Anne involuntarily tensed and pulled against the tightening ropes. Her muscles strained. The wheel spoke turned again. Searing pain shot through her arms and legs as they stretched beyond endurance. Anne bit her lip, closed her eyes, and forced her mind to focus on her Lord.

Lord Jesus, grant me Thy strength!

Wriothesley bent over the frame. "Now, tell us, mistress," he demanded. "Who were the members of your gatherings? Who gave you money?"

Blessed are they which are persecuted for righteousness' sake, for theirs is the kingdom of heaven.[28]

"Was it Lady Denny? Lady Hertford?"

Grant not, O LORD, the desires of the wicked; further not his wicked device, lest they exalt themselves.[29]

"Who visited you in the Counter? Who aided you in your trial?"

Set a watch, O LORD, before my mouth; keep the door of my lips. Incline not my heart to any evil thing.[30]

"How often did you meet in the queen's apartments? Who else was there?"

Every muscle in her body quivered in pain, yet Anne remained still, gazing up at the courtiers in silence. Wriothesley, holding his anger intact, leaned over Anne and stroked her hair. His lips smiled though his eyes remained cold.

"Mistress," he said quietly. "I have no wish to do you harm, but you force my hand. I assure you if you would but give us the names of those who aided you, you would be sent back to your cell. And, if you prove yourself a great help in this matter, I have the power to see that you are released and returned safely to your home. But you must tell us, madam, who took part in your meetings?"

Anne closed her eyes and said nothing.

In all his years at the Tower, Sir Anthony had never witnessed such serene determination and strength of heart. Awed by her resistance, he had had enough. Signaling the jailer to ease the wheel, he stepped forward to release her. Anne felt the searing pain subside and drew a thankful, quivering breath. The jailer, taking advantage of the moment, quickly left, unwilling to be a further participant in this hideous sport.

When Wriothesley realized that the ropes had gone slack, he turned in rage to Sir Anthony. "Just what do you think you are doing? We have not yet finished with this woman."

"Surely your grace realizes that what we do here is illegal," Sir Anthony said in defense.

"This woman is a condemned heretic! What does the law matter?" Wriothesley stormed. "Rack her again, and this time I want to hear bones breaking!"

"I will not, milord." Sir Anthony drew himself up straight, eyeing the Lord Chancellor directly. Wriothesley was astounded.

"You defy me? Do you not know that in defying me, you defy the king, who, I promise you, will not fail to hear of your insolence and disobedience."

"Do what you must, but I will not torment this poor soul further. I have not the authority to rack this woman, nor shall I be responsible for giving such a cruel order."

Wriothesley turned away for moment, his fist clenched in frustration. Then to the astonishment of Sir Anthony, the Lord Chancellor began to strip off his long outer coat. Pulling his arms free from the sleeves, he flung it across the room and stepped to the wheel of the rack. Following his lead, Rich, too, flung off his doublet and took his place on the other side. With a violent thrust, they turned the wheel. The rope straps snapped taut, Anne's body jerked in agony, an anguished gasp burst forth from Anne's cracked and bleeding lips.

"My Lord Chancellor," Sir Anthony protested, stepping up beside Wriothesley, "I beg you, do not continue in this evil deed!"

But Wriothesley merely shoved him aside. "I *will* get what I want from this woman!"

Excruciating pain screamed in every joint and limb as Anne felt her muscles tear and her joints pull from their sockets.

Grant me Thy strength, precious Lord. O, grant me Thy strength! She begged silently.

The rollers creaked again. The ropes burned against her flesh, and a bone in her ankle snapped. Her whole body quivered in revolt, and every fiber in her body begged for release. Anne felt herself slipping into unconsciousness. When Wriothesley saw her head fall to one side, he quickly eased back the wheel. Grabbing a ladle from a nearby bucket, he dashed cold water onto her face. Anne's eyes fluttered opened. Satisfied that she was again conscious, he pressed again. Anne bit her lip harder and tried to continue her soundless entreaties; but against the violent onslaught, all she could do was whisper the name of the One she loved more than life itself.

Lord Jesus, Jesus, precious Jesus...

"Milord, please! Enough of this! Much more and you will kill the poor woman!" Sir Anthony pleaded.

But Wriothesley did not care, nor did he want to stop. This wisp of a girl was making a mockery of him. He was Lord Chancellor of England! What audacity to defy him! He turned the wheel again. Anne's face contorted in pain, yet still she remained resolute in her silence though anguished tears slipped from her tightly closed eyes.

But finally, even Wriothesley realized that no matter how much pressure he applied, Anne would not speak. In anger, he stepped away from the rack. Sir Anthony quickly turned the wheel back until the cords laid slack. As he untied each one, he grimaced at the raw and bloodied flesh around each ankle and wrist. He released the neck shackle, then gently slipped an arm under her knees and around her shoulders and lifted her up. A soft groan escaped her lips. As he lowered her to the floor, he felt her body go limp. Anne had fainted.

Sir Anthony laid her broken body on the cold stone floor, then hastened to get some water and a rag. Dipping the rag into the water, he applied the damp cloth to her forehead and cheeks. Anne stirred. At her feeble stirrings, Wriothesley charged across the room and crouched beside her, shoving Sir Anthony away from the semiconscious Anne. He forced her to a sitting position and slapped her face to bring her to full consciousness. Rich and Baker huddled close by.

Sir Anthony looked on with disgust. When he realized that the gentlemen were totally focused on rousing Anne, he turned from them and slipped quietly from the chamber. The king would know of the afternoon's events, but not from Wriothesley. He raced up the stone steps, out of the Tower entrance, and across the grassy stretch to the Tower wharf. A bargeman, idly whittling a small figurine, glanced up when Sir Anthony hurriedly approached. Without waiting to ask whether the man had other business, Sir Anthony clamored aboard.

"Take me to Whitehall, man, with all speed!"

Though every muscle and joint in Anne's body throbbed, her tormentors would not relent. Unable to sit erect, she slumped painfully against the cold, damp stone floor while Wriothesley, Rich, and Baker continued for two hours to entreat her to give them the names of her "co-conspirators" and recant of her "erroneous opinions." But having endured the pain of the rack, Anne had no intention of giving in now. So as they continued to hammer her, she merely sat with her head bowed and her eyes downcast.

Wriothesley threatened to return her to the rack, but Rich and Baker persuaded him that it would be to no avail and that, in all probability, Anne would die. Finally, in exasperation, Wriothesley rose to his feet.

"I have tried to be patient with you, mistress," he hissed, "but you are obstinate and foolish! Do you really wish to die at such a young age?"

Anne could not lift her head, but murmured, "The vanities of this life hold no affection for me. I desire only to be with my Lord."

"Well, soon enough, you shall face your Eternal Judge, but you may not be as prepared as you think!" he snapped and turned to summon the jailer.

Sir John, who had been leaning against the wall beside Anne, straightened and said, "Your Grace, perhaps it would be wiser to house the lady in other quarters. You know how jailers gossip. I have an acquaintance with Lord and Lady Hildebrand. They could be persuaded to give her lodgings until we deem it appropriate to return her to the Tower."

"Aye, a wise observation, sir. 'Twould be best to keep her a safe distance from wagging tongues. Speak to your friends..." Wriothesley stopped abruptly and spun on his heels. "How long has Sir Anthony been gone?" he demanded.

Neither Baker nor Rich could answer. Wriothesley cursed, then sprinting toward the steps, he ordered, "I leave the matter in your hands, Sir John. Master Rich, we must ride with all haste to the king!"

Under the cloak of darkness, Anne was secretly carried to the modest home of Lord and Lady Hildebrand, where, for a week, she was at least provided with a comfortable bed and nourishing food, albeit no physician was called upon to help ease her pain. However, to Anne's great joy, Joane had been summoned and was allowed to wait on her mistress even though the poor girl could barely look upon her without breaking into sobs. An armed sentry stood guard outside her door, of which Anne wryly commented, "They pull me limb from limb so that I am quite incapable of standing, let alone walking; yet still they fear that I shall somehow escape their grasp."

Her words were true enough for even without a guard, Anne would have had no recourse but to stay where they had laid her. The injuries to her arms and legs were quite crippling; and without the ministrations of a physician, she could do little more than lie abed. But though terribly weakened and in constant pain, with the assistance of Joane, she secretly finished the account of her examinations and sufferings about which she stated, "with many flattering words they did try to persuade me to leave my opinion. But my Lord God, I thank His everlasting goodness, gave me grace to persevere." Then Joane, in a surprising display of bravery, smuggled the manuscripts out right under the nose of the sentry and delivered them to the hands of Anne's Protestant friends. Soon, to the embarrassment of the established faction and the frustration of Gardiner, the entire affair was well known throughout London, and Anne was elevated to the position of a Protestant heroine.

Perhaps in response to the widely circulated stories, but more likely, Gardiner's prompting, Wriothesley once again sent word to her that should she recant, she would at once be set free to go wherever she wished – even back to South Kelsey Hall. But Anne's heart no longer yearned for South Kelsey. A far more glorious home beckoned to her, and she kept her mind fastened on the moment when she would be ushered through that wondrous gate and into the arms of her Beloved Lord.

Chapter XIX

July 12, 1546

Somewhere amongst the branches of the wild cherry tree that brushed gently against the bedroom window, a skylark joyfully serenaded all who would listen, but Anne paid it no mind. For as she lay on her bed, her only thoughts were to console Joane, who sobbed uncontrollably as she knelt beside her mistress' bed, her face buried in her arms. Anne lifted a weakened hand and gently rested it on her maid's head, her fingers stroking the fine black hair.

"Hush, sweet friend, 'tis for the best," Anne crooned. "Francis and Betsy have need of you with them. And I trust you will serve them as well as you have served me."

Joane looked up, her eyes swollen and red. "Oh milady, I beg you. Do not send me away. Let me go with you and stay with you at Newgate. I cannot bear the thought of you being alone in that dreadful place."

"I shall not be alone, Joane. Do you not know that the Lord God, who has been with me every moment of my life, will be even more so as I go unto my death?"

At the mention of the upcoming execution, Joane dropped her head once again into her arms and dissolved into new tears. "I would... that I could take your place," she stammered between sobs.

"I would not wish it so. This life no longer holds any affection for me. Rather, my life is now in heaven with my sweet Savior."

Footsteps sounded outside the room. There was the familiar jangle of keys and the door opened. Four guards entered, toting a chair supported by wooden poles. Beyond them in the hallway stood Lady Hildebrand, her face ashen and grim.

242

"We have orders to take you to Newgate, madam, where you are to await your execution," one guard announced.

"I fear you will have to lift me as I am quite incapable of walking," Anne responded quietly.

The guard moved toward Anne, but before he reached her, Joane threw her arms over Anne's body and cried, "No, I shan't let them take you!"

Surprisingly the guard stopped. For a moment, compassion registered on his face, then he remembered his duty. He stepped forward, but unlike so many others before him who had come to escort Anne, this one showed a genuine tenderness for the condemned woman and her distraught maid. Gently but firmly, he pulled the sobbing young woman away from Anne and steered her toward the other side of the room out of his way. Unable to bear the sight of her mistress being taken away, Joane turned her face to the wall, her sobs muffled in her hands.

The guard bent, hoisted Anne into his arms, and set her down gently in the chair. Anne involuntarily winced as she settled into the hard wooden seat, but smiled kindly at her escort. As they lifted the chair, Anne spoke once more to her weeping maid.

"Joane, when you return to South Kelsey, you will find a gift from me waiting for you. I wrote to Francis and asked him to keep it until you returned. I shall pray that it will come to mean as much to you as it has to me." She then nodded that she was ready.

July 14, 1546

Wriothesley sat staring out the window in his private chamber, still chafing under his recent failure to bring the queen to ruin. His failure was particularly monstrous to him as it was so unexpected, and he scowled as he remembered with humiliation the scene as it had occurred. For up until the very moment he entered into the royal gardens and served the king the warrant for the queen's arrest, he was fully confident that the king heartily endorsed the action. He had had no way of knowing that the evening before, the queen had prostrated herself before her royal husband, begging his forgiveness for her most unbecoming behavior, and that Henry, wanting nothing more than an opportunity to display his great mercy, had eagerly forgiven her and restored her as his loving and faithful wife.

Therefore, when Wriothesley arrived, strutting into the garden with confidence that the king himself had instilled, he was completely taken off guard by his sovereign's reaction. Snatching the proffered warrant from the confused Lord Chancellor, the king bellowed, "Knave! Arrant knave, beast, and fool! Have you and your conspirators nothing better to do than to bring false accusations against a lady who surpasses each of you in virtue? Depart from my sight lest I give orders for your own arrest!"

Wriothesley did depart and with great haste. But the sting of the humiliation lingered, and now he stewed as the memory relived itself once again in his mind.

A polite knock sounded on his door.

"Come in," he grumbled. His young assistance, Ralph Wadloe, strode in.

"My Lord Chancellor," he said, bowing before the disgruntled man.

"Well, what is man? Can you not see that I am busy?"

The perplexed Wadloe glanced at the clear desk, but only replied. "Forgive me, my lord, but I was told to deliver to you these two letters." He stretched out his hand that held two sealed parchments. "One is addressed to you; the other, the king."

Puzzled, Wriothesley took the letters and glanced at the writing. He did not recognize the shaky script.

"If there is nothing else, my lord…"

"Yes, yes. Be gone with you," Wriothesley said impatiently as he broke the seal on the letter addressed to him. He read:

> *May the Lord God, by whom all creatures have their being, bless you with the light of His knowledge. Amen.*

As you are the king's Lord Chancellor and, therefore, a man of duty, I hope that it will well please you to accept this request and move on behalf of one who makes such bold request. My request to your Lordship is that you will be well pleased to be an intermediary for me to the king's Majesty, that his Grace may be fully aware of these few lines which I have written concerning my belief which, when it be truly compared with the harsh judgment given to me for the same, I think his Grace shall well understand me to be weighed in an uneven pair of balances. But I remit my matter and cause to Almighty God, who rightly judges all secrets. And thus, I commend your Lordship to the governance of our Lord God and to the fellowship of all true saints.

Your obedient servant,

Anne Askew

Wriothesley snorted in disgust. *Help that wretched heretic. I rather doubt it*, he thought as he broke the seal of the letter addressed to King Henry. He read:

I, Anne Askew, to whom God has given unto me the bread of adversity and the water of trouble (yet not so much as my sins have deserved), desire to make known this matter unto your Grace. For inasmuch as I am by the law condemned for an evil-doer, I here take heaven and earth to record that I shall die in my innocence. According to what I have said first and will say to the last, I utterly abhor and detest all heresies, but as concerning the Supper of the Lord, I believe just what Christ has said within the Holy Scriptures, which He also confirmed with His most blessed blood. I believe that He has willed me to follow Him, and I believe all that the true Church does teach concerning Him. For I will not forsake the commandment of His Holy Words, for what the Lord has charged me in His Word, I keep in my heart. I, therefore, most humbly beg your Grace to look kindly upon my unfortunate circumstances.

Your most obedient and humble servant,

Anne Askew

Wriothesley stared at the parchment as he considered the matter. In light of the king's most recent and abrupt change of heart toward his own lady, if His Majesty were to see this letter, he may very well be disposed to show mercy to this woman as well.

The Lord Chancellor rose purposely from his seat. He crossed the chamber to the fireplace on the other side and stood gazing into the small flickering flames. He glanced once more at the letters in his hand, then slowly crumpled them in his fist. He smiled wryly as he tossed the crumpled parchment into the fire and watched with satisfaction as the flames licked the unfolding letters, blackened them, and quickly turned them to ashes.

As it is with your letters, so may it be with you, Wriothesley thought with grim satisfaction.

July 16, 1546

"I am not afraid, dearest Lord," Anne whispered again, "for Thou art with me and shall be with me even as I pass through the fire."

She glanced again toward the prison window and realized the afternoon shadows were lengthening. It would not be long now. She thought of her sister, Martha; her brothers, Christopher and Thomas; and her beloved father. Would they all be waiting to greet her? With her whole heart, she hoped so; but, in truth, theirs were not the faces she longed to look upon. There was only One whose presence she delighted in, and He would be with her in the fire.

For the last time, she heard the jangle of keys and the squealing of iron on iron hinges as the door swung open. Four guards entered, with them the chair Anne had been carried around in for the last two weeks.

"'Tis time, milady," one guard solemnly announced. Anne startled him by flashing a joyous smile and quietly submitting as he settled her into the chair. Once she was secure, the guards hoisted the chair from the floor and started down the dark passageway. Anne's heart sang with joy as she realized that she would never again see these dank and dingy walls. In the courtyard, Anne's chair was momentarily set down as the guards waited for the other condemned prisoners and their escorts. In only a few minutes, the prison door opened and two of Anne's fellow prisoners appeared. John Hemsley, who Anne had known from several of the gatherings, stepped out first, followed by John Hadlam, the young tailor. Anne gave each man an encouraging smile, and the three exchanged greetings. Then a fourth figure emerged. John Lascelles stepped into the afternoon light. Anne's heart leapt at the sight of her old friend, and he came immediately to her, knelt before her chair, and clasped her hands.

"God shall be with you, my dear sister," he whispered.

"And with you," she replied softly.

A guard yanked John to his feet, wrestled his hands behind his back, and bound them with a rough rope. The two other men were likewise bound. The group assembled, the captain of the guard gave the order to proceed to Smithfield, just a short walking distance from Newgate. Anne's chair was once again hoisted by four men. The three male prisoners went out first with Anne being carried behind. Once outside the prison courtyard, curious onlookers crowded the narrow streets to catch a glimpse of the grim procession. Because both John Lascelles and Anne had become rather famous throughout London, people jostled each other and pressed against the guards to catch a glimpse of them as they passed. But Anne saw neither the sea of faces that stared nor heard the voices that jeered, for her mind was fixed firmly on her Lord and the glorious rapture that awaited.

The narrow lane ended and opened into the grassy arena of Smithfield, now trampled by the gathering crowd. On one side of the field rose St. Bartholomew's Church, its massive gray arches and stones stained with streaks of black as though it mourned each death it had been forced to witness. In front of St. Bartholomew's arched entrance a temporary stage with awning had been erected to seat the prominent dignitaries. As the condemned prisoners drew closer, Anne could see the all too familiar faces of Thomas Wriothesley, Bishop Bonner, Bishop Gardiner, Sir Martin Bowes, and other members of the king's Council. She could also see Nicholas Shaxton, trying very much to look as though he were in complete agreement with this solemn event. Summoning her remaining strength, Anne sat up as straight as she could and gazed evenly at the men on the scaffolding as she was carried forward. None returned her gaze.

As the procession of prisoners and guards filed onto the field, the eager spectators all craned their necks in effort to see them. The air crackled with anticipation as friends chattered amongst themselves, exchanging the latest gossip heard about the condemned. Parents held their little ones aloft for a better view, and jugglers and tumblers stopped their antics when they realized that the attention of their audience had been diverted to the main entertainment. To a casual bystander, it would almost appear to be a festive occasion as food vendors wended their way through the crowd and children whooped and hollered as they scooted around legs.

The procession continued into a large roped-off area. The three Johns walked with their heads erect, ignoring the jeers of the surrounding crowd; although John Hadlam, the young tailor, faltered a bit when first confronted with the horrifying reality of three solid, eight-foot wooden stakes rising from the center of the arena—stark reminders of the fate awaiting them. At the base of each stake, bundles of straw and sticks had already been placed. Three mounted soldiers rode continually around the outskirts of the arena in a constant effort to keep the jostling and rambunctious crowd behind the roped line.

When Anne was carried into the arena, an unexpected hush fell over the crowd. She looked so young and her body so weakened from her recent tortures that even the most hard-hearted among the gatherers was moved to pity. Adding to the astonishment of the onlookers was the sight of a small band of loyal friends walking bravely beside the condemned, offering them encouragement and comfort. Such open support was tantamount to treason as it spoke clearly to the authorities that these sympathizers opposed the judgment passed on the four individuals.

From the crowd, a deep voice bellowed out a warning. "You are all marked men who come to give them comfort. Take heed to your own lives!" But the warning fell on deaf ears and the friends gathered closer to pray one more time with the victims.

At a signal from the Lord Chancellor, guards shoved their way into the small group, pushing the sympathizers aside, effectively ending the prayer meeting. Three guards grasped each of the Johns and dragged him to a stake. Hadlam and Hemsley were bound back to back to the middle stake, and John Lascelles to the one on the left. Anne watched in prayerful silence, beseeching the Lord that neither she nor her friends would lose heart. A guard stepped up beside her. Anne looked up and was surprised to find herself confronted by the same man who had escorted her from Lord Hildebrand's home to Newgate only four days prior. His face was stern, but as he bent to lift her, she heard him whisper, "Forgive me, milady, for I know you are innocent."

Anne smiled softly at him. "There is nothing to forgive, for you are surely God's instrument to help me on my way to my precious Lord. For me, only glory awaits."

Their eyes met momentarily, and Anne saw compassion mixed with deep sorrow. He then gently lifted her from the chair and carried her to the remaining stake. Another guard waited with heavy chains. The kindly guard, his face white, lowered her feet while maintaining his grip on her waist. He then held her upright as the second man wrapped the heavy chains around her chest and thighs, binding her to the stake. When she was secured, the guard let go, but he winced as he watched Anne slump against the chains, unable to sustain her own weight. The chains dug cruelly into her flesh, but Anne uttered no cry of pain. The guard paused a moment as if torn by indecision, then spun on his heels and walked away, refusing to look back at the sagging form.

Another guard approached Anne. In his hand, he held a pouch suspended from a short, looped leather strap. He hung the pouch around her neck.

"Gunpowder," he explained in answer to Anne's inquisitive look. Anne breathed a prayer of thanksgiving. Her suffering would not last long.

All four victims were now securely in place. A hush fell over the crowd as Nicholas Shaxton lumbered up the steps leading to the open-air pulpit. He knew full well why he had been chosen for this occasion, but he clearly looked uncomfortable and carefully avoided the eyes of Anne and John Hadlam, who had been tried along with him. He cleared his throat and began to address the condemned.

"Friends, by your own choosing you have been brought to this place on this most tragic of days..."

"'Tis tragic indeed when one who had known the truth turns his back on it." Anne's voice rang out loud and clear. Shaxton's face reddened, but he ignored her remark.

"As we gather in this place, we hold forth our earnest hope that you give heed to this final warning and repent of your grievous and misguided ways. For should you remain steadfast in your erroneous opinions, eternal damnation awaits your immortal souls."

"Did not our Lord say, 'He who hears My words and believes Him who sent Me, has eternal life and does not come into judgment but has passed out of death into life'? Of what 'erroneous opinion' do you therefore accuse us?" Anne challenged him again.

Shaxton was visibly disconcerted, but tried again to assert himself.

"The Lord also said on the very night in which He was betrayed, 'This is My body which is given for you' thereby proclaiming Himself in the sacramental host."

"He also said, 'I am the vine.' Does He now live in every vine in every vineyard? If that be so, woe to him who cuts down the vine to plant a new one!"

Shaxton cast an angry eye at the outspoken young woman and was tempted to cease his preaching at that very moment and step down, but a penetrating look from Gardiner warned him it would be unwise for him to do so. So the hapless former bishop stumbled on through his rehearsed sermon, trying his best to ignore the running commentary by the condemned woman. The crowd, charged by Anne's boldness, urged Anne to continue, laughing and jeering at the preacher's obvious discomfiture. Finally, Shaxton reached his last point and hurriedly descended the stairs.

The crowd again fell silent as Lord Chancellor Wriothesley rose from his seat on the scaffolding and came to its edge. In his hand he held a parchment. Staring with disdain down at the four, he raised the parchment above his head and declared, "You have been charged with the most odious crime of heresy, which is not only a crime against your most benevolent Prince but more so against the Holy Church of God. Yet, even now, we offer mercy.

If any of you would now recant and put your signature on this document of faith, you shall even now be made free."

A messenger ran forward, took the parchment from the Lord Chancellor, and hurried down to present it to the condemned. He offered it first to each man, but in turn, each refused to even read it. Coming to Anne, the messenger extended the parchment to her.

A strange feeling swept through Anne. Rising anger mingled with overwhelming joy flooded her every sense. With her last ounce of strength and ignoring the pain that shot through her limbs, Anne forced herself into an upright position. She raised her head, looked straight into the eyes of Wriothesley, and announced in a voice resonating with a strength borne of her conviction, "I came not hither to deny my Lord and Master."

Their fate was sealed.

The last bundles of sticks and straw were piled around each stake. The hooded executioner, holding a lighted torch, stood by awaiting the signal. Sir Martin Bowes stood and moved forward. He studied once more the four individuals before him, a strange mixture of pity mingled with respect welling up inside. Then he cleared his throat and spoke loudly the final words, "Fiat Justitia!"

The executioner moved forward and tipped the torch to the bundles at John Lascelles' feet. As he moved to the next stake, John Lascelles called out to his friends, "Die well, beloved. We go to be with our Sovereign Lord!"

Anne responded, "Give thanks to the LORD for He is good. His lovingkindness is everlasting.[31]"

When the masked executioner came before Anne, he hesitated but a moment before moving quickly to perform his duty. Avoiding her eyes, he thrust the torch among the twined branches.

The fire around each stake smoldered, crackled, then flared. An anguished cry pierced the air. But as the flames leapt higher, the cry gave way to earnest prayer. Awed spectators listened in astonishment, not to painful screams but to voices of praise ascending above the roar of flames.

Refusing to watch the demise of her friends, Anne leaned her head back against the stake, gazing heavenward.

Lord Jesus, be Thou my strength.

The flames ignited her clothing and the smell of her own burning flesh assaulted her nostrils. She clenched her fist against the searing pain.

Oh God, grant me courage!

Scorching, black smoke billowed up around her, making each breath an agony.

Who shall separate us from the love of Christ? Shall tribulation, or distress, or persecution, or famine, or nakedness, or peril, or sword?[32]

Fire engulfed her and licked hungrily at the sack of gunpowder.

But in all these things, we overwhelmingly conquer through Him who loved us. For I am convinced that neither death...[33]

The sack exploded.

At long last, Anne Askew was in the arms of her Beloved Savior.

The last rays of the setting sun over the Lincolnshire hills sent fiery hues of red and orange cascading across the purpling sky. Joane sat under the willow in the gardens at South Kelsey Hall, gazing forlornly out across the horizon. Above her, a lone red kite serenely circled the darkening sky. As she watched, the graceful bird momentarily dipped, then suddenly soared upwards until it was lost from sight.

"'Tis over," the young woman whispered, a solitary tear falling from her cheek onto the well-worn book she clutched to her heart—Anne's beloved Bible.

Epilogue

If the members of the established faction held hope that Anne's death would undermine the Reformation movement, they were sorely disappointed. Within six months of Anne's death, her manuscript detailing her trials and torture was published and widely circulated throughout London and England. Anne was quickly elevated to the position of Protestant heroine, and the Reformation flourished.

In January 1547, Henry VIII died, and his son, Edward VI was crowned king. During Edward's brief reign, Protestant doctrine became firmly established in the Church of England with Holy Communion replacing the mass. Although under queen Mary, England returned briefly to a Catholic state; once Queen Elizabeth I ascended the throne, Reformation theology was again restored as the doctrine of the Church of England.

As to other Askew family members, surviving records indicate that all became dedicated followers of Reformation doctrine. Edward died in 1558, during the reign of Mary I. Sir Francis died of natural causes in 1564, leaving his vast estate to his son William. Anne's sister, Jane, was the only one of William Askew's daughter to find happiness in marriage. Married twice to men of strong Reformation conviction, she outlived both her husbands and died in December 1590.

Scriptural References

1 Psalm 27:1
2 Psalm 27:6
3 Philippians 4:6, 7
4 Psalm 46:10a
5 Psalm 73:25,26
6 Psalm 42:11
7 Exodus 20:12
8 Ephesians 6:1
9 Philippians 3:20 & 21
10 Ephesians 5:25, 26a
11 I Peter 3: 1, 2
12 I Peter 3:4
13 John 15:4
14 Matthew 5:10, 11
15 I Corinthians 7:15
16 Acts 7:48 and 17:24
17 I Cor. 14:8

18 James 5:16a
19 I Cor. 14:34
20 Hebrews 13:5
21 Romans 8:31b
22 Psalm 118:5, 6
23 Psalm 118:7-9
24 Psalm 139:7, 8
25 Psalm 140:1
26 Isaiah 41:10
27 John 15:18, 20b
28 Matthew 5:10
29 Psalm 140:8
30 Psalm 141:3, 4a
31 Psalm 118:1
32 Romans 8:35
33 Romans 8:37, 38a